The
Beloved

The
Beloved

ALISON RATTLE

HOT
KEY
BOOKS

First published in Great Britain in 2015 by Hot Key Books
Northburgh House, 10 Northburgh Street, London EC1V 0AT

A CIP catalogue record for this book is available from the British Library.

ISBN: 978-1-4714-0379-8

1

This book is typeset in 10.5 Berling LT Std using Atomik ePublisher

Printed and bound by Clays Ltd, St Ives Plc

www.hotkeybooks.com

Hot Key Books is part of the Bonnier Publishing Group
www.bonnierpublishing.com

ALSO BY ALISON RATTLE

The Quietness
The Madness

For my Beloved Mum

Wild was the wish, intense the gaze
I fixed upon the murky air,
Expecting, half, a kindling blaze
Would strike my raptured vision there . . .

Anne Brontë, 'Severed and Gone'

I am Alice Angel. I am sixteen years old. I am not mad. But I am a bad person.

I have done some terrible things lately. I want to be forgiven.

I want to be a good person, the person they all expect me to be.

I have seen you and I have heard you talk. I think you understand.

Can you help me?

You are my only chance to make things right.

Bridgwater, 1848

One

'Alice? Are you asleep?' Papa's voice is like soft, warm feathers tickling my ear. I smell the familiar weight of brandy and tobacco on his breath – rich and hot – and I am reminded as always of steamed fruit puddings and the scent of polished wood. I open my eyes and the closeness of his face startles me a little. I can see the stiff white hairs protruding from his nostrils and the yellowed edges of his moustache.

'No Papa, I am not asleep,' I say. 'I cannot get comfortable. Please can you talk to Mama?'

'Oh Alice,' he says, standing back up. 'If I thought it would do any good I would go down to the drawing room this instant.' He sighs. 'But you know what she is like. When her mind is set, there is no one in this world who can persuade her to change it.'

Papa strokes my wrist where the leather strap chafes at my skin. 'Besides,' he says, 'I am certain it is all for the greater good. Your mother may have her strange ways, but she loves you very much.'

'Does she?' I whisper. I think of how Mama looks at Eli, how her eyes shine and how her voice grows soft. She has never looked at me that way.

3

Papa smiles down at me. 'My darling girl. I am glad you have your own mind, but you must never question your mother's motives. She loves you and Eli more than anything. You must always remember that.'

I try to roll and stretch my arms to relieve the ache. 'But it hurts so much! Does she mean me to be in such pain?'

'Alice,' Papa warns.

I relax my arms and I wince as the leather straps bite into my wrists. 'Be brave, my dear Alice,' says Papa. 'It will not be for much longer.' He leans in to kiss my forehead and his bristles catch at my skin and set off an itch that I know I shan't be able to scratch.

'Now Alice, I have to travel to Bristol tomorrow and will be away for most of the week. Please be good while I am gone. Can you promise me that? It will make my life a lot easier if I know I can trust you to behave in my absence.'

My heart sinks. I hate it when Papa is not in the house. 'Please, Papa!' I try again. 'Please speak to Mama before you go!' I blink hard and it is not difficult to summon tears. I look straight at Papa as they roll from the corners of my eyes. I see how his face softens. I see how his hands are itching to unbuckle the straps around my wrists. 'Please, Papa,' I murmur.

But then the fear comes into his eyes and shrouds his face like a dark cloak and I know I've lost him. He will never stand up to Mama. He will never go against her wishes. I love Papa so much, but his weakness spoils everything. Why can he not see Mama for what she really is? Why does he have to love *her* so much?

He looks at me tenderly and sighs deeply. 'Goodnight, my darling girl. Sleep well,' he says. Then he blows out my candle.

I do not reply. I turn away from him and stare into the darkness of my room. Papa walks out and closes the door gently behind him. I lie still for a moment, frozen by the anger that sits heavy and cold in my belly. I want to scream out loud and shatter the windows with my fury, but instead I begin to beat my feet and legs on the mattress, harder and harder, faster and faster, until the bedlinen falls to the floor. I pull and wrench and turn my wrists inside the leather straps. But Mama is never careless or inattentive. She has done the buckles up tight as usual. I groan and spit harsh whispers into the night air. 'I hate you!' I scream silently at Mama. I twist my head from side to side, trying to rub my forehead against the top of my arms. The itch that Papa's kiss set off is infuriating me now.

Suddenly, I stop. Tiredness washes through me and I feel empty and numb. I know none of this flailing around is of any use. I lie still and catch my breath. My nightgown has ridden up my legs and the night air is cold against my skin. The steel bones of my stays crush my insides as cruelly as Mama tries to crush my spirit. I start to shiver and I know I have no choice now but to call Lillie.

Lillie is my lady's maid, but in reality she is Mama's little lapdog. She is thin and spiteful and carries with her a sickly sweetness that is only surface deep. And like the ruinous pollen of the flower she is named after, Lillie will drip her own poison wherever she can. Mama will not hear a word against her. She came highly recommended by Lady Egerton, you see, and as Mama is impressed beyond reason by true gentry, Lillie can do no wrong.

Lillie sleeps in the bedchamber next to mine and thinks herself very fine. Behind her back the other servants call her 'the toffee-nosed tart'. I am glad it is not only me who dislikes her.

'Lillie!' I call. 'Lillie!' She will make me wait, I know it.

Lillie is a constant annoyance to me, like an unpleasant clump of horse manure that I cannot wipe from my shoe. She wakes me in the mornings, she helps me to dress, she brings me fresh water to wash with and she lights my fire. She is always in my room, fiddling and neatening and tidying. She is supposed to take good care of my gowns, but I know she deliberately tears the lace of my cuffs, then reports it to Mama who sees it as another example of my careless disposition.

'Lillie!' I shout again. I am sure the whole household will have heard me by now.

At last, the door opens and Lillie greets me with a reluctant 'Yes, miss?' She stands over me and the light of her candle accentuates the dark hollows under her eyes. Her black hair hangs loose and lank around her shoulders. I remind myself she is only a servant and not some ghoul just risen from its coffin. 'Yes, miss?' she says again. Her eyes glide over the leather straps that hold my wrists to the bed and a smirk plays around the corner of her mouth. She is as ugly as a turnip.

'I am cold, Lillie. You can cover me up.' Lillie walks around my bed, her bare feet slapping hard on the wooden floors. I remember the first time Mama strapped me to the bed, and how I foolishly thought I might be able to appeal to some soft part of Lillie's nature. I soon learned there was no soft part to Lillie's nature.

She heaves my bedlinen from the floor and flings it roughly over me. I am too tired to ask her to do it tidily. I just want to sleep now and for morning to come. 'Anything else, miss?' she asks.

I ignore her and close my eyes. Lillie huffs loudly and slams the door on her way out.

The creak of Lillie's bed springs settles, and the small sounds of the night echo inside my head. The servants are closing up downstairs. I can hear doors being softly shut and the air stirs as the last of the maids creep up the back stairs to their rooms at the top of the house. Wooden floorboards scrape overhead. The plane tree outside my window taps a bare branch against the shutters and I think of its yellow-scabbed trunk and the small hole at the base that I made by digging out the crumbling wood with my fingers one long, boring afternoon in the spring when I was supposed to be stitching my sampler. The long-case clock down in the hall chimes eleven. I have eight more hours to pass before my hands are released.

I have learned in recent weeks that if I try hard enough I can go to a place that is outside of my body and this bed and this room and this house. It is a place where I can no longer feel the pain in my wrists or the stiffness in my sides and back. I wish for this place and sometimes it comes to me easily. Sometimes it does not come at all and the night is long and hard and cold as stone. Tonight I am lucky. Tonight my place is there ready and waiting for me behind my eyes. It is a meadow of the brightest green and I am alone in the centre of it with not another soul to be seen. I am wearing a loose shift and my hair is flying about my face as I move and stretch and run through grass that smells as sweet as freshly made butterscotch. No matter how far I run, the meadow never ends. I run faster, and the grass swipes at my bare ankles, and then I run faster still and faster and faster until my feet leave the ground and I am flying towards the morning.

Two

Temperance Angel ran her hands down the sides of her bodice and looked herself over in the full-length mirror that stood to one end of her dressing room. She was satisfied with what she saw. Jane, her lady's maid, had done well this morning. Temperance's hair was parted neatly down the centre and drawn back over her ears into a most pleasing arrangement. She would have the girl add some flowers later on, before Lady Egerton paid her long-awaited call, but for now it would suffice. Temperance's skirts fell flatteringly over her new crinoline cage; a French one that she had ordered especially on the advice of Lady Egerton. It was wider than any she had worn before and she knew she would have to take great care not to cause herself any embarrassment. She had heard terrible stories of women exposing themselves when they sat down too carelessly and the cage flew up in their faces. Worse still, she had heard tell of a fashionable young woman in Paris who had burned to death after a lighted cigar had rolled under her voluminous skirts. Temperance shuddered. She would never allow anything like that to happen to her.

Temperance was a beautiful woman and she was well aware of the fact. But she never took it for granted. She knew it was only her pale, almost translucent skin, her fierce green, almond-shaped eyes and her rich auburn hair that had got her where she was today. She turned heads. Arthur Angel would never have looked twice at her if she had been ordinary-looking. He certainly would never have married her. Temperance was not born stupid, only poor. She knew that no matter how beautiful she was, she would never have enticed a titled gentleman into marriage. There were limits to what the daughter of a lowly clerk could achieve. So Temperance had set her sights on the next best thing. A man of ambition.

Charles Angel was a man to be reckoned with in the small town of Bridgwater. He owned the local flour mill and had amassed a small fortune for his troubles. He was one of the new breed of industrialists who had gained respect in the town, not from his breeding, but from his wealth. He had a troupe of plain daughters who, despite the richness and fine cut of their gowns, could not hide from the world their unfortunate resemblance to a herd of farmyard pigs. But Charles Angel also had a son. Arthur was the youngest of the family and, although not a handsome man, he wore his plainness with a determination that somehow managed to organise his muddled features into a pleasing order. He was set to inherit the mill from his father and throughout the whole of her seventeenth year, Temperance had contrived to cross paths with him at every opportunity. In a town as small as Bridgwater, this wasn't a difficult thing to arrange.

Temperance timed her daily errands so that she was passing the Angel household (a magnificent red and yellow brick house known locally as Lions House, due to the lion-topped gateposts that flanked the front steps) at the exact time Arthur was leaving on his way to the mill in the mornings. She discovered that Arthur and his family attended the church of St Mary's on the other side of town to the church she and her father usually attended. So, much to her father's consternation, she insisted on making the extra twenty-minute journey there every Sunday morning, even though it meant her father had to go without his customary Sunday lie-in. But as Temperance had been running the household since the death of her mother five years earlier, her father had little choice in the matter.

It wasn't long before Arthur Angel began to tip his hat at Temperance. She wasn't at all surprised. She blushed at him prettily and lowered her eyes. But that was all. She didn't encourage him. She wanted to reel him in slowly. She wanted to be certain that when she finally caught him, there would be no chance of him slipping from her grip.

The months passed. Temperance made the best of her limited wardrobe by trimming her gowns with fresh pieces of lace she bought cheaply at the market and by pinning artfully arranged flowers in her hair. Arthur Angel, along with tipping his hat, began to greet Temperance with a polite *Good morning* or *Good afternoon*. She did not reply of course; decorum dictated that a young woman out on her own must never acknowledge the attentions of a man. Even so, she began to let a comely smile pass across her lips. A smile that would not fail to set Arthur Angel's heart beating fast.

Eventually, on a stark Sunday morning in the autumn of that year, when the sun shone weakly on the mulch of fallen leaves in the churchyard, Arthur Angel approached Temperance's father and introduced himself. Temperance stood to one side and was relieved that she had shined her father's only good shoes and mended the hole in the elbow of his ancient Sunday suit. She could not remember exactly what was said that day. She was distracted by the way her father kept pulling nervously at his collar and at the way his face flushed a ridiculous red. But whatever he said cannot have been too awful, because the next thing Temperance knew, Arthur Angel had taken her gloved hand and brought it to his lips.

After that, they met every Sunday in the churchyard once the service had finished. But now it was Temperance's father who stood to one side while Temperance was wooed by Arthur Angel. As was only right and fitting, Arthur left it a good few weeks before asking permission to call upon Temperance at home. This was the moment Temperance had feared the most. This was the real test. Could she entrance Arthur Angel so much that he would fail to notice the shabbiness of the tiny terraced house she shared with her father? Temperance spent the days before Arthur's visit scrubbing the house from top to bottom. She washed threadbare curtains, swept the floors until there was not a speck of dust to be seen, polished the windows to a shine and begged and borrowed from neighbours until she had a decent choice of plates and teacups, and a teapot that poured without dribbling.

On the morning of the day Arthur was due to call (it was raining, much to Temperance's annoyance. Wet weather always made the house look bleaker), Temperance was up before dawn. She dragged the old tin bath in front of the kitchen fire and poured in kettle after kettle full of steaming water. The water was hot enough to turn Temperance's skin a bright pink as she sat in the bath and methodically rubbed the washcloth between every toe, around her feet, up her legs, across her hips and onwards, not missing an inch of flesh. Then she dried herself carefully and put on the second- or third-hand brocade gown she had found after rummaging around in the back of the pawn shop on Corn Street. It fitted her perfectly and its green velvet bodice complemented her eyes much better than she could have hoped for. She disguised the musty smell of the old velvet by sprinkling it with the last few drops of lavender water from her dead mother's only perfume bottle.

Once satisfied with her own appearance, Temperance called her father and instructed him to clean himself thoroughly in the now tepid bathwater. She supervised his dress, combed his hair flat and bade him sit quietly in the small front room she had temporarily transformed into a parlour. With the tea laid out on the table and a few small fancies on a good china plate, all that was left to do was to wait. Temperance knew that the rest of her life depended on the next few hours and she had never been as nervous or as excited or as terrified. When the knock finally arrived at the door she almost choked on her own heart.

Little did Temperance know, but she needn't have bothered to go to so much trouble and effort. Arthur Angel was already frantically in love with her. He wouldn't have cared less if he'd had to pick his way through the worst of slums to get to her.

When Temperance answered the door to him the rest of the world fell away. Arthur could have been in a palace or a hovel. He didn't notice the damp in the corner of the room, or how threadbare the rug was. He didn't notice how the delicate china teacups that Temperance poured the tea into didn't all match. He barely noticed her father sitting quietly in the corner of the room and he certainly didn't taste the sweetness of the pastries that Temperance had gone to so much trouble choosing. All he noticed was how Temperance shone. He feasted his eyes on her long white neck and drank in the greenness of her eyes. He had never wanted something so much in his whole life and within half an hour of his arrival he was down on his knee asking for her hand in marriage.

As luck would have it, Charles Angel, who was not entirely in agreement with his only son marrying so low, met with a nasty accident while observing the installation of a new roller at the mill, leaving his entire fortune to Arthur and giving the inhabitants of Bridgwater a reason to gossip when St Mary's church hosted a funeral and then a wedding within two days of each other.

Temperance took to running Lions House as if she had been born to it. Arthur agreed with her suggestion that a newly married couple should enjoy complete privacy in the early days of wedlock, so the Angel sisters and Charles' widow were dispatched to a small but adequate cottage on the outskirts of town. Temperance looked at her grand new home, at the fine furniture and large army of servants it contained, she looked at her costly trousseau, that had all been handmade for her by a Bristol dressmaker, and she could not believe how easy it had been to get the life she had always dreamed of. Arthur, for his part, could not believe how lucky he was to have the wife he'd always dreamed of. Neither of them could have been more satisfied with the way things had turned out.

Within a year, Temperance had produced a son they named Eli and a year later a daughter named Alice. If Arthur was puzzled by the change in Temperance that came about after the children were born, he never said a word about it. He adored his wife and if she was not as enthusiastic in the bedroom any more, well maybe that was to be expected after the rigours of childbirth? When she moved out of their bedroom altogether, he meekly accepted it as her right to a good night's sleep. He grew used to containing his passion for her and counted his blessings instead: that he was fortunate enough to have the most beautiful wife in the whole of Bridgwater.

Temperance's beauty dominated the Angel household. It drew everyone towards her and made them want to please her: from the lowliest maid-of-all-works to all of Arthur's business associates. By the time any of them recognised the dark truth behind Temperance's perfect façade, it was too late. She had them caught in her trap, and none was brave enough to speak out against her. No one, that is, except for her daughter, Alice Angel.

Alice saw straight through her mother. From the moment she was born, Temperance was aware of the baby's small black eyes following her around the room. Temperance found it disconcerting that a mere baby could make her feel so uneasy. She would dream of the child's miniature fingers digging into her face and peeling back the skin to reveal the ugliness of the blood, bone and muscle underneath. Temperance spent as little time as she could with the child. She called her difficult, awkward and wearing, although the nanny she engaged to look after the child found Alice to be nothing but sweet and lovable. In truth, Temperance could not bring herself to even like her daughter. Temperance felt different towards her eldest child, Eli. If love made your insides turn soft for a moment, then Temperance assumed she loved her son. She could feel his adoration of her: it poured from him. He would hold his arms out to her and when she picked him up he would press his velvet cheeks against hers as he wrapped his little arms around her neck. He was a beautiful boy. He had inherited Temperance's auburn hair and green eyes, and Arthur's soft nature. Eli grew into a gentle and caring young man and, best of all, his love for Temperance never wavered.

Alice, on the other hand, grew worse the older she got. Once the girl learned to speak, there seemed to be no way of training her tongue. She questioned her mother endlessly and challenged her on every decision. *But, why must I wear that? Why can't I play outside with Eli? Why can't I go and see Papa now? Why do you love Eli more than me?* The girl was insufferable. She didn't act at all like a young lady should; she was ridiculously untidy and raced around the house like a common street urchin. Temperance despaired of her. She could barely bring herself to look at the girl at times. It didn't help that Alice looked so different. She hadn't inherited her mother's ethereal beauty, but neither did she take after her father's side of the family. Alice had an intensity to her. Everything about her was more than it should have been. Her hair was blacker than coal, her

16

skin creamier than the freshest milk and her eyes sharper than a kitchen knife. If Temperance believed at all in changelings, she would have sworn that Alice had been swapped for an otherworldly creature at birth.

It was Alice that Temperance was thinking about as she stood admiring herself in the mirror. The damned girl was suffering from hysteria, she was sure of it. She was sixteen now and should have long since ceased to be a thorn in Temperance's neat side. But she was so wilful. Everything with her was a battle. She should have been completely corset trained by now. But no, Alice being Alice, she would take the thing off at night, complaining that it was too uncomfortable to sleep in. Of course it was uncomfortable. A good, straight and comely posture could not be gained without a modicum of discomfort. But Temperance had got her own way as usual. She saw to it herself that every night now, Alice's hands were strapped to her bed. There was no tampering with corset laces now. A few more weeks should do it, then hopefully Alice's wayward mind would be restrained, along with her figure.

Temperance checked the clock on her mantelpiece. It was seven o'clock. Time for the day to begin in earnest. She would go and untie Alice first, say goodbye to Arthur before he left for Bristol, then instruct the cook on exactly what was needed for Lady Egerton's visit.

Three

I smell Mama before she even enters my chamber. The cloying scent of her lavender announces her arrival at my door. My body tenses and I am aware that I am holding my breath. I turn my face away from the door and listen as the key clunks in the lock. I hear the rustle of her skirts as she walks to my bedside. She lifts the covers from me and runs her hands down the length of my body to feel the sheet beneath me. I feel the cool of her fingers on my wrists and she makes a tiny grunting noise as she pulls at the buckles and frees my hands. Then she is gone. Without saying a word. But she's left her lavender scent behind and I need to rid my room of it.

First though, I pull the chamber pot from under my bed and relieve myself, thankful that I didn't wake to cold wet sheets again. Whenever I have disgraced myself in this manner, Mama has me carry the bundle of sodden linen down to the kitchens so all the servants may witness my shame. I am spared this at least today.

I sit on the edge of the bed and rub at my wrists. The skin is red and sore and there are welts where the straps have cut into me the deepest. I reach under my pillow for the pot of ointment hidden there. I open it and scoop out a fingerful of the oily cream to smooth on both wrists; it's cold and soothing. I stole the pot from Mama's room. It is called Rowlands Kalydor and the label declares it to be 'a cooling and refreshing milk for the face, hands and arms'. Mama has a dozen of these pots and has not noticed that one is missing yet. Just in time, I hide the pot back under my pillow. The door opens and Lillie comes in with my wash water. 'Can you open the windows?' I ask her.

'But it's so early,' she says, looking at me disapprovingly.

'What of it?' I say. 'Open the windows please.'

Lillie tuts and makes a great show of tugging the curtains across and pushing the windows open a crack.

'Open them wider,' I tell her. She looks at me as though I am mad, but pushes the windows open anyway so that a welcome rush of air and the smoke of early morning fires comes swirling in. I feel better now I cannot smell Mama any more.

Lillie is breezing around the room now. She opens drawers and cupboards and lays an assortment of underclothes on the end of the bed. 'What gown will you be wearing today, miss?' she asks me.

'Whichever one,' I tell her. 'I don't really care.'

Lillie tuts again. I stand and stretch to try and relieve the aches and soreness in my sides and under my ribs. I pull my nightgown off and walk stiffly to the washstand to begin my morning toilet. Lillie watches me closely. Most of me despises having to wear these dreadful stays, but there is a small part of me that is glad the cursed thing inspires envy in Lillie. She would give her right arm, I know, to be tight-laced, and to swan around in a well-made gown.

19

I stay silent as Lillie dresses me in a blue silk. I am so exhausted I can barely lift my arms to push them through the sleeves. Lillie brushes my hair and tugs hard on the knots. I won't give her the satisfaction of complaining. Eventually I am ready and it is time to go down to breakfast. I hope that Eli will be there. It is too unbearable to think I may have to dine alone with Mama.

I hear his voice as I near the door to the dining room and the knot in my stomach loosens. It is the first good thing of the day. And every good thing, no matter how small, makes each day easier to live through. As I open the door, I hear him telling Mama of his plans. How he is going for a ride on the moors this morning before lessons with his tutor begin. He stops mid-sentence as I come in the room and he greets me warily. 'Good morning, Alice.'

I bend to kiss his cheek and catch my breath as a bone in my stays jabs under a rib. Eli's brow creases in concern. 'Are you well?' he asks.

'She is quite well,' says Mama tersely. She ignores me and feasts her eyes on Eli, as if he is the only person in the room. 'Now,' she says to him. 'Finish telling me of your plans.'

'Yes, Eli,' I say brightly. 'Tell us of your plans. It is a beautiful day for riding.' Mama's face hardens for an instant. She will punish me for this later. She will punish me for speaking to my own brother and for taking his attention away from her. But I don't care. I want to hear Eli describe how he will ride like the wind across the wide, open space of the moors into the shadows of the Quantocks; how he will look out for wading birds and maybe stop for a while to watch the peat gatherers. All of me aches to be able to join him. Even though I have never even sat upon a horse, I can imagine the feel of it and the power and the freedom. Eli does not know how fortunate he is.

I spoon some eggs onto my plate and push them around as I listen to Eli talking. It is easy to pretend that everything is ordinary while there is his voice to hide behind. Ordinary is what I wish for. Ordinary is what everyone else takes for granted. But for me, to be ordinary would be so very special.

I watch how easy he is with Mama and how easy she is with him. I sigh. It will be a long week without Papa here to soften the edges.

Eli wipes his mouth on his napkin and beckons one of the maids over. 'Will you let the stable boy know that I will be ready to leave in twenty minutes?' She scuttles off to do his bidding and I turn cold inside as he pushes his chair back and stands to leave. 'Have a good day, ladies,' he says. He kisses Mama on the cheek, but doesn't see how she glares when he comes over to me to do the same. Eli leaves the room and suddenly the air turns cold too. Mama doesn't speak for a moment. She sips her tea and looks out of the window. I chew and swallow my eggs quickly, though they are rubbery and tasteless; I may not get the chance to eat again today. I let my cutlery fall clanking onto the empty plate. I might as well let it begin now, so it will be over all the quicker.

Mama whips her head around at the noise. 'Will you *never* learn?' she hisses. 'You dare to interrupt me when I am talking to Eli, and you have the table manners of a ruffian!'

'I am sorry, Mama,' I say. 'I did not know it was a crime to be interested in my brother's life.'

Mama puts her hand to her head. 'You dare to be so insolent to me,' she says through clenched teeth. 'You will go back to your room and stay there! It was too much to hope that you could have taken tea with Lady Egerton today. Too much to ask that you would not continue to embarrass me.' She lunges across the table and slaps me hard across the cheek.

I blink in shock, but I won't let the tears come. I take a deep breath. 'Lady Egerton is nothing but a primped and powdered old windbag,' I say. 'Why would you want to impress her?'

Mama's face turns white with rage. 'Get out!' Her voice trembles and I am glad to see her perfect brow crinkle into ugly creases.

I have been in my room but a minute, when I hear the key turn in the lock. Mama isn't taking any chances. I go to the window and press my head against the glass. My room looks out over the street, and I can see that the day has barely even begun. It is mid-July, but the sun has not yet lit the pavements yellow. The few people that are scurrying about their business are the early risers: servants, hawkers and dustmen. Lady Egerton would not be seen dead out and about at this time of the day. Her sort is rarely seen about before midday. I hate it that Mama thinks more of the woman than she does of me. I bang my forehead slowly against the window and the rhythm comforts me. It is going to be another long day.

I pass an hour or so writing in my journal. It soothes me to lose myself in words. I write of happy things: of sitting on Papa's knee in front of the fire when I was small and giggling as he sang me nursery rhymes; of chasing Eli around the flower beds in the garden; of picnics in the summer and of tending to a small grey pony called Rose. I write of a mother who loves me. A mother who shows me kindness instead of scorn. A mother who does not stick pins into my arms because my sampler stitches are less than perfect. It is all nonsense of course. These things are only wishes. Pages and pages of wishes that have never come true.

I hear a clattering from outside, so put down my pen and go to the window. It is Eli, back from his ride. He dismounts and hands the reins to the stable boy. As he turns towards the house he looks up at my window. When he sees me looking down at him, the exhilaration on his face slips and turns into disappointment. He cannot understand why I continue to anger Mama so much. He tries his best for me, I know. But like everybody else, Eli is blind to her faults.

I sit in my chair for a moment, listening carefully. I knew it would come, and soon there it is; a small knock at my door and the sound of the key turning. Eli comes creeping into the room. He closes the door quietly, then looks at me seriously, with Mama's green eyes. 'What has happened, Alice?' he asks.

'Just the usual,' I tell him. 'I shouldn't have talked to you at breakfast. You know how Mama hates me taking your attention away from her.'

'Oh, Alice,' he says. 'She wouldn't punish you for *that*. What really happened? What have you done now?'

'You honestly don't see, do you?' I shake my head. 'It's so different for me than for you, Eli.'

'Well, of course it's different, Alice.' He drags his hand roughly through his hair. 'I am a man and you are a girl. A young lady now, in fact. I hate to say it, but maybe it's time you started acting like one.'

'And how should I do that, Eli?' I challenge him. 'Should I allow Mama to tighten this thing . . .' I jab my fingers at my waist, '. . . so much that it cuts me in half? Should I never say what I think or feel? Should I just sit quietly in some corner with no mind of my own?' My voice has grown shrill and Eli puts his finger to his lips and looks nervously at the door. 'What's the matter, Eli?' I say stiffly. 'Are you afraid Mama will lock you in your room too, if she finds you in here with me?'

He looks at me sadly.

'Or,' I continue, 'are you afraid she will stop loving you?'

'Alice.' Eli sighs. 'I cannot talk to you when you are like this.' He digs around in his pocket and brings out a packet. 'Here, take this.' He holds the packet out towards me, but I don't move. 'You will be grateful for it later,' he says as he throws it onto the bed. 'Please, Alice.' He looks at me as he opens the door to leave. 'Please see sense. Apologise to Mama for whatever it is, and let us have a good week while Papa is in Bristol.'

Then he is gone. I stare at the back of the door and listen as Eli turns the key in its lock again. I would laugh if I did not feel so wretched.

I go to the window once more. The glass is warm now the sun is finally soaking the world outside. The street is busy with the comings and goings of people who have lives. They pass

24

beneath the spread of trees that are now throwing twisted shadows on the house-fronts opposite; delivery boys with baskets of bread, suited men sweating in hats and stiff collars, and women swaying along the pavement with silk and lace parasols shielding their complexions.

Lady Egerton will be here soon and Mama will be in her element. Perhaps Eli will join them for tea, and perhaps her Ladyship will be taken with Eli's handsome features and will think him a good candidate for one of her daughters. I snort at the idea. How much more insufferable Mama would be if that were ever to happen. I think of Lady Egerton's smug face and her hook nose, which she dabs at with a succession of embroidered handkerchiefs, and of her judgemental eyes and thin slash of a mouth. As people grow older, they get the faces they deserve. Lady Egerton certainly got the face she deserved. She is not as pious as she would have the world believe. Mama's beauty will fade one day too, I am sure of it. The ugliness inside her will worm its way out and spoil her features for good. Then everybody will see what I see.

I would ruin the whole day for Mama if I could. If I were not locked in my room, I would interrupt her little party and have some amusement of my own. Perhaps my cup of tea, accidentally knocked from its saucer, could spill onto Lady Egerton's skirts. Or I could ask her Ladyship, very politely, if she has ever considered consulting a doctor about the broken veins on her high and mighty cheeks. How Mama's nerves would be tested at that! But better still, I wish I could prevent Lady Egerton from coming here altogether. How devastated Mama would be then!

I close my eyes and I imagine her Ladyship descending the great stairway of Bridgwater Hall on her way to the carriage that will bring her here. I see her bony foot, clad in a satin slipper, catching the hem of one of her petticoats and sending her tumbling in a heap of squashed crinoline and broken bones. I even hear her Ladyship's squawks, as loud and indignant as a parrot knocked from its perch. I see her lying at the foot of the stairs as clearly as if I were standing next to her. I wish and I wish for all of this to happen. I wish so hard that I tremble with the effort.

I'm surprised then, and horribly disappointed, that when I eventually open my eyes, Lady Egerton's green and crimson liveried carriage is pulling up on the street below.

I throw myself on the bed in a huff and land on the package that Eli left there. Pulling it from under me I rip it open; a piece of bread and a slab of greasy cheese falls out. For some reason this makes me laugh. Great bubbling gulps of laughter burst out of me. I laugh until my ribs hurt and I cannot stop, not even when Lillie unlocks the door and pokes her head in to see what all the noise is about.

Four

Temperance Angel wrung her hands. It was not like her – this pacing up and down and fretting. But then, she had never waited on a visit from anyone of Lady Egerton's status before. Temperance had been to the window so many times she was worried she would soon wear the pile on the new crimson Turkey rug. She stopped pacing and looked critically around the drawing room. Everything had to be just so. Not a single detail could be overlooked. Temperance knew what Lady Egerton was like. She found fault in the smallest of things. Temperance had overheard her on many occasions complaining that Frances Cooper served tepid cups of tea, that Cordelia Sprigg's table linen was a disgrace and that Agnes Hawthorne had no control over her servants. Temperance had no wish to be added to that list of unfortunate women. She had worked hard for this day: donating large sums of Arthur's money to Lady Egerton's various philanthropic causes, attending each and every meeting of Bridgwater's Ladies' Committee (set up by Lady Egerton to help prevent unfortunate young women from taking to evil ways), suffering the stench of the workhouse on a number of rescue missions and visiting the low parts of town with various members of the Committee. On one of these visits Temperance was forced to pass by the end of the street where her father lived. She was horrified to see him in the distance, shuffling along the pavement. She feigned a dizzy spell and Cordelia Sprigg immediately escorted her home, thus preventing a hideous and embarrassing encounter. Although Temperance occasionally sent her father money (in a bid to keep him quiet rather than from any sense of guilt), she had not seen him since the day of her wedding to Arthur Angel, and wanted to keep it that way.

Temperance walked to the window yet again. Her hands were sticky and her upper lip damp. She flipped open her fan and flapped it furiously in front of her face and at the open neck of her bodice. She hoped the flowers that Jane had arranged in her hair had not wilted. Everything had to be perfect. She had threatened the servants with instant dismissal if they so much as put a foot wrong. And, of course, Alice was locked safely away at the other side of the house. Temperance sent out a silent prayer. Today would be her biggest success yet. Lady Egerton would be impressed by all that she saw. There would not be a single thing to complain about. And Temperance would finally be accepted into the upper echelons of society.

As the carriage pulled up outside, Temperance hastily arranged herself on the couch with a book of poetry open on her lap. She did not want to look too eager when Lady Egerton was shown into the room. There was a knock on the door. 'Come,' said Temperance as calmly as she could.

'A message from Bridgwater Hall for you, Ma'am.'

Temperance was puzzled. She looked behind the maid, who was holding a tray with a letter on it. 'Where is Lady Egerton?' she hissed. 'You haven't left her standing in the hallway, have you?'

'Oh no, Ma'am,' replied the maid. 'Just a servant from the Hall came, and asked for this to be passed to you.' The maid held the tray out towards her mistress.

Temperance snatched the letter and ripped it open. Her hand flew to her throat and she gasped out loud.

'Is everything all right, Ma'am?' asked the maid.

'No, it is not,' breathed Temperance. 'Fetch me a glass of water.' As the maid hurried to do her bidding, Temperance looked at the letter again. It was the very worst of news. Lady Egerton was not coming. All that waiting, all that work, all that planning: all for nothing! Temperance screwed up the letter and threw it across the room. It would be a long while before another visit could be arranged. The stupid, stupid old bitch had fallen down the stairs and broken her ankle!

Five

Mama has not come to my room to strap my hands to the bed. It is not like her to be late. Lillie is keeping tight-lipped. The mistress is indisposed, is all she will say when I ask after Mama. For all her sharpness and spite, though, Lillie can be quite dull at times. I realise, with a tiny thrill, that as she leaves my room, she has quite forgotten to lock the door.

I savour the feeling of freedom for a while, but I dare not close my eyes. Mama is bound to come soon, and if she finds I have fallen asleep untethered, there will be another day of punishment tomorrow. I turn this way and that, I plump up my pillow, and I listen to Lillie moving about in her room. Soon though, I am bored with waiting. The thought that I could get out of bed if I wanted to, and even leave my room, nags away inside my head. I am curious about what could have happened to make tonight so different. Mama is never forgetful or shoddy in her intentions. Will it make matters any worse if I creep out of my room to find Eli?

I climb from my bed and put a shawl over my nightgown. I take a lighted candle and open the bedroom door softly, so as not to alert Lillie, and then I am out. I stifle a giggle as a joyous rush of possibilities sets my skin tingling and my heart racing. I don't know what to do first. Should I go straight to Eli? Or should I go to the kitchen and see what I can find to eat? I wolfed down Eli's thoughtful package of bread and cheese an age ago, and now my mouth is watering at the thought of some thick ham, or cold potatoes, or even a spoonful of honey eaten straight from the jar. I creep barefooted down the back stairs and make my way to the servants' territory. I flit along the kitchen corridor feeling like a wraith on a haunting mission. The lowest of the maids will still be on duty, I know. But they pose no danger to me. I slip into the kitchen. It is hot and steamy and a small girl is on her knees scrubbing the flagstones in front of the great fire. She jumps when she sees me and clutches her brush to her chest. Her frock and cap are wet and soiled and her apron is filthy with ash stains. I put a finger to my lips as I walk past her to get to the larder. The cool air inside is filled with the smells of good things. There are muslin-covered jars lining the shelves, a cooked ham glistening with fat and a huge pie with a golden crust that looks thicker than my arm. I put down my candle and pick up a knife that is lying near to the pie, then I cut myself a generous slice and eat it with my fingers. Mama would be struck down by apoplexy if she could see me now. The pie is delicious. It is full of jelly and meat juices that dribble down my chin, and creamy slices of potato and salted bacon. I swallow great mouthfuls of it and am thinking of cutting another slice when I hear voices in the kitchen. I am sure it will be no one of any importance, at least no one who will report me to Mama. But I decide to stay where I am just in case. And besides, I want more pie.

The voices in the kitchen are low and furtive. I wonder if the girl by the fire will tell the newcomer that I'm in the larder. I quickly fill my mouth with pie. 'The mistress is in a right state tonight,' says one of the voices. 'By all accounts, she is upset beyond reason by Lady Egerton's mishap. Though why she should take on so, I really don't know.' I stop chewing and move closer to the door. There is the sound of water being sloshed around and the clanking of metal on metal. 'Hurry up with that, Ivy,' says the voice. 'I want to get to my bed before midnight, if you don't mind.'

I am curious. What mishap are they talking about? I stay still – listening – but nothing more is said. Brushing pastry crumbs from the corners of my mouth, I go back into the kitchen. The girl is still there, on her own, wiping around the inside of an enormous copper pan. She looks to the floor as I walk by. I hope she doesn't get the blame for the missing slices of pie.

I tiptoe through the house, my ears straining to every creak and knock. My heart hangs motionless for a moment as I walk past Mama's room to get to Eli's. There is a flickering sliver of light coming from the gap under her door and a whiff of fusty lavender. I hold my breath until I get to Eli's room, then I tap my fingers lightly on the door – thrice, then twice, then once, like we used to when we were children. I wriggle my toes in expectation and wait. 'Is that you, Alice?' I hear him whisper. I tap again and Eli opens the door and beckons me inside. He looks at me warily. 'What are you doing?' he asks as soon as he's closed the door behind us. 'Why are you not in your room?'

'I was just looking for Mama,' I tell him. 'I have not seen her since this morning.'

'No,' he says slowly. 'She was very distressed earlier when Lady Egerton failed to keep her appointment. She has been in her room ever since.'

'But I saw Lady Egerton's carriage arrive,' I tell Eli.

'It was a servant who came in the carriage,' said Eli. 'To pass on the news of Lady Egerton's accident.'

'What accident?' I ask.

'She tripped on her petticoats and fell down the stairs at Bridgwater Hall. I believe she has broken her ankle.'

I catch my breath and reach out to a nearby chest of drawers to steady myself.

'What's the matter, Alice?' says Eli. 'You've gone quite pale.'

'It's nothing,' I manage to reply. 'Just these hideous stays. They rob me of my breath sometimes.'

Eli colours slightly. 'The perils of being a woman,' he murmurs. Then he frowns. 'Maybe I should check on Mama. It's unusual for her to have kept to her room for so long.'

'No, no,' I say. 'Don't do that. I am sure she is fine. Wait for the morning, Eli. Let her rest.'

He looks at me and narrows his eyes. 'You will not take advantage of the situation, will you Alice?'

I shake my head.

'You will go straight back to your room and do as you are supposed to do?'

'Of course I will! What do you think of me?'

'You know quite well what I think of you, Alice. You are my sister and I love you, but I wish you would not cause Mama so much heartache.'

Sometimes I want to hit my brother hard in the face. Maybe the pain of a bloody nose would open his eyes to the truth. 'Don't worry,' I say instead. 'I'm going. Back to my room.'

Eli smiles at me. 'I'm glad to hear it, little sister,' he says. He leans towards me and kisses me tentatively on the cheek. 'You should learn to trust Mama. She knows what is best for you.'

Usually, I would snort with derision at his remark and ask him how he can be so foolish as to believe that, but I am desperate to be on my own so I can think about the miracle that has just happened.

Back in my room, I take a candle and stand in front of the mirror. I stare into my eyes. I stare for so long that all around me blurs into misty shapes and colours. Only my eyes remain clear: dark and shining; floating in the candlelit mirror. I put the palms of my hands on the glass to stop them from shaking. My wishes have never come true before. What did I do that was so different this time? I look deep into my eyes once more, trying to see if something has changed. I see nothing but a long, empty darkness. Then my breath, heavy with expectation, mists the glass, so I walk away and go to my bed instead.

It is late now; I feel how the air in my room has cooled. Mama will certainly not come now. I am free to do as I like. But, strangely, this unexpected gift of liberty has me at a loss as to what to do next. I pace the room for a while, thinking of Lady Egerton and her broken ankle. I need to wish again, I decide. It's the only way I will ever know for sure that her mishap was of my doing. I need to test myself. A small wish. Just to see.

But there are so many things to wish for. Where do I begin? I pick up my journal and flick through the pages.

I could wish for a horse of my own so I could ride out on the moors with Eli.

I could wish for Papa to see the truth of what is under his nose.

I could wish for him to stand up to Mama.

I could wish to be allowed to study the things that Eli studies.

I could wish never to have to complete another piece of embroidery.

I could wish for Mama never to hurt me again.

My mind races with all the possibilities. There is so much that I wish for that I cannot decide where to begin.

I sit on the edge of my bed, and as always, my stays take my breath away with their steel grip. Just one night, I think. What bliss it would be to have one night when my body is not tortured by Mama's ambitions.

I hear a small cough from the room next door. Lillie is safe in her bed. No one will know. I can easily remove the stays myself, and if I am careful to tighten them as much as I can in the morning, who will be any the wiser?

I push my nightgown up over my hips and reach my hands around to the knot of laces at the back of my stays. I pick and pick at the knot, until it eventually loosens and I am slowly able to pull the stays apart. I gasp out loud at the aching relief. After a moment, when I have got used to being able to breathe normally again, I stand and peel the loosened stays from my body. Then I step out of them and kick them across the floor.

I run my hands over my body where the stays have kept it prisoner. My skin is sore and bruised and as I lift my nightgown and chemise, I see the steel bones have left deep red marks. Suddenly, a hot rage ignites inside me and before I know what I am doing, I have taken the stays from the floor and pushed them into the fireplace. They are immediately smudged and streaked with old ashes. I take my candle and with shaking hands hold the flame to the stiff fabric. It singes but will not catch. I look around my room desperately, for something that will help set the flames. Seizing my journal again, I rip some clean pages from the back of it and then crumple them into the fireplace. The pages soon burn and, with them, the stays at last burn too. I watch the flames turn blue and green, and listen to the sizzle and cracks until there is nothing left in the grate but steel bones: twisted and strange like some monstrous carcass. My rage dies with the flames; I blink hard as if waking from a dream and look in horror at what I have done.

I hug my knees tightly. Suddenly I am afraid, very afraid. I cannot imagine what Mama will do to me now. My eyes are drawn to the three small scars on my forearm: ragged circles of pale skin, each one the size of a threepenny bit. I remember, it was my eighth birthday and Papa had given me a book as a gift. 'You can read well enough now,' he had said proudly. It was a beautiful book, bound in soft buttery leather. I read the words on the front cover, *Household Tales, The Brothers Grimm*, and a shiver of terrified delight ran through me as I weighed the book carefully in my hands, sensing the power of the stories that lay within. A book! All of my very own.

But Mama had been furious, and had snatched the book from me before I had even opened a page. 'How could you, Arthur?' she had raged. 'This is not suitable reading for a girl! Especially not for *Alice*.' She threw the book onto the drawing room table and Papa raised his eyebrow to me in apology. 'I forbid you to read it,' said Mama. 'Do you understand me, Alice?'

I nodded at her mutely, but I already knew I would disobey. The book was *my* gift. It sat there on the table, all fat and stretched tight with hidden treasures. My fingers itched to turn the pages.

I waited until after dark, when the house had stilled and I was sure everyone was asleep. Lighting a candle, I crept from my chamber through the shadowy house until I was back in the drawing room. There was my book – still on the table where Mama had left it. I picked it up and caught the sweet scent of leather and ink. It made my heart beat fast. I clutched the book tightly to my nightgown and padded back to my chamber as quickly as I could, the flame of my candle dancing nervously across the walls. I clambered back into bed and placed the candle on the table beside me. I laid the book on my lap and when I had recovered my breath and my heart had stopped racing, I ran my hands over the cover, feeling how each letter sank into the leather and I could read the meaning with just my small fingers. I balanced the book on my raised knees to be closer to the candle flame, and then I opened the cover and smoothed the pages inside. The paper, yellowed by candlelight, was thick and as crisp as bread crusts. Words danced in front of my eyes and my mouth began to water as I started to read.

A certain king had a beautiful garden, and in the garden stood a tree which bore golden apples. These apples were always counted, and about the time when they began to grow . . .

I didn't hear her come in. I had been so enthralled with my gift. But suddenly, the book was snatched out of my hands, and I yelped before I knew what was happening.

'You little thief!' she whispered. 'This is what happens to sneaky children who defy their mother's wishes.' She pulled my arm towards her, her hand locked tight around my small wrist. Then she lowered her candle and tilted it over my bare skin. One. Two. Three drops of hot wax splattered onto my arm. I clenched my teeth together, so as not to cry out. But the tears rolled out of my eyes before I could stop them and it was then I looked up at her and saw the satisfied turn of her lips.

I never saw that book again. I wonder what she did with it as I brush my fingers tentatively over the faded scars. Did Mama burn it in the fire? I look again at the charred remains of my stays, and my heart turns ice cold.

I jump as the door opens. But it is only Lillie. She stumbles in, rumpled-haired, clutching a shawl around her pokey shoulders. 'I smelled smoke, miss,' she says as she rubs her eyes awake. She walks over to where I am still sitting by the fireplace. 'If you had wanted a fire, you had only to call me,' she says testily.

I stand quickly and try to block her view of the grate. But I am too late. Lillie's stare flicks from my unfettered form, to the burned mess behind me. Her hand flies to her mouth in disbelief. Then she stiffens and sniffs. 'I'll have to tell the mistress of this,' she says, her weasel eyes glinting.

'But you don't, Lillie. You don't have to tell her anything,' I say, knowing as I speak that my words are wasted.

Lillie's mouth twitches. 'Oh, I do,' she says defiantly. 'And I will. First thing in the morning.'

I look hard into her face – at her eyes, like two shrivelled currants pushed into a ball of raw pastry – and, suddenly, I know how I can stop her. 'As you like,' I say to her. 'But remember, Lillie. Everyone gets what they deserve in the end. Everyone.' Lillie makes a noise at the back of her throat, like a disgruntled dog, then turns on her heels back to her room.

I laugh bitterly. I will make her regret this. Somehow, I will make her pay for her spitefulness. I know I cannot hide my burned stays from Mama, but I will not give Lillie the pleasure of tattling. I will teach that piece of poison a lesson she will never forget.

I climb into bed and try to clear my mind of all thoughts, except one. I lay my head on the pillow and close my eyes. I concentrate as hard as I can on my next wish. I imagine Lillie's pale, pinched face, her eyes gleaming with delight as she rushes to Mama's room to tell of my terrible sin. I imagine Lillie opening her mean little mouth and finding to her horror that there is no sound to come out of it. I imagine her voice, shrivelled to a black lump, rolling off her tongue and falling to the floor. I wish and I wish as hard as I can, and as I fall asleep, all that is in my head is a picture of Lillie with her mouth, empty of words, gaping wide like a goldfish.

Six

Temperance Angel woke from a fitful sleep. As she came to her senses, the terrible feeling of having been snubbed descended upon her again. As she thought of Lady Egerton, her throat filled with bitter bile and her temples ached. She had banged her fists so many times on her dressing table the night before, that she had grazed her knuckles and Jane had had to bathe them with salted water. She glanced at them now. They looked hideous. She would have to wear gloves for the foreseeable future.

Temperance never knew that disappointment could be so crippling. It was as though she had lost control of everything. Her vision of what should have been had come to nothing. And she couldn't bear it. She tried to reassure herself. Lady Egerton had been badly injured, so of course she could not have kept her appointment. It hadn't been a deliberate snub. But no matter how Temperance thought of it, and broken ankle or not, the result was the same. Without the gilded presence of Lady Egerton in her drawing room, Temperance would not be accepted into the tight inner circle of Bridgwater's finest ladies. Her delicate features tightened into a sour grimace. She would not be beaten, she decided. She would allow herself this one slip only. She shook herself slightly, like an injured bird fluffing its feathers, and set her mind on the day ahead.

Alice, she suddenly remembered. The girl had been left to her own devices all night. She was bound to have stepped out of line. But even if she hadn't, Temperance could always find an excuse to vent her wrath. It would take her mind off Lady Egerton at least. Temperance was slightly cheered by this notion, and she reached out to pull the bell for Jane.

Down in the kitchens, Lillie's mind was doing somersaults. She couldn't wait to see the mistress and spill the beans on what had happened last night. Alice Angel was a strange one all right, but there was a part of Lillie that could not help admiring her. It was as though she really didn't care about anything. Taking off her stays was bad enough, but what Lillie had seen in the grate late last night had set her heart pounding with a mixture of fear, awe and excitement.

Alice had still been asleep when Lillie had gone into her room first thing – curled up like a cat and snoring gently. Lillie had drawn the curtains back, but when that had not woken the girl, Lillie had decided to leave her be while she went to the kitchens to fetch warm water for the girl's morning toilet. As soon as she was done with her duties, she'd go and find the mistress. Lillie could barely contain herself. Being the bearer of terrible news filled Lillie with a delicious self-importance and she held her head high, ignoring the other servants in the kitchens as she filled the water jug and snatched at a piece of bread to eat on her way back upstairs. The bread was fresh from the oven and still steaming gently as Lillie popped it in her mouth and began to climb the stairs. Then two things happened at once. First, the knot in Lillie's apron strings slipped, causing her apron to drop to the floor where it caught on her right foot just as she was lifting it to climb another stair, and second, she flicked out her tongue to lick a stray breadcrumb from the side of her mouth. Before Lillie had time to close her mouth she had crashed onto the sixth step up and landed heavily on her chin. The jug of water flew from her hands and smashed into pieces on the hall floor below. But worse, as her chin hit the stair, the force of the fall clamped her teeth shut onto her protruding tongue and she bit the end of it clean off.

Seven

I am torn from sleep by the most dreadful screams. I sit bolt upright. The walls of my room tremble with the sounds of running feet and shouts and the banging of doors. I jump from my bed and rush to the door. 'Fetch the doctor!' someone shouts. As I reach the landing I see the stairs are crowded with servants. The screams have stopped, and instead there is a loud keening noise, like nothing I have ever heard before. I think of wild animals and of a kitchen cat we once had that made a similar sound before it gave birth to six dead kittens. But this is worse. I want to put my fingers in my ears to silence it. Suddenly I think of Mama and how she didn't come to my room last night. Something terrible has happened to her, I am sure of it. My first feeling is one of relief. Now perhaps she will never have to know that I burned my stays.

Then Eli is standing next to me, hastily belting up his dressing gown. 'What has happened, Alice?' he asks me quickly.

'I . . . I don't know,' I stammer. 'I think, Mama. Maybe?'

Eli pushes past me and begins to take charge of the chaos. 'Move out of the way. Let me see,' he orders. The clamour quietens and the servants step back to make room for Eli. There is a moment of silence.

'It's all right, Alice,' he shouts back up to me. 'It is not Mama. It is only Lillie.'

Disappointment clutches at my stomach briefly. I peer over the banisters and the first thing I see is blood. It is smeared all over a kitchen maid's apron and hands and is splotched onto the pale rose-covered paper that runs up the stairwell wall. Lillie is slumped against the wall and a blood-soaked cloth is being held to her mouth by another servant.

'What has she done?' asks Eli. 'Do we really need to call for a doctor?'

'She's bit her tongue off, sir,' says the servant with the cloth. 'Look. Here it is.' She opens her hand and I see what looks like a small piece of red meat resting in her palm. Eli recoils and starts walking back up the stairs towards me.

'Get her into a bed,' he says. 'And yes, indeed, please call Dr Danby.' His face has paled. 'Don't look, Alice,' he tells me as he reaches the landing. 'Go back to your room and let them deal with it.'

But I cannot move. I hold on to the banisters and I cannot tear my eyes away as Lillie is helped to her feet by the grave-faced servants and led away, her moans echoing down the hall.

'Alice!' hisses Eli. 'Don't be so ghoulish. Come on.'

He doesn't understand.

I don't understand.

I made this happen.

My wish came true.

I turn from the stairs and start to walk slowly back to my room. I am dreaming all of this, surely?

44

The floor feels soft beneath my feet, and the walls on either side of me are closing in. I think that if I were to touch them, they would give beneath my fingers, like melted wax. My bedchamber is at the end of the corridor, but it seems much further away. My belly is rolling around inside and I have to move faster, although it is hard to lift my feet. My belly forces its way up into my throat and suddenly I am in my room and vomiting into the bowl on my washstand. Now I know I am not dreaming. I see again the small piece of meat in the maid's hand and I shiver.

I wanted Lillie silenced. But not like this.

As I catch my breath and reach for a towel to wipe my mouth, I hear a small noise. A quiet, shifting, stirring sound. I lift my head from the bowl and my throat tightens as I see Mama. She is standing by the fireplace. She has the poker in her hand and is swirling it around in the ashes. Every now and then it clinks on the charred steel bones of my stays. She has her back to me, but I can see by the movement of her shoulder blades – sharp as elbows through the thin silk of her robe – that she is breathing deeply. 'How dare you,' she says quietly, her voice quivering slightly. I retch into the bowl again.

'Unforgivable.' Her voice comes closer. I look over the rim of the bowl. She is standing next to me and I see the poker still clenched in her hand. It has left a trail of soot on the pale pastel of her morning robe. 'One night,' she says, in a voice so calm it makes the base of my skull prickle. 'For one night I leave you. And look what you do.' She aims the poker under my chin and slowly forces me to lift my head from the bowl. 'I was quite convinced it was *your* screams I heard just now,'

45

she says. 'It is the sort of thing I have come to expect from you. But no. Jane told me it was Lillie. A foolish accident, I believe?'

She slides the poker out from under my chin, and instead of leaning to the bowl again, I get to my feet and dare myself to look her in the eyes. The green of her irises is a little too bright and the narrow furrow between her brows twitches a heartbeat. I think it is best I keep quiet for now.

She strolls back towards the fireplace. 'I was pleasantly surprised to find it was not you shrieking like some vile creature,' she says. 'But then I come to your room, and what do I find? That you have spent an unremarkable night sleeping? That although I was remiss in not coming to check on you last night, all would be in order? All would be well?' She places the poker back in its companion set and wipes some imaginary soot from her hands. 'How foolish of me to think that.' She sighs heavily. 'Not only did you defy me by removing your stays, but you saw fit to burn them.

'It is my fault,' she says, still so strangely composed. 'I should never have listened to your father. He said you would change as you grew older. That you would calm down, and become more biddable.' Mama laughs, but it is forced and hard. 'I should have done what needed doing years ago.'

She turns to the window and stands looking out, with her hands clasped neatly over her belly. The butter-soft light of the morning catches in the pale down on her cheeks. I wait for her to say more. To explain what she means. *What* needs to be done?

In the silence that follows, I think of Lillie again. There was so much blood. I never wished for blood. Will she bleed to death?

Then Mama clears her throat. 'Such a beautiful day,' she murmurs to herself.

I don't know why this bothers me, but it does. It bothers me that Mama can make even a beautiful day sound so wrong and sinister.

My throat is tight and bitter with the aftertaste of vomit. I want to ring for Lillie to bring me tea. I want her to clear the mess I have made and bring me warm water so I can wash the staleness and fear from my skin. I want Mama to leave now, to tell me what my punishment is and to leave. But I know, even as I think all this, that none of it will be.

Nothing will ever be as it was.

Suddenly, Mama turns from the window and fixes me with a determined glare. 'I believe I heard that Dr Danby has been called?'

'Yes,' I say quietly. 'To attend to Lillie.'

'Good,' she says. 'Then I shall have him come to attend to you afterwards.'

'But I am not ill,' I say. I glance down at the froth of vomit in the bowl. 'It was only the shock of seeing Lillie. And the blood. I am recovered now. There is no need to bother the doctor on my account.'

'Oh, but it is not on your account, Alice. It is for my sake he will attend you.' She smooths back a wisp of hair from her forehead. 'You will stay in your room from now on. It would not be safe to have you running loose in the house.' She flicks her gaze around my room. 'There will be no more fires in here and, of course, no candles.' She looks back at me and shudders slightly as her eyes fall on the washstand bowl.

47

'I will send a maid up. You will wash, and ready yourself for the doctor.'

'But there is no need for the doctor, truly, Mama. Why do I need a doctor?' A thread of fear is stitching my insides tight. I had expected anger, coldness and the usual blank disappointment. But a doctor?

'Do not question me, Alice!' she says through clenched teeth. Her composure disappears and she is now the Mama I know best. 'You are always questioning, questioning, questioning.' Spots of dangerous red have marked her pale cheeks. She grips her robe tight at her throat and sweeps from the room, slamming the door behind her. I hear the thunk of the key in the lock, and my heart drops like a stone into my empty belly. My sentence has been passed, but I have no idea what my punishment will be.

I sit on my bed and wait. There is nothing else to do. My head is a muddle of thoughts that I cannot untangle. I think of Lady Egerton and her broken ankle and Lillie and her severed tongue. But the edges of my thoughts are tinged red with Lillie's blood. I want Papa to come back from Bristol and make everything better. And I want Eli. He has always cushioned me from Mama's wrath. But where is he? Why has he not come to me? When I was little, he would always come; as sure as the long-case clock in the hall chimed each hour, Eli would find a way to offer me small comforts.

I remember a summer long ago when I was confined to my room for some misdemeanour that I cannot now recall. But I remember how I longed for the outside world, for the feel of the sun on my skin and for the scent of grass and roses and the taste of fresh air. Eli would sneak into my room and bring the outside to me. He brought me feathers, soft downy ones, which I imagined the garden sparrows had shaken from their tails. He brought me polished pebbles, 'jewels for a lady,' he would say, and once he brought me a rose head in full bloom that I pressed between the pages of my Bible. Even after the petals had dried and crumbled to dust, I could still smell the sweetness of that rose whenever Mama instructed me to read the scriptures.

I have heard the long-case clock strike twice now. Eli is not coming this time.

Eventually, my door is unlocked and a young maid with red-rimmed eyes and a plain face scuttles into the room carrying a large jug and bowl. 'Water for you, miss,' she says shyly.

I look at her closely. I am not certain I have seen her before. But maybe it is just that she has never been upstairs. 'Can you tell me how Lillie is?' I ask, as she covers the soiled bowl with a cloth and replaces it with the new bowl and jug of water.

The girl looks at me and her eyes fill with tears. 'Oh, miss,' she says, sniffing loudly, 'the news ain't good. She's gone 'alf mad with the pain she has. And the blood . . . she won't stop bleeding. They say . . . they say Lillie might bleed to death.' On the word *death*, her voice rises to a wail and the tears she has been trying to control come tumbling down her face.

'I . . . I am sure she will not die. I am sure she will be fine,' is all I can think to say to her.

'I hope so, miss,' says the girl. 'Doctor says she's to be taken away. There's nothing more can be done for her here.' She takes up her apron and messily wipes her face. 'Sorry, miss, sorry,' she says. 'Must be terrible for you, miss. Her being your lady's maid an' all.'

'Yes,' I manage to say. 'Yes, it is terrible.' The girl stands there, twisting her apron around in her hands. 'Is everyone so upset?' I ask. A dreadful guilt is pressing hard on my chest. 'Was she well liked downstairs?'

'She weren't, miss, I'm sorry to say. She had a wicked tongue on her – oh.' The girl realises what she has said and she clasps her hand to her mouth as though she can stuff the words back in.

I smile at her and nod gently, to tell her it's all right. I don't mind.

The girl clears her throat. 'Like I said, miss, she weren't well liked – nasty piece she was, beg your pardon – but biting off her tongue! You wouldn't wish that on your worst enemy, would you?'

I don't answer. How can I? I rub at the goose pimples on my arm. I am cold all of a sudden and sick to the stomach again. *It wasn't my fault. I didn't mean Lillie any harm.* There's another voice, nagging behind my temples. *You did this, Alice*, it says. *You wished Lillie to be silenced. You did this, Alice, and you meant it to be.* 'You can go now,' I tell the girl. 'I should like to get dressed and I can manage well enough by myself.'

The girl sniffs loudly, then takes up the bowl of vomit and leaves, locking the door behind her.

I don't want to think any more.

I pin my hair up and strip naked. The water the girl brought is cold on the washcloth. I quickly wipe and rinse my skin and I'm surprised at how good the sharpness of the water is. I splash my face several times and gradually my skin begins to feel tight and clean and the layer of night sweat and the slick of fear that covered me are washed away. I dress loosely in chemise, drawers, petticoat and a plain gown. I examine myself in the mirror and think I look well enough. The absence of stays has not harmed my posture.

I sit at my desk and take up my journal. I tidy the edges of the pages that I tore last night and I put pen to paper. I write nothing of any sense; only words that are in my head and I want out of it.

Blood and tongue and silence

Mama and cold and hatred

Eli and envy and anger

The words pour onto the paper and I have filled a whole page when I hear the key in the lock again. This time it is Mama and Dr Danby. They stand in the doorway and Mama says something in the doctor's ear and directs her gaze towards the fireplace. The doctor looks and nods gravely, then pats Mama reassuringly on the shoulder. 'Now then, Alice,' he says. 'I hear you have been quite unwell?' He walks towards me. There is a shock of blood on his collar.

'You have been misinformed,' I tell him. 'I am quite well, thank you. But tell me, how is Lillie?'

'She is being taken care of,' he says. 'Now would you mind coming to the bed so I can examine you?'

I don't move.

'But how serious is her condition?' I ask. 'Will she recover?'

The doctor sighs. 'That I cannot tell you. She has been taken to Bristol. To the infirmary. She will be in good hands.'

I point to the blood on his collar. 'Is that hers? Is that Lillie's blood?'

'Alice!' hisses Mama. 'You see, doctor? She is like this all the time. I can do nothing with her.'

'Perhaps, Mrs Angel,' says Dr Danby, 'it would be better if you stepped out of the room while I examine Alice. And perhaps you should take a glass of claret to calm your nerves. You have had a most trying morning.' He takes Mama by the arm and guides her out of the door. 'There,' he says, as the door closes and there are only the two of us left in the room. 'Perhaps we will get on better now.'

'Perhaps it is Mama who needs your services, not me?' I suggest.

Dr Danby frowns. He has a lot of eyebrow, so much that his eyes are almost invisible under the tangle of black and granite. 'I think that is for me to decide,' he says brusquely, and proceeds to take a selection of gleaming instruments from his battered leather bag. He lays them in a neat row on my bedside table 'Now, please. Come and lie on the bed.'

I feel myself shrivelling inside. I don't want this man to prod me with the tools of his trade. I don't want him anywhere near me. 'Dr Danby,' I say. 'There is nothing wrong with me. I've never felt better. I do not need you to examine me.'

The doctor raises his eyebrows – as much as he can – and picks up something that looks to me like a small trumpet. He runs his fingers over the glossy brass surface. 'I would suggest your refusal to cooperate is a symptom of your condition.'

There is a button come loose on his frock coat, a black thread dangling. I think if he puffs his chest out any further, the button will pop off altogether. I fix my gaze on the button. I look at how polished it is and how it is crimped around the edges like a pie crust. Dr Danby prowls around my room tapping the small trumpet in the palm of his hand. I glance over at the other objects laid out on the table: scissors, knives, long silver needles, and small brown bottles with faded labels. I am filled with a squirming horror.

'Now, Alice,' says Dr Danby. 'You have been menstruating for over a year, your mother tells me. Are you regular with your bleeds?'

I feel my face flush hot. *What business is it of his?*

'Alice,' he prompts. 'Did you hear me?'

'I heard you,' I say. 'But I do not care to answer you.'

Dr Danby sighs heavily and puts the small trumpet away in his bag. Then he takes out a notebook, and reaches into the inside pocket of his coat for a pencil. He turns a page in the notebook and slips out the tip of a fat, livery tongue to lick the end of the pencil. My belly heaves again. I turn from him and stare instead at the words I have written in my journal. They are just black lines and flicks and curls of ink now. Dr Danby scratches in his notebook, grunting now and then with the effort. 'What about the fire, Alice? Will you talk to me about that?' he says. 'Why did you burn your stays?'

He is impatient now. I can tell by the way he spits his words out. He wants to get home, I think, to his wife who will fetch him a fresh, clean collar and a cool drink for him to sip in his study while he smokes on his pipe. I am not one of his submissive patients. He will get nothing out of me. I pick up my pen and dip it into the ink pot. I let a drop of ink fall from the nib onto a clean page of my journal. I idly put the pen nib into the centre of the blot and pull it into spider legs.

'Are you writing down your answers, Alice? asks Dr Danby. 'Would you rather write them than speak to me?'

Why is he still here, when he can see I have no need of him? I press my pen hard onto the page; so hard that the nib snaps off. Clean off, like Lillie's tongue. I am furious that my pen has broken and that this maddening man is still in my room. I turn to him suddenly and the pen leaves my hand and flies across the room. 'Get out!' I shriek. 'Leave me alone!'

The pen hits the doctor high on his chest. He blinks, startled. I hold my breath. His collar is splattered with ink now, as well as blood. A drop of ink has found its way onto his weathered cheek, and it is sliding down slowly, like a dark tear. He wipes his hand across his cheek and the ink smears into the loose crepe of his face. He looks at his hand, then back at me. I see the knot of veins at his temple throbbing angrily through the thin stretch of skin.

'Your mother was right to call upon my services,' he says, gathering his instruments and putting them back in his bag. 'You are indeed a disturbed young lady.' He throws me a look of pity, takes up his bag and leaves the room.

I let out a breath and go to retrieve my broken pen from the floor. I hope this is the last I will see of Dr Danby, but something in my bones tells me otherwise. I hold the pen in my hand and a stain of ink spreads across my palm. I squeeze my hand shut and when I open it again, the ink has altered and I am disturbed to see instead the face of a strange man, with a full beard and piercing eyes. I wipe my hand quickly on the skirts of my gown. With all that has happened, I think, my imagination is playing tricks on me.

It is then that I hear low voices outside my door. I press my ear against the wood and listen closely.

Eight

Temperance paced the corridor outside Alice's room, waiting for the doctor to emerge. It had been the most trying of mornings. Everything she had strived so hard for seemed to be slipping away. Her usual tight rein on matters had loosened and been replaced by mess, anguish and inconvenience. Of all the staff to suffer such an unspeakable accident, why did it have to be Lillie? The one servant that Lady Egerton had particularly recommended and the only servant she was ever likely to ask after. Temperance felt as though she had been entrusted with a beloved pet and had failed utterly in her duty to care for it. And as for Alice – Temperance closed her eyes and took a few slow breaths – the girl had surpassed herself in wickedness. It was insufferable. No mother could be expected to raise a child like that.

She thought again of the terrible moment she had seen the burned stays in Alice's fireplace. It had taken all her strength to resist the urge to strike Alice with the poker – straight across her disobedient face. Temperance shuddered at the memory. She was glad Arthur was away on business. He was too protective of Alice, and too fond of making excuses for her behaviour: she was high-spirited, she was unusually intelligent for a girl, she needed more to occupy her mind. He was soft on her, and Temperance had let it go on for far too long.

The door of Alice's bedroom opened and Temperance gathered her features into a semblance of motherly concern.

'It is not good news, I'm afraid,' said Dr Danby, as he closed the door behind him and turned the key.

'Oh,' said Temperance, and she put her hand to her throat in what she hoped was a suitable response. She felt her heart fluttering excitedly beneath the silk of her morning robe. 'What happened in there?' she asked. 'What has happened to your face?'

'Your daughter attacked me.' Dr Danby brought his fingers to his face and touched his ink-stained cheek. 'In an unprovoked violent outburst.'

Temperance caught her breath. This was better than she could ever have wished for. This was solid proof that Alice was quite out of control. And it had all been witnessed by a respected medical man. Arthur's arguments would mean nothing now. 'This is most dreadful, doctor,' she whispered. 'What can be done with her?'

'You need to prepare yourself for the worst,' he said. 'It is my opinion that Alice is suffering from a disease of the nerves. She is displaying all the classic symptoms of hysteria. A refusal to cooperate or conform to the expectations of society, a tendency to cause trouble, a melancholic demeanour and, of course, the violent outbursts – the burning of her stays and the attack on me.' He paused for breath. 'If she were a little older,' he continued, 'I would suggest you find her a husband. The married state is often the best cure for cases such as this. But as it is . . .' He tailed off.

'But what, doctor?' asked Temperance. 'What is the answer then?'

Dr Danby cleared his throat. 'Would you rather discuss this elsewhere? It is a delicate matter.'

Temperance shook her head. 'No, doctor. Please continue.' She knew what he was going to suggest, and she didn't want to wait another minute to hear it.

'Well,' he said. 'There is a place in Bristol. Brislington House. It is a private lunatic asylum. Most discreet. And is run by a Dr Fox.'

'You can secure a place for Alice there?' asked Temperance, trying to keep the elation from her voice.

'I can certainly have a word with Dr Fox. I have recommended other patients to him in the past.'

'And do you believe he can cure Alice?' asked Temperance. 'Will she ever behave as she should?'

'Well, obviously every patient is different.' Dr Danby lowered his voice as a maid hurried by with an armful of linen. 'Some take to treatment better than others,' he continued. 'But I must tell you, to allay any fears you may have, that Dr Fox does not practise the traditional methods of treating the insane.'

'And what are the traditional methods of treating the insane?' Temperance felt vaguely insulted. 'I have had no previous experience in these matters.'

'No, no . . . of course you haven't,' Dr Danby stuttered. 'What I mean to say is that rather than using mechanical restraints, for example, or bleeding, purging and forced vomiting, Dr Fox uses much gentler methods on his inmates. What he practises is known as moral therapy.'

'I have no interest in what it is called,' said Temperance firmly. 'Only that my daughter will be cured of her . . . her madness, and that she will cease to be an embarrassment to me.'

'I have high hopes that she can be cured,' said Dr Danby. 'Dr Fox has an excellent record. He runs his asylum like a well-ordered household. He believes a patient's sanity can be restored through self-discipline and a strict regime of punishment and reward.'

Temperance nodded impatiently. 'Yes, yes. But how soon can you arrange for her committal?'

'I will make some initial enquiries today,' said the doctor. 'But I presume you will wish to wait for your husband's return to discuss the matter with him?'

'Make your enquiries, please, Doctor. And rest assured that my husband will be in total agreement with your diagnosis and my decision. In matters concerning our children, he trusts me implicitly.' Temperance held out her hand. 'Now, I bid you a good morning and I hope to hear from you soon, regarding all necessary arrangements.'

Temperance hurried back to her room. She felt light on her feet and wonderfully refreshed. If the doctor was true to his word, Alice could be out of the house by the morning. Arthur would be incensed, of course. But she would deal with him when he came home. She would make him see that sending Alice away was for her own good and, more importantly, would help protect the family reputation.

She sat at her dressing table and studied her face in the mirror. Admiring her near perfect features was one of Temperance's greatest pleasures. She was ageing well, and was still by far the most attractive woman in her circle. But she was overly critical, and as she stared at her pale skin, she could not help noticing the faint trace of lines that had recently appeared around her eyes and at the corners of her mouth. She frowned. It was all Alice's fault. All the trouble and worry that girl caused was bound to leave its mark.

Temperance reached for her toilet chest and opened the polished walnut lid. Inside, the chest was lined with dark green velvet and nestled into various pockets were numerous silver-topped glass bottles and pots, a small pair of silver scissors and a pair of mother-of-pearl tweezers. Her little box of magic, she thought guiltily. It was much frowned upon for any lady of good standing to embellish her face with cosmetics. It was a vulgar practice, only indulged in by vile creatures who sold themselves on the streets and the painted ladies of the stage. But Temperance was shrewd, and excelled in the subtle application of certain ingredients that enhanced her beauty and disguised any signs of ageing. Her beauty had, after all, served her well so far, and deserved to be protected.

Hidden in the toilet chest, amongst bottles of respectable medicinal treatments, were Temperance's pots of wonder, and in particular, her precious pot of Crème Celeste – obtained from a discreet chemist in Bristol. She unscrewed the lid, and in a moment her blemishes and small lines disappeared under a coat of the waxy paste as she smoothed it deftly over her face. The paste smelled pleasantly of sweet almonds and rosewater, and the scent relaxed Temperance as she moved through her daily routine: a touch of carmine to her cheeks, a slick of beeswax to her lips and a drop of lemon juice in each eye. She felt calm, her balance of mind restored, and as her face bloomed back at her from the mirror, her mind filled with thoughts and plans. Once Alice was out of the way, she would be able to concentrate fully on the smooth running of the household and her work with the Bridgwater Ladies' Committee. She would let it be known that Alice had been sent to relatives in the north, and as for Lillie . . . well, even if the girl survived she could not come back to Lions House. There would not be a position for her once Alice had gone, and besides, a mute servant was of no use to anyone.

Temperance plucked a stray hair from her brow. She would organise an arrangement of flowers to be sent over to Lady Egerton, the most elaborate that money could buy. The situation could be salvaged. After all, her Ladyship could hardly blame Temperance for Lillie's accident when she herself had succumbed to misfortune. Temperance smiled into the mirror. A last dusting of ground pearl powder to her cheeks and a dab of lavender behind each ear, then she would ring for Jane to come and dress her.

Nine

I pace my room. From the window to my bed and back again. From my dressing table to the door, to the end wall and back to the window again. Mama cannot mean it. She cannot mean to have me sent to an asylum. The word fills me with horror. It is where the mad are sent: wretches with no minds of their own. It is the sort of place that people only speak of in a whisper. *The madhouse.* I shake my head. Am I dreaming this whole morning? If I am, it is a nightmare. I pinch my arm hard.

But I heard them outside my door. Mama and Dr Danby. Although muffled, I heard it all. I heard the doctor call me mad and I heard Mama, only too eager to have me sent away. Even though I know it is still locked, I pull and turn the door handle. Someone must come to me soon. To explain it all away. To tell me what I heard was a mistake. I bang on the door with my fists. 'Eli!' I shout. 'Eli! Eli!'

But no one comes.

What have I done to deserve this? Nothing, I think. Nothing, but to be myself.

I pace some more, but my legs are weak now. They tremble, and my head feels light. It is only hunger, I tell myself. It is not a symptom of madness. Even so, I walk to the bed and lie down, curling myself into a ball. I close my eyes and I think back to when I was small and how I used to curl like this into Papa's lap when Mama allowed me and Eli down from the nursery. She would scold me for running across the drawing room and jumping into Papa's arms. 'Alice! Walk. Do not run!' I would bury myself in his lap and fold up into the smallest ball I could, thinking that if I could not see Mama, then she could not see me. But I could always hear her. As Papa stroked my hair and rocked me gently on his knee, Mama would spoil every moment of it. 'You indulge her too much, Arthur,' she would say. 'It will do her no good in the long run.'

Eli would sit quietly with his hands folded neatly on his lap. 'And what have you been reading today?' Mama would ask him.

'I have been looking at the atlas,' Eli would reply. 'I know where Africa is now.'

I remember Mama clapping her hands in delight. 'See, Arthur? See how clever our little boy is?' I would wait, trembling, in Papa's lap, knowing it was my turn next. I pushed my face deep into the tired tobacco musk of his waistcoat, until my breath was moist on my hot cheeks. 'Alice! Get down from there.' There would be Mama's accusing voice. 'She is not a dog, Arthur. Please do not treat her like one.'

Then Papa's legs would shift and he would sit forward and grip me around the waist. 'Come on, Alice. Enough now. Do as your mother says.'

But I wouldn't let go. I never wanted to let go. And Papa would have to stand up and peel my small hands from their grip on his jacket. When he finally managed to set me on the floor, I was so angry with Mama that when she asked me, 'So, Alice. Tell me what you have learned today,' I would screw my face up tight and refuse to speak a word.

'You see, Arthur?' Mama's shrill words would follow me out of the room when the nanny came to usher me away. 'You see how you've spoiled her? She is like a little wild animal!'

A noise outside my room pulls me sharply away from my memories. I look around, hoping to see Eli's face appear as the door opens. But it is just the maid again, from earlier. This time she is carrying a tray which she sets down on my bedside table. She looks at me warily, then turns to go.

'Wait!' I say. She stops. But her hand reaches for the doorknob, and she lets it rest there. 'What is your name?' I ask her.

'Sarah, miss,' she says. 'Me name's Sarah.'

I sit up and swing my legs off the bed. I see Sarah's hand tighten its hold on the doorknob. She looks to be the same age as me – sixteen or so – but her plain face still has the touch of a child to it, despite the tired circles under her eyes. 'Do not look so frightened,' I tell her. 'I only want to know if you have seen Master Eli today.'

'Oh no, miss.' She shakes her head. 'I only normally works in the kitchens. First time I've done upstairs duties is today.'

'Well then,' I say. 'Do you think you could do the kindest of favours and take a message to him from me?

Her eyes widen. 'Don't think I could, miss. I wouldn't know how.'

'It's simple, Sarah,' I tell her. 'I will write a note and all you have to do is take it to his room. It is the fourth door on the right, down the corridor.'

64

She shakes her head again, vigorously. 'I couldn't, miss. Sorry, miss. But I'm to go straight back to the kitchens. Got me orders, you see.'

'But it would only take you a moment. Look, I'll write the note now.' I fly across to my desk and tear a page out of my journal. I pick up my pen and, too late, I remember it is broken. 'Sarah . . .' I turn to her. 'You will have to *tell* Eli my message instead.'

But Sarah has already opened the door. She looks close to tears. 'I'm sorry, miss,' she says. 'I can't do it. The mistress would have me guts for garters if I'm caught, I have to go.' With that she leaves the room, and once again I hear the key turn in the lock.

A blade of fear slices through my insides.

I swallow hard. Eli won't allow anything to happen to me. He won't allow Mama to send me away. He won't, will he? And besides . . .

I am not mad.

I am not mad.

I am not mad.

I chant the words over and over to myself. And as I do, I see Lady Egerton again, tumbling down the stairs, and I see Lillie's gaping mouth, empty of words but full of blood. I did those things. I wished for those things to happen. And like a miracle, those wishes came true. For a brief moment, I forget my fear and am filled instead with a wonderful sense of power, as though the sun is caressing my bones from the inside. But the feeling is only fleeting. Soon, the dread is back, and I have to stand and walk again. I follow the same path as earlier: from the window to the bed and back again, from

65

the dressing table to the door to the end wall and back to the window again. Nothing will happen until Papa comes home, I tell myself. Papa would never let Mama send me away. I am not mad. Papa knows that I am not mad.

I see the tray that Sarah left on my bedside table. I lift the white linen cloth and there is the usual cup of beef tea and bowl of watery gruel that Mama sees fit to punish me with. I spoon out a small amount and put it to my lips. It tastes of nothing. It is invalid food. I spit the gruel back into the bowl and throw myself on the bed.

Then the tears come, taking me by surprise. A torrent of them, bubbling up from some place deep inside me that I never knew I had. They keep coming, robbing me of my breath and soaking my pillows. I cannot stop. I cry until my throat hurts and my tongue grows thick in my mouth. I cry until my head pounds and my stomach turns inside out. Then a shaft of sunlight creeps from the window and slides across my legs, covering me like a warm blanket. And gradually, with great shuddering gulps, I fall into an exhausted sleep.

Grey light filters through my eyelids. How long have I been sleeping? I ease one eye open, but it aches so much that I have to close it again. For a brief, blissful moment, my mind is empty of thought. But then I try to open my eyes again and I feel my face tight with salt and suddenly everything comes rushing back and my mouth turns dry.

Where am I? I look around wildly, staring into the gloom. Strange shapes loom in the shadows. There are bars at the window. I sit up and my breaths turn to gasps.

It is too late. They have taken me while I was sleeping. My heart batters against my ribs as the horror of it all dawns on me. I am locked in a cell. In the *madhouse*.

I push back against the headboard, my knees drawn up to my chest. *Oh God!* Mama did it. She finally got rid of me. And she didn't even wait for Papa to come home.

I press harder against the headboard, praying the solid oak will stop me from falling down the dark hole that has opened beneath me. As I struggle to make sense of my surroundings, I suddenly hear a sound in the distance, a familiar sound, a sound I have heard every day of my life. I half laugh, half sob with relief as I count the long-case clock down in the hall strike eleven times. I look around the room again, and the strange shapes rising up from the gloom room reveal themselves to be my wardrobe, my washstand, my desk, my dressing table and chair, and the bars at the window to be simply the folds in the curtains.

My hand shakes as I reach out to my bedside table and feel for the cup of beef tea. It is cold, and a film of grease coats my teeth as I swallow it hurriedly. The liquid swirls nastily in my stomach, but it is nourishment, at least. After a while, when my nerves have calmed and my stomach has settled, I climb from the bed and pull the chamber pot from underneath. A pungent smell catches at my nostrils and tells me that no one has been to empty it since I relieved myself earlier. I squat over the pot, knowing that I will have to bear the indignity of its contents for the rest of the night. Someone will surely come to attend to me in the morning. When I have finished, I walk over to the window. There is no means of lighting a candle, but the moon is high and silver and I can see the empty street below my window almost as clearly as if it were daylight. There is a yellow gaslight spluttering at the end of the street, but other than that, there is no other movement.

I am gripped by a sudden and horrible sense of loneliness. Is there no one in this world that I can turn to? Is there no one in this world who understands me? Only Papa, I think, but he is not here. Eli has abandoned me and as for Mama, she has never wanted me from the moment I was born. I am not the daughter she wanted. But how can I be someone else? How can I be anyone other than me? I lean my forehead against the glass. Would it help if I opened the window and screamed for help? Would anyone answer me? And if they did, would they too think I was mad?

I have already slept for so long that when I eventually return to my bed, all I can do is lie there and count the hourly strikes of the clock, and watch how the grey light darkens to thickness in the dead of the night, and how it gradually pales again as dawn approaches and another day begins.

Ten

It is early morning. The clock has only just struck six. I am restless, hungry and longing for someone – even if it just Sarah – to come and open my door. My mouth is watering at the thought of toast and a pot of hot tea. Will I be permitted to breakfast downstairs? I could see Eli then, and tell him what I overheard between Mama and Dr Danby. But even as I pretend to myself and imagine that things could go on as before, there is a much bigger part of me that knows with a hard and cold certainty that nothing will ever be the same again.

I climb out of bed and stretch. I look down and realise I have slept in my gown. I have never done that before. This small thing somehow helps. It is as though there are no rules any more; and that from now on, anything is possible.

Time passes slowly. Hunger grinds at my insides and boredom weighs heavy on my shoulders. If I shouted and banged and kicked at the door, surely someone would come. *You could wish for someone to come. You could wish for someone to come*, a voice in my head tries to persuade me. I shake it away. I dare not wish for anything, not after what happened to Lillie.

I walk to the window. It is going to be another beautiful day. A day when, if I wasn't me but somebody else altogether, I could sit in the garden at the back of the house with a parasol to shade me from the sun when it grew too hot. There would be a jug of lemonade by my side, with chips of ice inside it, bobbing and sliding between stray lemon pips. Ice – all the way from the mountain lakes of Norway – that Papa paid the ice-man to deliver in a block, every day. There would be cucumber sandwiches too, cool slivers of cucumber, salty butter and wafer-thin bread. Eli would come and sit next to me and we would read to one another or play backgammon. I would beat him, of course, and he would feign disappointment before smiling chivalrously and chasing me across the lawns.

But I am not somebody else. I am only me.

I start from my daydream. There is a cab rumbling down the street. It is a black, plain affair, much like the one Dr Danby uses. My heart catches in my throat as I watch it draw nearer and nearer. I close my eyes, praying that when I open them again, the cab will have passed by, taking its early-morning travellers to a destination that is anywhere but here. But it is not to be. I do not need to open my eyes to hear the cab jangle to a halt outside the house. Who would call at this hour of the day? My heart pounds in the back of my throat. It can only be Dr Danby.

He has come to deliver the news of my fate.

I open my eyes and watch as the driver steadies the horses. Then the cab door opens, but instead of Dr Danby's thatch of salt and pepper hair, it is the thinning flaxen hair of Papa's valet, William, that emerges. How can that be? I must be seeing things. Then, as William holds the cab door open, the familiar and solid shape of Papa climbs down the cab steps and alights on the pavement. Before I can stop myself I am banging on the window until the glass rattles in its frame and I am shouting, 'Papa! Papa!'

He rubs at the back of his neck wearily, then looks up at me and raises his hand in greeting. Papa is home! And I did not even have to wish it. Before I can grasp the full marvel of it all, the bedroom door opens and I turn to see Mama, and Sarah, struggling under the weight of a laden tray, following close on her heels. Mama looks stern, her lips set in a tight line. As she crosses the threshold, her nose wrinkles in disgust. She takes a handkerchief from her sleeve and puts it to her face. Then she gestures to Sarah. 'Open the window, girl. Air this room and get it cleaned up.'

Sarah begins to bustle around the room. I am glad to see her remove the soiled chamber pot from under my bed. I look back at Mama. She is staring at me as though I am a stranger. 'And you,' she says. 'You are a disgrace. You will wash and change your gown immediately. Illness is no excuse for uncleanliness.'

'I am not ill, Mama.' I hate the whine in my voice. 'Why do you insist on saying that I am?'

Mama raises her eyebrow in a small, triumphant arch. 'But it is not only me who says you are ill, Alice. If you remember, you were examined by Dr Danby only yesterday. It is his opinion that you are ill. And we cannot argue with a doctor, can we?'

I cannot bear that she looks so pleased with herself. So I walk over to where she is standing and cross my arms over my chest as I look her straight in the face. 'And you would have me put in a madhouse, wouldn't you? I say.

Surprise, then annoyance, flash across her face. But only for an instant. She licks a shine of moisture across her bottom lip, and her face settles back into its usual perfect blankness. 'Sarah!' she barks. 'Please leave us now.'

Sarah scuttles out of the door, her face flushed red.

Mama glares at me. 'Do not talk of such things in front of the servants!' She crosses her arms over her bosom too. 'If Dr Danby recommends that you are sent away to be cured, then that is what will happen.'

I want to shake her. I want to take her by the shoulders and rattle her so hard that her teeth knock together and her eyes jump in their sockets and her tightly coiled hair comes loose and hangs in trembling tatters around her face. I want to shake her until her beautiful, hard shell cracks and the pieces smash to the floor and all that is left behind is a soft and ordinary woman who will put her arms around me and love me like a mama should. But I won't do that. Not because I don't dare to. But because I am scared that if I do crack her shell, I will find there is nothing inside but a hollow space.

And then what would I do?

'Papa won't allow it!' I scream at her. 'He will never let you send me away!'

She smiles at me pityingly. 'But your father is not here, Alice. And therefore the decision falls to me.'

'But . . .' I quickly glance back to the window. *Does she not know he has returned?* A smile slides across my face. Now it is my turn to be triumphant. Before she can stop me, I push past Mama and rush out of the door. I hear her gasp as she stumbles against the door frame, but by then I am at the top of the stairs and I am flying down, taking two steps at a time and calling out 'Papa! Papa!' As I turn the last curve of the staircase, there he is, standing in the hall, pulling his gloves off, finger by finger.

'Alice?' Papa has no time to brace himself, before I fling myself at him and wrap my arms tight around his waist.

'What a greeting! But do let me take my coat off first.' The reassuring tone of his voice soothes me like a cooling ointment on a cut. I cling to the firm comfort of him and for a moment I am lost for words.

'Arthur! You are home unexpectedly. You should have sent word and I would have had the servants prepare for your arrival.'

I turn my head and there is Mama gliding down the staircase towards us. She has her eyes fixed upon me. 'Papa, Papa,' I whisper urgently into his shoulder. 'She wants to send me away. She wants to send me to the madhouse. Please don't let her. Please!'

Papa pulls my arms from around his waist and studies my face. His brow wrinkles in concern. 'Calm down, Alice. Why are you so excitable? What do you mean you are being sent away? Temperance, what is the child talking about?'

Mama is beside me now; the cloying scent of her lavender hangs between us. She takes my wrist and squeezes it tight. 'Alice needs to go back to her room,' she says. She tries to tug me away. 'Come on, Alice. I have to talk to your father.'

'No!' I slap her hand from me and grab Papa's arm. 'Please, Papa. Don't listen to her. She wants me in the madhouse.' Papa looks at me, his eyes wide and puzzled. Then he looks back at Mama.

'Take her to her room, Arthur. You can see she is hysterical. Please take her now, and then I will explain everything to you.'

73

'Yes . . . yes,' murmurs Papa. 'I think that is a good idea.' He puts his arm around my shoulders and takes one of my hands gently in his. 'Come on, my darling girl,' he says. 'Let's get you upstairs and comfortable, then we will see what the problem is.'

'I told you!' I hiss. 'She wants rid of me.'

He presses his hand into my back and I lean into him, suddenly exhausted, as he leads me up the staircase and back into my room. 'Now,' Papa says as he settles me on the bed. 'I will have some tea sent up to you, and you will stay here and calm yourself, while I go downstairs to talk to Mama.'

'Don't leave me, Papa.'

Now he is here, I cannot bear for him to go. I hold tight to his hand. Panic grips at my heart and sets it racing. 'She will tell you things that are not true. She hates me, Papa, she hates me!'

'Oh, Alice,' Papa kisses me gently on the top of my head. 'You know that is not true.' He sighs deeply. 'Let me go now.' He eases his hand away from mine. 'And please don't worry yourself. I will sort out this problem, whatever it is.'

'Promise me, Papa?'

'I promise,' he says. He smiles at me, and because he looks so sincere and because of the way his eyes crease so kindly around the edges, my heart steadies and I allow myself to believe him.

Eleven

Arthur Angel listened patiently as his wife recounted the events of the last two days. He watched as her white, tapered hands gestured and pressed to her breast. He gazed at the green of her eyes as they flashed hard then grew soft with tears. He was always amazed that, whenever he came back to her after being away for any length of time, her beauty had the power to shock him all over again.

He had been glad to cut short his business trip when he had been taken ill on the first night. A piece of rotten meat, no doubt. His stomach had always been sensitive. He was glad to come home because, in truth, it was where he wanted to be the most; as near to Temperance as he could be, and with his children as solid evidence of her love for him.

But his surprise homecoming had not been as he had imagined. As he listened to Temperance tell him of Dr Danby's visit a great sadness twisted at his heart and brought beads of sweat to his forehead. His darling girl was severely disturbed, that much was clear; he had seen it for himself. And Temperance, normally so calm and collected, was at her wits' end.

But an asylum? It was such a gruesome word. One he had

always associated with pitiable unfortunates or the lowest of criminals. How could he agree to send poor, sweet Alice to a place like that?

He could not deny that Alice needed help. For some reason, her temperament was not as it should be. He had been soft on her. He knew that. As a young child, her wild spirits had amused him, but he had always assumed she would grow out of it. That she would settle down and embrace her position in life. But it had not happened. She had attacked the doctor, for God's sake! Arthur reached for his handkerchief to mop at his face. He did not feel as steady as he should. The illness that had afflicted him the other night had obviously not left his system. He would call for William, to bring one of his brandy tonics.

'Arthur? Are you listening to me?' Temperance slapped her hand lightly on the polished oak of his desk.

'Of course I am, my dear.' Arthur adjusted himself in his chair. He did not feel comfortable at all. He took a deep breath and turned his attention back to Temperance. As he let his eyes travel from his wife's pearly pink lips, down the length of her white throat and into the soft shadows of her bosom, she told him about a place in Bristol – 'a *private* asylum, Arthur,' – that promised to offer a cure for Alice's affliction. 'No one need know,' she impressed upon him. 'And if we don't act now . . .' She left the sentence unfinished and Arthur felt the weight of responsibility fall upon his shoulders.

Could he truly send his only daughter to a lunatic asylum? Could he send her to a place where she would have to endure all manner of unmentionable treatments? Arthur pinched the top of his nose and rubbed his hands over his face. But what was the alternative? To lock her in her bedchamber, or hide her away in the furthest corner of the attic – Arthur grimaced – and watch her grow worse every day? His hands felt clammy, and he wiped his handkerchief across his palms. 'There must be something else we can do,' Arthur said hopefully. 'A second opinion at least. Or we could send her to Bath, to take the waters.'

He knew his feeble suggestions had fallen on deaf ears when he saw a pink flush spread across, and mar, the perfect creaminess of Temperance's décolletage. 'If you do not agree to this, Arthur, I shall never speak to you again.'

Arthur knew then that he really had no choice in the matter.

Twelve

I cannot believe what I have just heard. I wish I had stayed in my chamber now, instead of sneaking down to listen outside Papa's study door. Eavesdroppers never hear any good of themselves.

If I had stayed in my chamber, I could have remained ignorant and carried on pretending – for a while at least – that Papa might protect me. But he didn't even try. I want to hate him, but I can't. All my hate belongs to Mama. It is easy to hate Mama. It is a straightforward feeling with clean, sharp edges, all neatly packed in a box. But I can't hate Papa, not even now. What I feel for him is muddled and cluttered and it spills out of me in an untidy mess. I do know I am ashamed of him though, because the thought of what he has done makes my toes curl and my face burn hot. He has betrayed me. He has made it as clear as polished glass that Mama comes first every time.

I want to fling the door open and spit my venom at them both, but isn't that what a madwoman would do? I won't give Mama the satisfaction. I learned a long time ago how to harden my face and my feelings against her. But Papa . . .

I always thought that when it really counted, he would step in to save me. He has only ever done it once, but I have held onto that all these years, thinking and praying that he would do the same again when the time came.

I was only five. It was a cold winter and snow had fallen thickly onto the back lawns. It weighed down the branches of trees and sat in small drifts at the base of each windowpane. It had fallen onto the street at the front of the house too, but had soon turned brown and sludgy under the wheels of carriages and the hurried footsteps of well-wrapped pedestrians. I had never seen snow before and as I pressed my nose against the chill of the nursery window, I wanted nothing more than to run outside and touch this strange white stuff that had iced my world so prettily. But Mama had forbidden me to go outdoors.

'Only fools and thieves go out in this weather,' she said.

I knew that wasn't true because I had seen the gentlemen in their thick overcoats going about their business and the servants were still in and out all day, the hems of their frocks flapping wetly around their ankles. So I waited until Mama was busy with her household books and I slipped the catch on the double doors in the library and stepped out into the dazzle of the gardens.

My boots crunched into the whiteness and I was amazed at how soft it was and how deep my boots sank into it. I bent down and touched it with my fingers. It was cold, but my fingers burned. I took some more steps, then I stopped and looked behind at the trail of footprints I had left. I was dismayed to see that I had ruined it all. I had spoilt something that had been so perfect. I didn't know how I was going to fix it, but

79

before I could even try, there was a shout from the house and I turned to see Mama standing at the library doors. Her face was quivering with anger. At first I thought it was because I had made all those footprints in the snow and that it was as bad as if I'd walked mud across one of the expensive rugs in the drawing room. But it wasn't that at all.

I had disobeyed her and gone outside.

She made me take off my boots and my stockings then she shut the library doors in my face and locked them. I was out there for hours. Eli came to look at me once. He pressed his face against the library window and his breath frosted the glass. He waved at me sadly before he turned to go, leaving a small hole of clear glass where his nose had been.

I stood where Mama had left me. I didn't dare to move in case I messed up more of the snow. But I was so cold. Too cold to even shiver. After a while I stopped caring about messing up the snow and I lay down in the softness of it and tried to pretend it was a pile of warm blankets and that it was all right for me to go to sleep.

That is how Papa found me. Half asleep and half frozen in the back garden. He picked me up and carried me indoors, and I cried bitterly when the hot flames from the fire brought the feeling back to my toes and feet.

'Never do that again,' he said to Mama in a strange, tight voice, as he wrapped a blanket around my shoulders.

'She had to learn a lesson,' Mama had said. 'I was just about to fetch her in, in any case.' She left the room without saying another word and Papa held me to him for a while.

'I am sorry, Alice,' he said.

I thought then that he was saying sorry for what Mama had done to me, shutting me out in the snow to half freeze to death. But I know better now. I understand what he really meant. He was saying sorry for loving her better than me.

A hand on my shoulder startles me. 'You shouldn't be listening at doors, Alice,' whispers Eli.

I turn to face him. 'And what of it?' I whisper back. 'Have they told you what they are planning to do to me?'

Before he can answer, there is a shift of noise from inside the study and Mama's voice moves closer. I don't want her to find me here, so I push past Eli and run back upstairs to my chamber. But I don't miss the guilt that flashes across Eli's face, like a rat running for cover.

Thirteen

Arthur spent the rest of the day in his study. He felt too guilty and too unwell to see Alice again. How could he face her, knowing what he was condemning her to? He ate a light lunch at his desk and spent a pleasant hour with Eli, going through the mill accounts. The boy was bright and Arthur was confident that before too long, Eli would prove to be an asset to the business. They didn't talk about Alice, although the unspoken words hung in the air between them and made them squirm uneasily in their chairs.

As the day came to a close, Arthur felt a great weariness descend upon him. He drained his glass of brandy and took up a candle to light his way to bed. William had turned his sheets down and laid his nightgown out. There was a small fire burning in the grate, warm water on his washstand and a fresh glass of brandy beside the bed. It was good to be home. It would be better still if Temperance was lying in the bed waiting for him, her auburn hair spread across the pillows like a carpet of autumn leaves. Maybe when all the trouble with Alice was resolved, Temperance would be more generous with her affections. Arthur could only hope.

He climbed into bed and settled himself against the feather pillows. As he reached for his glass of brandy – a final tot before sleep – he felt a weight press upon his chest. A weight so heavy, he thought, it could have been the great roller at the mill and he could have been a solitary grain of wheat being crushed and ground into flour. The glass of brandy dropped from his hand and smashed onto the floor. It was the first thing that William saw when he went to try and wake Arthur Angel the following morning.

Fourteen

Something has changed. As soon as I open my eyes, I can sense it. An emptiness. A blankness. As though this new day is the first page in a book full of clean, white pages. It is not an unpleasant feeling and I lie in my bed and soak it up as I watch the morning light steal through the gap in the curtains. I don't want to move. I don't want to break the spell. I want to stay here forever so that nothing will ever happen and the pages of the book will never have to get written upon.

After a while, I realise there is a strange quietness too. I have not heard the usual sounds of the day beginning.

'I am Alice Angel,' I say out loud, to reassure myself that I have not been struck deaf.

I hear my voice quite clearly inside my head and outside too. So I begin to wonder then, why the house is so quiet. Even though I do not want to wonder or think about anything. But it is too late now, I can feel the spell begin to break. Bit by bit the cracks appear. They spread like tentacles across the surface of the day. Then, like a broken mirror, the spell shatters into splinters of glass and comes crashing down around me.

Fear and despair creep through me, as stealthily as the sun

sneaks across the wooden floor of my chamber. Will today be the day that I get taken away? Will it be Dr Danby who comes for me? Or will it be rotten-toothed men, snarling like dogs, who rattle through my door with clinking chains to fasten my limbs together and with knives to hack off my hair? I torture myself, imagining dark, damp cells crawling with cockroaches and infested with lice. I imagine filth-caked women with long, yellow fingernails and breath that reeks of dead things. And I imagine a long oak table covered in white linen that is laid out with gleaming scissors, knives, scalpels, metal hooks – all the hideous tools I saw in Dr Danby's leather bag, and more besides. Soon, I will be laid out on the table too, and a faceless doctor with ice-cold hands will plunge each gleaming tool into my soft flesh and I will be helpless to resist.

I shake my head, in a bid to fling these terrible notions from my mind. But they refuse to leave. They cling on tightly, inside my head. And soon they are joined – by the one thing I have been trying my hardest not to think about. And my heart is crushed and twisted once more when I remember how easily Papa agreed to send me away.

I am scared. So scared. I am not good enough as I am. That much is clear. Mama, Eli and now even Papa think I am not the person I should be. So I have to be sent away. I have to be cured of being me.

I hear noises now. Doors opening. Doors closing. Feet on stairs. They are coming for me. I wrap my arms around the bedpost and hold on tight. I will not make it easy for them. My heart is kicking furiously in my chest and throat and ears. All I can think of is this moment and what I can do to get rid of the fear. So despite what happened to Lady Egerton and Lillie, I close my eyes tight and I wish and I wish with all my heart and soul that something, *anything*, will happen to prevent me from being sent away.

I keep my eyes closed as I hear my chamber door opening. The floorboards creak as someone enters. I tighten my grip on the bedpost and ready myself for rough hands to rip me away. But nothing happens. Instead I hear shaking breaths and a familiar voice speaks my name. I open my eyes and there is Eli, in his nightgown with his hair still tousled by sleep, standing in the doorway. His eyes are swollen and red, and tears are pouring down his face. 'Alice,' he says again, and half chokes on the word. I am surprised that he has come to say goodbye. But he isn't trying to help me, so I hate him too.

'Go away,' I tell him. 'I don't want to see you.' It hurts me to say that when I love him so much. But he has not been the brother he should have, and I want him to know that he has failed me.

'No, Alice,' says Eli. 'You need to listen.' He comes closer and reaches out a hand to me. I shrug it away. Eli takes a deep breath. 'It's Papa, Alice,' he says. 'It's Papa. He . . . he's dead.'

I stare at Eli. Why is he being so cruel? Saying such things?

He wipes at his eyes with the back of his hand. 'Alice?'

I blink. 'What . . . what are you telling me, Eli?'

'William has just found Papa in his bed. And he has gone, Alice. He is dead.' Then he turns, and after taking a minute to set his shoulders square, he leaves my bedchamber.

Everything is still. Even my heart, it seems, has stopped beating.

Then the long-case clock begins to strike. One. Two. Three. Four. Five. Six. Seven times. Eli has left the door ajar.

Papa's bedchamber is next to Mama's, a few doors away from mine. I walk along the corridor. Daylight never reaches this part of the house when all the doors are closed. There are usually lighted candles in the sconces on the wall, but this morning there are none. So the corridor is a hazy grey tunnel, the floor cold on my bare feet and the air as stale as morning breath. I push at Papa's door. Inside, his chamber is full of shadows; the curtains shut tight as sleeping eyelids. A single candle burns on the dresser. The flame trembles.

They are all in here. There is Mama, sitting beside the bed. Her head is bowed and her hair swings loose across her lace-dressed bosom. Her long white hand rests on the eiderdown. Eli is standing behind her. His face is pale and his shoulders are twitching. William is standing to one side with his hands clasped neatly behind his back.

And there is Papa. His head is resting on a pillow, his greying hair brushed back from his forehead. There is a linen handkerchief folded under his chin, the ends fastened in a knot at the top of his head to keep his jaw fastened shut. The candlelight plays on his skin, which shines damp, although his worry lines have softened and he looks as well as I have ever seen him. I would swear he was sleeping, if it were not for the two silver coins balanced on his eyelids.

I walk to the bed, the opposite side to Mama, and I stand in silence and stare down at Papa. The eiderdown is stretched tightly across his chest. I watch carefully. There is no movement. His arms have been placed on top of the eiderdown and they lie peacefully by his sides. I look at the lace cuffs of his nightgown. One has ridden up and the grey hairs on his wrists spill untidily from underneath. His gold rings seem too big for his fingers now. His hands are yellow and withered and I notice the nail on the little finger of his left hand is torn at one corner.

My eyes flick to his face: to his mouth, which is partially hidden by the brittle growth of his moustache and his beard. His lips are cracked and dry and there is a white stickiness at the corners of his mouth. As I study the yellowing edges of his moustache, I realise with a twist of my heart that Papa will never smoke another cigar. He will never lick his lips moist again, nor trim his beard. He will never taste another morsel of food nor utter another word of comfort to me. I reach my hand out to straighten the cuff of his nightgown.

'Don't touch him!'

I snatch my hand away and hold it to me as though it has been burned. Mama is glaring at me. 'He is not to be touched,' she says again, but calmer this time. She tucks a lock of hair behind her ear. Then she leans over Papa and kisses his forehead. Her lips linger there and for the first time in my life, I see how Mama loves him. My heart twists tighter. I thought he was only mine to love. Mama has always had Eli, and I have always had Papa. To see her kiss him like that rips at my insides. I turn away and push the heels of my hands into my eyes to stop the hot tears that are spilling down my face.

'Now,' says Mama. 'There is much to be done.'

I turn back and she is on her feet. Her face is composed, though full of purpose. She sweeps from the room and William follows close behind, like a lost dog looking for a new master.

It is just Eli and me now.

'What happened?' I whisper.

He shakes his head.

'I cannot believe he is gone, Eli.'

'I know,' he whispers back.

We stand there, either side of Papa, not knowing what to say, while Papa lies on his deathbed listening to our silent grief.

Eventually Eli moves. He comes to my side and puts his arm around my shoulder. He turns and leads me out of Papa's chamber. 'I think the doctor is here,' he says. 'I will talk to him. I am the man of the house now.'

I stop, and feel the blood drain from my face. 'He has come for me, hasn't he?' I say.

Eli glances at me and frowns. 'He has come to see Papa,' he says.

'He has not come to take me to the asylum then?' I whisper, hardly daring to believe.

'Alice.' Eli's voice is full of disappointment. 'How can you think of yourself at a time like this?' He lets his arm slip from my shoulder. 'I am sure Mama has much more important things to consider now.' He looks at me hard. 'And I hope *you* will start to consider Mama now and curb your behaviour. It is not going to be easy without . . . Papa.' He stumbles on the final word, then turns from me and heads to his chamber. I turn towards my chamber too. I am shaking now and my head is spinning with a terrible realisation.

I sit in my chair by the window and grip onto the arms. I dig my fingers hard into the chintz fabric. It is not the shock of Papa's death that has knocked me off my feet. It is something much worse. I swallow the howl that rises to my throat. Then, with unsteady legs, I stand and walk to the mirror and stare at the girl who looks back at me. Her face is pasty and greasy as pig's lard. It looks all the worse framed as it is by ropes of dark, unkempt hair. But it is her eyes that frighten me the most. They are black and glittering and wild. Like the eyes of a madwoman. Like the eyes of a murderer.

'You did it, didn't you?' I say to the creature in the mirror. 'You murdered Papa.' The girl's lips move in time to my words. 'You wished this to happen,' I say. 'You wished for something, for anything to happen, so you would not be sent to the asylum.' The girl in the mirror widens her eyes. 'Don't look so surprised,' I tell her. 'What did you expect?'

She looks back at me at steadily, with her bold accusing eyes. But she doesn't answer. So I take the poker from by the fireplace and I smash it into her face, until she shatters to the floor in a hundred pieces.

Fifteen

Mama has taken to mourning with a passion. I think perhaps she was born to be a widow. The word slips over her head and fits her as neatly and as perfectly as the most costly gown in her wardrobe.

By midday, she has had every mirror in the house covered in black crepe. The pendulum has been removed from the long-case clock in the hall and the time has been stopped at six, the nearest hour to Papa's passing. She has instructed that every window in the entire household is to be covered. Not a chink of natural light is to penetrate Lions House. She has banished the sunshine until further notice.

I slip through the house unseen. No one has bothered to lock my door. No one seems to remember I exist. Everyone is too busy dealing with the business of death.

The dressmaker comes and Mama orders a selection of modestly cut gowns made in the finest of black silks. She also chooses a dozen black veils of intricate lace and a selection of exquisite mourning jewellery fashioned from the finest quality jet. She sends William to purchase a sheaf of writing paper, edged in thick black, with matching envelopes. I watch through

91

the door as she sits with a straight back at her desk in the parlour, scratching with a pen across one sheet of paper and then another. The notes are sent from the house to all those of any importance in Bridgwater, to inform them of Papa's death.

Eli will not come out of his room. I have knocked a few times, but all he will say is, 'Go away, Alice,' in a weary old man's voice. I wander down to the kitchens. No one notices me there either. It is all hustle and bustle. Cook is rolling out a rich, yellow slab of pastry on the kitchen table. Some other girl is polishing crystal glasses. And another is drawing hot water from the copper and setting aside clean rags. It is as though nothing terrible has happened at all. The only difference between now and before is that all the servants are wearing black armbands.

It is my fault, I think. *He is only dead because of me.*

I stand with my back to a wall and watch all the comings and goings. The smell of hot fruit – gooseberries perhaps – drifts towards me. But instead of making my mouth water, the green sweetness makes my stomach lurch. I think I will never eat again.

Sarah scurries into the kitchen. She bobs quickly when she sees me standing there. Then she hurries over to the kitchen fire and fills a bowl with water from the large kettle and picks up a pile of washcloths and clean rags. *For the laying out*, I think I hear her say to Cook. *Missus has asked me to help.* She passes by me again on her way out, but now her face is rigid with concentration and she doesn't acknowledge me again. I follow her through the house and up the stairs. She walks carefully, steadying the bowl of water in her hands. The bundles of cloths are thrust under her armpit. It is only when we reach Papa's bedchamber that I understand what she is about to do.

'Are you coming in, miss?' she asks.

I shake my head. 'I can't,' I whisper.

She tuts in sympathy then nods at the door. 'Would you mind opening it for me, miss?'

I do as she asks and she slips past me and into Papa's chamber. The smells of lavender and burning wax coil out of the room. And another smell too: the warm comfort of Papa's tobacco. I find that I cannot close the door on it. So I leave it open, but just a snatch, and I stand still and watch.

I see Mama first. She is hovering at the foot of Papa's bed. Then I see William. He is stripping Papa of his nightgown from under the modest covering of a sheet. He pulls the nightgown over Papa's head and hands it to Sarah. I watch, with my heart sliding around in my chest, as William then packs freshly laundered rags into Papa's mouth and deep into his nostrils. I let out a breath. Then Mama ushers Sarah to the bed. She brings with her the bowl of water and bundle of washcloths.

Sarah wets one of the cloths and wrings out the excess water. Then she reaches under the sheet and begins to wash Papa's body. She washes him from his neck down to his feet and not once does she baulk at her task. She might as well be wiping down a table. I can't help but wonder what it must be like to touch Papa now. Is he still warm? Or is his body already cold and stiff like the pig carcasses I sometimes see hanging outside the butchers on Friarn Street? I shiver in disgust, but I can't help feel a pang of envy that Sarah is able to be so close to him.

William brings a set of clothes over to the bed and with Sarah's help he dresses Papa for the final time. Between them, they put Papa in a white shirt with a high, starched collar and then they bend his arms into a low-cut embroidered vest. They pull a pair of tapered woollen trousers onto Papa's useless legs and then they button him into a matching frock coat with velvet lapels. Finally, William ties a black cravat softly at Papa's throat and tucks Papa's gold pocket watch into his vest.

I swallow hard. Papa looks so handsome now. Except his hair is ruffled from where William and Sarah moved him. I want to go and smooth it back. It is the least I can do for him. I push at the door gently. It whines at the hinges. Mama whips her head around and she fixes me with a glare. *I haven't forgotten about you*, she says, without even opening her mouth. Then, as though she has read my mind, she walks to Papa's side and smoothes his hair flat again.

Sixteen

Sarah comes to help me clear the mess of broken mirror from my floor. I tell her it was an accident and she says to never mind, miss. All the mirrors are covered anyway. And she hangs a piece of black cloth over the empty frame. I am to dress now, she tells me, for the photographic artist, Mr Gibbs, is on his way and I will need to look my best. I ask her if she has had much practice arranging hair, and she tells me that as she used to plait the mane of her father's horse in readiness for the springtime fair, she's sure she could manage.

Sarah helps me into a green shot-silk gown. You will do very well in this one, miss, she tells me, until your mourning gowns arrive. She brushes my hair to a shine and with a simple twist, she pins it to the back of my head. 'There,' she says. 'I think you are ready.'

I walk through the house towards the front parlour. Everywhere there are candles burning and whispers hanging in the shadows. I walk by the long-case clock and it is strange to see it so still. The door to Papa's study is ajar. I catch a whiff of brandy and smoke and it stops me in my tracks. I cannot resist pushing the door open to see if Papa is there, sitting in his chair with his papers before him and his brow furrowed in concentration. But of course his chair is empty. I drift into the room and run my hand across the pile of papers on his desk. I hold it there for a while, imagining Papa's hands shuffling through the pages only hours since. There is an empty glass on the desk too. I pick it up and hold it close to my face. I see the trace of sticky lip prints on the rim. Papa's lips. I press my mouth to the glass. A last kiss. But I feel no comfort. I place the glass back on the desk, and as I leave the room I whisper, *I'm sorry, Papa. I am sorry for my wickedness. I never meant for you to die.*

I hear noises and voices coming from behind the door to the front parlour. I do not want to go in. I cannot face them all. I stand outside, hesitating, one hand on the doorknob. I want to go back to my room. I want to go back in time, to before any of this happened. If I could, I would be a small child again and I would try to be who they wanted me to be from the very beginning. Then maybe Papa would still be here. But I can't go back in time. I know that. The very best I can do is to change. I have to be the person they want me to be now. That other person, the other me, is no good. She hurts people. She made Papa die by wishful thinking.

I take a deep breath and close my hand around the doorknob. But before I have the chance to turn it, the door is pulled open from inside. I jump back. It is Eli. Relief crosses his face when he sees me. 'I was just coming for you,' he says. 'We have been waiting. Mr Gibbs is ready for us.'

I swallow hard. 'I am ready, too, Eli,' I say.

The light in the front parlour blinds me for a moment. The room is ablaze. There are candles on every surface and an oil lamp burning in the centre of the table. I peer into the light and I see a bespectacled man standing in front of me. He is fiddling with a large contraption, a box on long spindly legs. 'This is Mr Gibbs, Alice.' Eli introduces me. I nod to the man. There are beads of perspiration dancing on his forehead. 'Ah, good,' he says. 'We are all here then?' He gestures for us to move to the other side of the room.

I see Mama at once. She is standing stiffly with a black half-veil shading her face. And then I see Papa and I start to tremble. He is sitting in a high-backed chair with a large bowl of gaudy roses on a table at his side. The light of the candles shine harshly onto his face and his skin is grey and stretched. I stop and look to Eli. 'Go on, Alice,' he says. 'It is all right.' But Papa's eyes are wide open and he is staring at me. Eli gently pushes me forward. As I move closer, Papa's eyes look stranger still, like the eyes of the china doll that sits upstairs on a shelf in the old nursery.

Mr Gibbs begins to fuss around us. He arranges Mama so she is standing behind Papa's chair, then he directs Eli and me to stand either side of Papa with our hands placed upon his shoulders. 'Yes, yes. That's good. That's good.' I am squashed next to the bowl of roses. But even the thick sweetness of them, combined with Mama's powdery lavender scent, cannot disguise the stench of old bacon that is rising from Papa. My hand sits on his shoulder, my fingertips trembling against the velvet of his lapel. Mr Gibbs adjusts Mama's skirts. He suggests that Eli puts his free hand in his trouser pocket, and he asks me to move an inch closer to Papa. 'Perfect,' he says. He returns to his box and bends down to peer through it. 'Now,' he says.

97

'I would ask that you all remain perfectly still until I tell you otherwise. Exposure will take about ten minutes.'

And so we stand, this little family of ours, while Mr Gibbs captures our likeness forever.

It is hot in the room. My skin is prickling in the heat and I can feel Mama's quick, shallow breaths on the back of my neck. Mr Gibbs is humming quietly. He checks his pocket watch and nods encouragingly at us. 'A moment more, if you please,' he says. Under my bodice, a bead of sweat rolls slowly down between my breasts. Suddenly, a weight falls onto my arm and my hand slips from Papa's shoulder. I look in horror to see that Papa's head has rolled from its position and is hanging awkwardly over the side of the chair. I move away and in my haste I knock into the table and send the bowl of roses crashing to the floor. Mama yelps, Mr Gibbs rushes forwards and in that moment I see why Papa's eyes look so strange. His eyelids are closed, but someone has fashioned upon them, in paint, the crude likeness of an open eye. It is this, as much as anything, that sends me fleeing from the room.

I dash out into the hallway, desperate for air. But it is, of course, all shadows and dark corners. Where can I go? Every room in the house is smothered and in gloom. The whole place is like a tomb. I look to the great double doors at the end of the hall, the ones that lead outside. I know I shouldn't, I know it is the bad Alice that wants to go outside. But I have no choice. If I don't leave this house now, I think I might die too.

I tug the door open and step out into the remains of the day. I walk down the steps, through the iron gates and out onto the pavement. The evening air is soft and warm and I swallow great mouthfuls of it. It has been so long since I have tasted fresh air, I am dizzy with the pleasure of it. I look around and see the street is empty. I should go back inside. My head tells me *that* is the right thing to do. But the thought of the darkness and the scent of roses and lavender, mingled with the stink of Papa and the heaviness of my guilt, is too much to bear. I find myself walking away from Lions House, listening to my boots slapping the ground. I come to the end of the street and I walk faster. A cab passes me on the road, sending up clouds of dust in its wake. The thick plod of horse hooves echo in my ears. Further on and there is a pair of gentlemen, strolling along deep in conversation. Then there is a girl carrying a basket of wilted flowers. She is scuffing her feet along the pavement as though she has nowhere in particular to go. As I walk on, the streets grow busier. I pass an alehouse. A group of factory workers lean casually against the walls, their caps on the floor and pots of beer in their hands. There is colour everywhere now. In the bonnets and gowns of scurrying women and in the fruits and fancy goods piled up outside the shops.

I stop and listen to all the noises: the hum of voices, the rumble of wheels, the clatter of crates and doors. I turn this way and that, seeing everything, soaking it up, feeling the aliveness of it all. A trail of people walk by and turn the corner towards the town square. More follow, and before I know it, I am carried along with them, curious as to where they are all going.

In the far corner of the square there is a tight knot of people. There are all types: gentlemen in top hats, dour women in plain dress, merchants, hawkers, flower girls and a smattering of painted ladies. I hover on the fringes of the crowd and watch how each person finds their own spot, then stands still and listens. There is a voice coming from deep within the crowd, from someone that I cannot see. But everyone is listening intently, so I move closer so that I can hear too.

'THE DAY OF JUDGEMENT IS ALMOST UPON US! THE LAMB OF GOD WILL WALK AMONGST YOU AND THE FAITHFUL WILL CLEANSE THEIR SOULS OF ALL EVIL!'

The voice is rich and powerful. I push my way forward, trying to catch a glimpse of who the voice belongs to. The crowd parts easily. Some are muttering under their breath and are already breaking away. There is a gap at the front, and I position myself between a young woman whose pale face is covered in a riot of freckles, and an older woman who has her hands clasped tightly to her bosom. I look to the speaker and am surprised by what I see. Instead of the grey, papery preacher I was expecting, there is a tall, broad man with hair and a beard as black as mourning crepe. His hair is swept back from his forehead and falls in ringlets past his shoulders. He is standing on a wooden crate and has his arms spread wide as though trying to embrace the whole of the crowd before him.

'ON THE DAY OF WRATH ALL PROPERTY AND RICHES WILL BE AS DIRT!'

He is dressed simply in a dark frock coat and I am taken aback to see that his feet are bare. Suddenly, he stops talking and he sweeps us all with his eyes. They are as blue as any eyes I have ever seen and are framed by long, black lashes.

'WHO OF YOU HERE CAN SAY YOUR SOULS ARE TRULY CLEAN?'

The woman next to me whimpers.

'My soles ain't clean!' shouts a voice from the crowd. 'I just trod in horse shit!' Laughter ripples through the air and the crowd thins out some more as the laughter eventually drifts away.

The man on the crate just smiles. 'What those unbelievers do not know,' he says to the few of us left, 'is that I am the Beloved Lamb of God.'

The woman next to me cannot contain herself. She steps forward, bends to her knees and kisses his feet. He speaks again, as though he hasn't noticed her.

'RECEIVE ME AS THE SON OF GOD AND YOUR FLESH WILL BE LIBERATED FROM SIN IN THIS WORLD!'

I cannot tear my eyes from his face: he is so earnest. And although I do not understand much of what he is saying, there is something true and comforting in his expression. He seems not to care what the dwindling crowd thinks of him. He is happy to be who he is.

The girl with the freckles puts her hand on my arm and turns to me. 'He is wonderful, is he not?' she says, her eyes shining with tears.

I nod, unsure of what to say. 'Who . . . who is he?' I brave.

She raises her eyebrows in surprise. 'It is him!' she says. 'Our Beloved.'

I am none the wiser, so I try again. 'I am sorry,' I say. 'But I have not seen him before. Tell me, what is his name?'

'Henry Prince,' she says dreamily. 'Our Beloved Lamb of God.'

The hairs on the back of my neck begin to prickle. I turn and see that this Henry Prince is looking straight at me. He gathers me up in the blue of his eyes and he holds me there while he says softly, 'Are you for saving, little lamb?'

I cannot speak. He is staring at me so keenly I fear he can see right inside my soul, that he can see the badness inside me. My face flushes hot and I look down to my feet. Then he begins to speak again.

'COME WITH ME AND I WILL SHOW YOU PARADISE ON EARTH!'

I turn swiftly and walk away, back across the square. I feel his eyes following me and I quicken my pace. It is not until I round the corner, to where he cannot see me any more, that I begin to breathe easy again. He has shaken me, and I do not know why.

The sun is orange and heavy in the sky. It is later than I thought. I hurry along the dusty pavements, nervous now, that I have been missed. An aproned butcher, unhooking the last pig carcass from outside his shop, turns to look at me. A tightly buttoned-up woman, pushing a squeaking perambulator, stares at me for longer than is comfortable. I realise I must look out of place. A girl out on her own, wearing neither bonnet nor shawl, is a cause for gossip.

It is not far now; I can see Lions House in the distance. My heart sinks as I see Eli too, standing outside the gate looking up and down the street. I slow my feet. I am in trouble again, and all for the want of fresh air. Eli raises his hand and comes hurrying to meet me. 'Alice! Where have you been? We have been worried about you.' His pale face looks tired and drawn and his eyes have lost their shine. Poor Eli, I think. He has the weight of the world upon him. I am glad to see him and I forgive him, as I always do. After all, I have no one else but him now.

'I am sorry,' I say. 'I did not mean to go. But that room, Eli. And . . . and Papa. I just needed some air.'

'It's all right, Alice,' he says. 'I did the same. Only I escaped to the gardens.' He smiles at me and reaches for my hand. I take it gratefully and we walk back into the house together.

'So. Mama. Is she very angry with me?' I ask.

He squeezes my hand. 'She is none the wiser,' he says. 'She is only glad that that the photograph was saved. Mr Gibbs has assured her of that.'

We stop in the hallway and look at each other. 'So where did you go?' he asks.

I hesitate. I think of Henry Prince and the blue depths of his eyes and how he called me a little lamb. 'Nowhere,' I say. 'I just wandered the streets for a while.'

He frowns at me. 'You are a funny thing, Alice. The streets are no place for a young lady, you know that, don't you?' He sighs. 'Just promise you will tell me next time you need to go out. I will be happy to walk you round the gardens.'

I nod. 'I'm sorry, Eli,' I say. 'I promise.'

He bends to kiss me. 'You and I,' he says, 'we must look after Mama now.'

As he turns to leave, I reach out a hand to stop him. 'Eli,' I say. 'Am I a bad person?'

He laughs, as though I have asked an amusing question. 'No, Alice. You are not a bad person,' he says. 'You have just not found your place in the world yet.'

I drop my hand, but as he walks away I know that he is wrong. I am a bad person. I am wicked. I am a lamb that needs saving. And all of it is of my doing: Lady Egerton's broken ankle, Lillie's terrible accident and especially, *especially* Papa.

Seventeen

The day of Arthur Angel's funeral dawned the hottest in living memory. By nine in the morning, the whole of Bridgwater was withering. Dogs lay sulking in the shade of doorways, the pavements hummed with heat and handkerchiefs were damp with the sweat of brows. The two mutes who had been standing outside the front door of Lions House since daybreak were melting in their heavy black cloaks. They consoled themselves by thinking of the jugs of ale that would soon be theirs after they had pocketed a few shillings for their morning's work.

An enormous hearse, topped with plumes of ostrich feathers, waited on the pavement below. The six horses, with their black flanks shining like glass, stood with their heads bowed. Other carriages, at least ten of them, stretched out in a long line behind. Suddenly, the front door opened and the two mutes moved aside as the ornate oak coffin containing Arthur was carried down the steps and loaded into the hearse. The mutes followed behind and joined the dozen other hired mourners, pallbearers and pages that stood waiting either side of the hearse. Then there was silence, save for the steady whisper of horse breath and the odd scrape of hoof on stone.

Temperance Angel emerged from Lions House into the glare of the day and, like an actress taking to the stage, she surveyed the waiting world with a mixture of apprehension and exhilaration. She was gratified to see such a turnout. She spotted Lady Egerton's carriage at once, and although she knew it was empty – Lady Egerton still being too unwell to attend – it swelled Temperance's heart with vanity to see that her Ladyship had at least sent her carriage as a mark of respect.

The funeral entourage stood still, waiting for Temperance's cue. Not a feather fluttered in the dead air. Then Eli and Alice stepped out of the house, and Eli offered his mother his arm. Temperance slipped her black-gloved hand through the crook of his elbow and with her other hand, she flicked open a large, black, ruffled fan. They both walked slowly down the steps, leaving Alice to descend on her own, trying hard not to tread on the hem of her mother's voluminous skirts.

The hired mourners stood to attention and waited until the family were seated in their carriage behind the hearse. Then the hearse driver flicked his whip and with a great creak and groan the funeral procession began its solemn journey. Temperance fanned herself feverishly. It was stifling inside the carriage and she wanted to keep her composure. It would not do, if she emerged from the carriage at St Mary's with a face as red as a farmer's wife. She glanced to Eli sitting opposite and her insides softened for a moment. He was so handsome and determined. He would not fail her, she was certain. Then she looked to Alice, and the familiar weight of disappointment and bitterness settled in her stomach like a bout of indigestion. Black did not suit the girl at all. She was beyond pale; sickly almost.

Her gown looked dreadful. It was too wide on the shoulders and too loose about the waist. Not that Alice cared an inch for her appearance, that much was obvious. Temperance turned away. She would not let Alice ruin the day. Instead, she looked out of the window and consoled herself with the view. She saw shopkeepers pause in their work to watch the procession. Some leaned on brooms and others put their baskets on the ground and touched their caps. The carriage moved slowly along the streets, and everywhere the pavements were lined with onlookers. Temperance had instructed the funeral director to lead the procession the long route to St Mary's. That way, not a single person in Bridgwater would be left unaware of the passing of Arthur Angel and the magnitude of grief felt by his beautiful widow.

Temperance was in her element. She gazed out of the carriage window and soaked up the attention. If it had not been so unbearably hot inside the carriage, she would have been happy to stay there forever. Parading up and down the streets, knowing with every second that passed, she was foremost in the thoughts of every bystander.

Eli shifted uncomfortably in his seat. He felt suffocated. His collar was tight on the damp skin of his neck, and he longed to tear it off. The scent of his mother's perfume was overbearing and the sight of Alice slumped in the corner of the carriage, looking for all the world like a lost waif, heated his blood and made him want to take her by the shoulders and shake her. It was time he stopped thinking of her as poor little Alice. It was time he stopped feeling sorry for her. Papa had spoiled her and had ignored Mama's efforts to correct things. If Alice couldn't behave as she should, then it was her own fault. It was time she grew up.

The carriage crawled towards St Mary's. And with every yard onward, Eli's anger grew. He was angry with his father for dying; angry that he had inherited the mill, when he might have wanted to do something different with his life; angry with having to become a man so soon and angry with having to sit in the airless carriage for such an interminable amount of time. Both Eli and Temperance were so absorbed in their own separate musings that neither of them noticed the barefoot man standing on the edge of the town square. Neither of them noticed the piercing blue of his eyes or the soft ringlets of hair that hung down his back. And neither of them noticed how Alice turned her head or the rapt expression on her face.

Eighteen

He is there again. Henry Prince. As we pass the town square, I see him standing before a small crowd. His arms are stretched wide. My heart jolts. I wish I could hear what he is saying. But the air in this carriage is so heavy it seems to muffle all sound from outside, except for the slow heavy creak of the wheels. I drink in the sight of him. He is like no one I have ever seen before. There is something about him, something in his eyes; something that I can't explain. But it makes me feel scared and thrilled all at the same time. As we pass by, the crowd turns to look at us. He turns too. For a moment, he looks straight at me, and it is just like before. It feels as though he has looked straight into my soul. I shudder. *Someone's just walked over your grave*, Eli would have said when we were little.

I follow Henry Prince with my eyes, craning my neck to catch a last glimpse of him. As he disappears from view I am left with an empty feeling; a hunger for something that I can't describe. I will see him again. I know I will. I will find a way to leave the house. I will walk to the town square and if I have to wait all day to see him again, then I will. Even if I have to go back day after day, I will find a way to see him.

I slump back in my seat, and look across at Eli. He is itching at his collar and scowling like a little boy. It is hard to imagine that he is the man of the house now. I wonder if Mama will even let him be the man of the house. I wonder if she will be different now that Papa has gone. Will grief soften her? Will she be grateful for what she has left? I look at her, wafting her fan and gazing out at the onlookers as though she is royalty or some such.

She turns her head to me and glares. 'Sit up straight, Alice,' she commands. 'We are nearly there now. All eyes will be on us in a moment, and you will *not* embarrass me. Do you understand?' Then as though she has read my thoughts, she leans towards me and whispers over the top of her fan, 'Just because your father has died, do not think things will be any different.'

She snaps her fan shut and traps a fly between the lacy ribs. And, like the fly, any hopes I had of a gentler Mama are crushed. The carriage jolts to a standstill. We have arrived at St Mary's, and although the sun floods into the carriage when the door is opened, I have never felt as miserable in my whole life.

Nineteen

The hole is bigger than I thought, and much deeper. It looks dark and cool at the bottom, where the soil is soft and damp. I step away from the edge. I cannot imagine how Papa will like it down there. Especially once the earth has been piled on top of him and the worms have eaten their way through his frock coat and shirt and into the flesh of his belly.

They are lifting his coffin over the hole now. The pallbearers' faces are greasy with the heat and the effort. The thick rope slides through their fingers, and there is a slight thud as the coffin hits the bottom of the grave.

'For as much as it has pleased Almighty God to take out of this world the soul of Arthur Charles Eli Angel, we therefore commit his body to the ground, earth to earth, ashes to ashes, dust to dust, looking for the blessed hope when the Lord Himself . . .'

Reverend Piggott's dreary voice drifts lazily around the churchyard. He must have said the same words a thousand times before. I wonder why God would be so pleased to take Papa when he was quite happy here on earth. I think perhaps Reverend Piggott is lying. It is my fault Papa is dead and not God's. God didn't want Papa yet, I know it.

111

Reverend Piggott's bare head is pink and there are dark patches spreading from under the armpits of his white surplice.

'... *shall descend from heaven with a shout, with the voice of the archangel, and the dead in Christ shall rise first ...*'

He throws a scattering of earth on top of Papa's coffin. I imagine Papa inside, squashed into the darkness, wondering where he is. Perhaps the earth landing on the wooden lid sounds to him like rain pattering on a roof? I wring my hands together. Does God know it is my fault? Does Reverend Piggott know it is my fault?

'... *we which are alive and remain shall be caught up together with them in the clouds to meet the Lord in the air ...*'

Reverend Piggott is looking at me now. His eyes are grey, dull and accusing. There is no forgiveness in them, and no understanding. My throat tightens. It is as though I am choking on the soil the Reverend is brushing from his hands. My temples throb. *I didn't mean it, Papa*, I shout inside my head. *Please don't leave me.* I think of the man in the town square again. I haven't been able to stop thinking about him. He looked at me too. But in a different way. As though he knows what I have done but will forgive me nonetheless.

'... *and so shall we ever be with the Lord, wherefore comfort ye one another with these words.*'

Mama throws a handful of earth onto Papa's coffin. She does it carelessly, as though she is discarding a soiled handkerchief, then she inspects her gloves to see they have not been marked. It is Eli's turn next. He throws the earth with force onto the lid of the coffin, so the bigger lumps explode into dust. Then he blinks hard, from the glare of the sun or the prickle of tears, I do not know.

All eyes are on me now. It is hard to breathe with the heat pressing down on me from all around. I stoop to the ground, my legs trembling. I reach out to the earth that is piled along the edge of the grave. It is warm and dry and crumbles to my touch. I close my hand around it and a trickle of powder pours through my fingers. I try to stand, but my head feels light: full of clouds. 'Eli,' I whisper. 'Please help me up.'

He bends to take my elbow and hisses in my ear, 'Compose yourself, Alice.'

His tone of voice stings me and I am horrified to feel hot tears gathering behind my eyes. I clutch at the grains of earth in my hand and move my feet forwards. I look down. I am so close to Papa now. Only a few feet of space and the thickness of the coffin lid separate us. I open my hand and let go of the earth. Then everything slows down. I see each grain of soil peel away from my palm and float gracefully, one by one into the grave. Suddenly, the sun strikes the brass coffin plate that is engraved with Papa's name and a knife of light blinds me. Silence pounds in my ears. The scent of dark earth and dead things fills my nostrils and I am hovering over the coffin, moving closer and closer. A long drawn-out scream breaks the silence.

Then everything turns black.

Twenty

'Miss? Miss? Try some tea, will you.'

There is a hand on the back of my head. I open my eyes to see Sarah leaning over me with the steam from a cup of hot tea misting in front of her face.

'There, there,' she says. 'Just a sip. A small sip.' She brings the cup to my lips and I take a drop of the scalding liquid. 'That's better,' she says and she lowers my head onto a pillow.

As the tea burns a trail to my insides, I look around and see I am in my bedchamber. I am lying on my bed, still dressed in my mourning gown. Except it is patched with smears of mud now.

'You didn't 'alf give everyone a fright,' says Sarah. 'Whatever made you do it, miss?'

'Do what?' I croak.

She looks at me oddly. 'Why, jump into your father's grave, of course. You've caused a right old stir, you have. The whole house is in uproar.'

I groan and close my eyes again as I remember: the heat, the earth, the light and Papa in a box, forever.

'I fainted, Sarah,' I whisper. 'That is all.'

'All?' Sarah's voice squeaks. 'You have no idea, do you miss?' She sighs. 'The whole town is talking about it. The mistress . . . well. She is in such a tizz. I've never seen the like. In fact,' she says, her eyes darting back to the chamber door, 'I shouldn't be here at all. Only no one was looking out for you, and I wanted to make sure you were all right. You won't tell on me, will you?'

I am not surprised that Mama and Eli have not been to see me, but I am touched that Sarah has thought of me at least. I struggle to sit and as I pull myself up, I lurch forward and knock the tea from Sarah's hand.

'Oh, miss!' She grabs the cup, but the brown liquid has already spilled on to the bed sheets. I watch as the stain spreads over the white linen. It is fanciful of me, I know, but I swear I see a face appear. A bearded face with staring eyes. I reel backwards. Papa! He has come to haunt me already.

'You've gone quite white, miss,' says Sarah. 'But don't worry yourself. It's only tea. It'll wash off, no trouble.'

And I think to myself that she is right. It is only tea. But when I look down again, the face is still there. But it's not Papa any more. This time, the face is smiling out at me from a halo of ringlets.

'Sarah?' I reach for her arm as she turns to go. 'I saw someone in the town square. Just after Papa died. A man with bare feet and black ringlets. He was preaching to a crowd . . . Do . . . do you know of him?'

Sarah laughs. 'Everyone knows of him, miss. He's a strange one, all right. Henry Prince is his name. He has a place in Spaxton. Where me Pa lives. Surrounded by high walls it is. The gates guarded by bloodhounds.' Sarah lowers her voice. 'They call it the Abode of Love.'

I want her to tell me more. I like the sound of it, *the Abode of Love*, but there are noises at the door and her eyes are panicked. 'Thank you for the tea,' I say. 'And don't worry, I shan't say a word.' She bobs to me, but before she can leave, the door opens and Mama, Eli and a man I have never seen before, enter the room. Mama looks daggers at Sarah who bows her head and sidles quickly out. I am so glad to see Eli that I don't at first wonder who the man is. I hold my hand out to my brother, searching his face for some sign.

But his eyes won't meet mine. He looks everywhere but at me. I turn cold then. I drop my hand and look to Mama. She still has daggers in her eyes and they are pointing sharply at me.

'So, this is Alice?'

I turn to the man and see he is talking to me. He has a slight curl of a smile on his lips.

'How are you feeling?' he asks, with his head cocked to one side.

'I don't know,' I answer. Because that is the truth.

'I am here to help you, Alice,' he says. 'My name is Dr Fox.'

Then everything happens at once. A thickset woman appears in the room and takes me by the arms. She pulls me from the bed and sets me on my feet. Before I have a chance to gasp, she wraps a shawl around my shoulders and holds me tight to her side. My nostrils fill with the smell of her: rotten meat and chamber pots. She marches me from the room and all I have the chance to do is to shout Eli's name.

'It's for your own good, Alice,' he calls after me. 'You'll soon see.'

Mama is nowhere to be seen.

I try to twist out of the woman's hold, but she is strong. She grips me so hard, I fear she might squeeze the breath out of

116

me. My feet barely touch the ground as she whisks me down the stairs. The man, Dr Fox, is striding ahead. 'Discretion, Mrs Abbot,' he says over his shoulder. 'Remember. Swiftness and discretion.' Although he is quick and wiry, he doesn't take after his name. He is more like a pigeon, with his grey suit, beady eyes and bouncing head. Then we are outside and there is a carriage waiting at the pavement, with its doors already open.

'Where are you taking me?' I manage to ask. But before the words are out of my mouth, I have been thrown into the carriage. 'Stop!' I shout. But the doors are banged shut and in a blink I find myself huddled on a hard wooden seat with the looming figure of Mrs Abbot sitting opposite me.

'Tis no use carrying on,' she says. 'What's done is done and you might as well sit quiet now.'

I look around frantically. The curtains are drawn, but not tightly, so daylight filters through and I see the interior of the carriage is shabby, the walls scuffed and the floors covered in dirty straw. The air hangs heavy and hot and is filled with the odour of Mrs Abbot. The carriage jerks forward and I grab the leather hand strap to steady myself. Mrs Abbot grunts as the horses take up a steady pace, and her chins jiggle with the motion.

'Where's Dr Fox?' I demand, trying to keep the fear from my voice. 'Where are you taking me?'

'He's up top with the driver. He doesn't like to ride with his patients.' Mrs Abbots blows her nose noisily on a large, grey handkerchief. She inspects the contents, and then looks to me as though I am of much less importance than what has just come out of her nose. 'Anyway, it is no concern of yours. Just settle quietly. We have a long way to go.'

117

The terrible truth hits me hard in the stomach. 'This isn't meant to happen!' I scream at her. 'Papa died so I wouldn't be sent to the asylum!'

'Did he, dear?' she says. 'Yes, yes. Well, I'm sure we'll soon cure you of that notion.' She smiles to herself.

'I am not mad,' I say firmly. 'I am not mad.'

Mrs Abbot fumbles in her skirts and takes out a small silver flask. She eyes me as she unscrews the lid and takes a sip of whatever is inside. She licks at the corners of her mouth. 'That's what they all say, dear,' she says. 'That's what they always say.' She folds her arms under her bosom and purses her lips.

'You can't do this,' I plead. 'You can't just take me from my home!' Mrs Abbot blinks lazily and purses her lips tighter.

I gesture to my mud-stained gown. 'Look at me,' I shout. 'I have just come from my father's funeral. I need to be with my family!'

Suddenly, Mrs Abbot leans forwards and slaps me hard across the face. 'Shut up!' she hisses. 'Or there'll be worse to come.'

I hold my hand to my face. My cheek stings with heat and furious tears; I am too angry to speak. Mrs Abbot holds out her grey handkerchief to me and I shake my head dumbly. 'Perhaps,' she says, 'we can have a peaceful journey now.' She shifts about in her seat, then sighs, as though she has found a comfy spot. But then the carriage swings around a bend and I am flung to one side, and Mrs Abbot is nearly thrown from her seat. 'Gently! Gently!' she screeches and reaches up to thump on the ceiling.

I stay in the corner of the carriage with my head knocking against the curtained window as the carriage lurches its way onwards. I watch Mrs Abbot settle down again. She folds her hands in her lap and rests her chin on her bosom. Then she takes out her handkerchief again and dabs at her forehead and at the crease under her chin where its folds meet her neck. 'Beastly hot, int it,' she mumbles.

I turn away from her and try to put from my mind frightful images of darkness and filth and cold stone; I want to close my ears to the dreadful screams of lunatics and madmen. It is as though I am falling down the deepest darkest hole and there is no way out. This is my punishment. The price I have to pay for wickedness, for being the wrong person and for letting Papa die. I press my head hard against the carriage wall, desperate to banish all these thoughts. The curtains hang in front of my nose, and I realise that from where my head rests, I can see a sliver of the outside world through a gap in the side of the worn velvet. There is an edge of blue sky, which disappears and reappears with the motion of the carriage. I see marching chimneys and pieces of rooftop. Then underneath all that are glimpses of brick, shop windows, the flick of a horse's tail, the shocking green of summer leaves and the passing faces of people I will never know.

I inch my fingers towards the curtains and lift a corner. A shaft of sunlight darts across my skirts. I see we are passing the town square, which is milling with people.

'Shut that curtain!' Mrs Abbot suddenly bellows, and my hand drops to my lap as though burned. I have only been in this carriage a matter of moments and already I have had more than a taste of what is in store for me. I lean back on the seat and close my eyes. If I can sleep, maybe I will wake up and all this will be a bad dream. The carriage rattles onwards, but of course, sleep won't come. Mrs Abbot's wheezy breath, the stench of her and the closeness of the air, remind me all too clearly where I am. Is the town square to be my last glimpse of Bridgwater? I think of Henry Prince, and I wonder if he was still there. My skin prickles as I recall his face, and how I seem to have known him before I even saw him. How could that be? And why? I puzzle over these questions and try to remember what Henry Prince said on the day that Papa died. What was it he wanted me to hear?

RECEIVE ME AS THE SON OF GOD AND YOUR FLESH WILL BE LIBERATED FROM SIN IN THIS WORLD!

The remembered words spark a flicker of hope deep in my belly. I think of the girl too, the one with the freckles. The one who had stood in front of Henry Prince and looked at him with such light in her eyes. *Our Beloved*, she had called him. *Our Beloved*.

I know what I have to do now. There is only one place I can go. And it won't be to the madhouse.

There is a low rumble from Mrs Abbot. I look across to see that her head has fallen into her bosom and the slack skin of her cheeks is jiggling to the rhythm of the carriage. I keep my eyes upon her as I dare to sneak my hand to the curtain again. I tweak it open. Mrs Abbot doesn't flinch. I turn to peer out of the corner of the window and I see we have left the town now. The horses have picked up their pace and we thrum past fat hedgerows and fields of wheat baked golden. I wonder which field of grain is destined for Papa's mill. Then an ache grows behind my heart as I remember it is now Eli's mill.

Time passes and Mrs Abbot keeps snoring. I can't sit still. The further away from home we travel the more my insides seem to fall apart and the more my head fills up with fragments of memories and lost things and broken hopes. My feet tap insistently on the floor, scuffing around the old bits of straw. My hands twist in my lap or fly upwards to grab strands of my hair that I pull and wind round and round my fingers. I am leaving myself behind. That is what it feels like. I hear Dr Fox shouting something to the driver. I hear the crack of a whip. Then I hear a low humming, a flat desperate sound that I realise is coming from my own throat. I clamp my hand to my mouth, not wanting to disturb the slumped form of Mrs Abbot.

I can't bear it any longer. I feel like Papa must feel, alone in the darkness, buried deep in the cold ground with the weight of the world above, and a mountain of earth pressing down on him. I want to escape. I want to smash through wood and stone, and claw through the earth to reach the light. I look out of the window again and see the hedges have flattened out to moorland and ditches, and there is a flock of birds wheeling and diving high up in the still, blue sky.

It is then that I do it. There is no moment of decision. There is just my hand twisting the brass door handle and pushing open the carriage door. There is the unsteady hovering of my boots on the edge of the doorway and a great rush of warm air on my face. There is a roar from Mrs Abbot and a roar from me as I throw myself away from the great snarling wheels of the carriage and land with a sickening thud on a grassy bank.

There is silence and panic as the breath leaves my lungs and there is none to replace it. There is the clattering and skidding of hooves and the creaking and squealing of wheels. There is shouting and cursing. There is a huge pain in my chest as I manage to steal a precious swallow of air. Then there are my legs and tangled skirts, and running and running, and more pain in my chest and the distant figures of Mrs Abbot with her hands on her hips and Dr Fox waving a walking stick in the air.

Twenty-one

It was Eli who received the news from a red-faced Dr Fox. 'What do you mean, she's gone?' he asked. 'Gone where?'

'She threw herself from the carriage. There was nothing we could have done.' Dr Fox unconsciously straightened his bow tie and wished he was back in the sanctuary of his office at Brislington House. 'She is obviously in a far worse state of mind than we at first presumed, but I have every faith that she will be back here by nightfall. After all, where else has she to go?'

'And if she doesn't come back?' Eli was at a loss. It wasn't right that he should bury his father and lose his sister all in the same day.

'She will,' said Dr Fox. 'And if you could see your way to allowing myself and Mrs Abbot to stay here this evening, then we will make sure this doesn't happen again.'

Eli installed them in the drawing room. Dr Fox sat gracefully in a chair by the window and picked up a discarded newspaper to read. It was, Eli realised with a pang, the last paper his father had ever read.

Eli wondered, in hindsight, whether it would have been best

to have Mrs Abbot wait in the kitchen. She didn't belong in a drawing room. It was fortunate that Mama was indisposed. The sight of Mrs Abbot seated broad and heavy on the delicate cream sofa would have proved the final straw for her.

The house was quiet and smelled of sadness and decaying flowers. Temperance lay in her darkened chamber, overcome with shock and shame. A small draught of laudanum had calmed her enough for Jane to help her out of her mourning gown and into a robe.

How could Alice have done such a vile and wicked thing? Every time Temperance closed her eyes she saw the same thing; Alice plunging headlong into Arthur's grave and the expressions of horror on the faces of the gathered mourners.

Temperance whimpered and tossed her head from side to side. Even the cool cloth that Jane laid upon her forehead did nothing to banish the terrible images from her mind. At least Alice was out of the way now, locked up safely, hidden from prying eyes and the gossip-mongering. But even so Temperance wondered, with fear clutching at her heart, could she ever undo the damage? Would Bridgwater's finest ever grace her drawing room now?

Eli thought it would be better not to inform his mother of Alice's disappearance. Not yet anyway. Alice would be back soon. Dr Fox seemed certain of it. And what was the point of distressing Mama further, if the problem could be dealt with quietly and discreetly?

Eli paced the house. He couldn't settle. He couldn't find a place to be. It was too lonely in his bedchamber, knowing that apart from Mama's room, all the others along the corridor were empty now. The library reminded him too much of Papa, with the cracked leather armchair still bearing his shape, and the books, half read, still open on the table. He couldn't bring himself to open the door of the study, knowing that inside would be the whole essence of his father: the sweat of him, the echo of his voice in the corners of the room, and the marks of his pen on a hundred sheets of paper. Eli couldn't bear the thought of the drawing room either; he had nothing to say to Dr Fox and Mrs Abbot.

So he found himself in the kitchen, sitting at the scrubbed wooden table, watching nameless servants going about their work. He was amazed. Life had come to a standstill upstairs, but down there, amidst all the scurrying and washing and kneading and stirring, you would never know the house was in mourning. He took some comfort in that, and tried for a while to imagine that nothing had changed, that his life was still as easy as it always had been. He ate a slice of sweet gooseberry pie that someone placed in front of him and drained a jar of beer. He wished he could escape on horseback to the moors and ride forever, and never have to face this new way of living. He knew that soon there would be lawyers and business meetings and he would have to prove himself in a man's world.

But for now, the kitchen was his haven, and he sat and watched the comings and goings and waited for Alice. The hours passed. The afternoon drifted into evening and still there was no sign of Alice. Candles were lit and the servants sat warily at the table and shared their supper of cold meat and pickles with Eli.

The kitchen quietened, and gradually emptied, until only a couple of servants remained, stoking the fire and scouring pots. Eli knew then that he couldn't hide any longer. With a heavy heart he climbed the stairs to the main house and made his way to the drawing room. Dr Fox was asleep in his chair, his legs still neatly crossed, his hands folded in his lap and his trim beard resting on his chest. Mrs Abbot was asleep too, sprawled out on the cream sofa, her chins shuddering with every snore.

Eli coughed loudly. Dr Fox's head jerked upright. 'She is back?' He looked hopefully at Eli.

'She is not,' said Eli. 'And I would like you both to leave now.'

Dr Fox raised his eyebrows. 'If . . . if you are sure,' he said. 'But is there nothing else we can do to help?'

'You have done enough,' Eli said. He was trembling with the effort of keeping his temper. He felt like a young boy again, who hadn't got his own way. He wanted to stamp his feet and yell loudly, then run to Mama so she could sweet-talk him and tell him everything would be all right. But he wasn't that boy any more and Mama was the one who needed him now. He reached for the decanter that sat sparkling on its silver tray, and splashed an inch of amber brandy into a glass. He took a deep breath and poured the burning liquid down his throat. He gasped, then turned back to Dr Fox. 'You have lost my sister,' he said, 'and unless you are going to search the streets and back alleys and poorhouses yourself, then I would like you out of my house!'

My house. It was his house now, Eli realised: the bricks, the mortar, the furnishings, the servants – all of it. He was responsible now, and the knowledge of that made him nauseous.

He nodded to Dr Fox and glanced over at Mrs Abbot, who was struggling to her feet. 'You can see yourselves out,' he finished. Then he dashed from the room and just made it to the potted fern that sat at the bottom of the stairs as the brandy surged from his stomach.

Twenty-two

There is just the quiet of this barn now, and the warm, dry, sunshine smell of straw. I have left Dr Fox and Mrs Abbot far behind and all that matters is that I am here, in this small dusty corner. I want to sleep, and so I do, burrowed safely under the straw. It is a dreamless sleep. When I wake the light has changed to a dusky orange and I am so hungry I feel my stomach has been ripped from me. I wince as I stand. My hip is bruised where I jumped from the carriage and my bones are stiff. I brush powdery stalks of straw from my gown and poke my head around the barn door. The farmhouse across the yard glows warm in the evening sun. I imagine a family inside sitting down to a supper of bread and pork and hot potatoes, and my belly growls.

I have no money, nothing to purchase food with. The only thing of value I have is the gold locket around my neck that Papa gave me for my tenth birthday. And I would rather starve to death than part with that. As I look out into the quiet of the farmyard, I realise that for the first time ever, I feel at peace with myself. Despite being dressed in a filthy gown, with nothing to eat and no place to sleep, I feel calm and full of purpose. I know where I am going now. I just need to find my bearings.

I limp across the yard and knock on the farmhouse door. As I wait, I hastily check my hair for any stray pieces of straw. A woman eventually answers. She is ruddy-faced but kindly looking. She looks me up and down and waits for me to speak.

'Good evening,' I say brightly. 'I wonder if you can help me. I am travelling to the village of Spaxton and I seem to have lost my way. Could you . . . could you point me in the right direction please? If . . . if it isn't too much trouble?'

The woman raises her eyebrows at me and considers for a moment. 'George . . . George!' she shouts over her shoulder. 'A young lady here wanting directions.' She leans on the door frame, waiting, her eyes flicking from my boots to my hair and back again.

Eventually, a man appears at her side. He is wearing thick brown trousers and a grubby shirt rolled up at the sleeves with a pair of braces dangling loose at his sides. 'What you hollering me for?' he says.

'This young lady,' says the woman, 'wants to know how to get to Spaxton.'

'Oh, yes,' he says. And he brings his face close and squints at me. He smells of tobacco and the edge of his white moustache is tinged with yellow. He reminds me of Papa until he coughs thickly and shoots a gobbet of spit out into the yard.

'If you don't mind me saying so,' he says, 'you don't look like the sort of young lady who ought to be out on her own at this time of day. And what do you want to be going to Spaxton for in any case?'

Although it is none of his business, I don't wish to offend him, so I think quickly. 'It is my sister Sarah,' I say. 'Yes, Sarah. She lives there you see, and . . . and she is not well. So I am going to visit, and . . . and help with the children.'

'Oh, yes,' he says again. 'Right you are then.' He glances at the woman, who I presume is his wife, then he points his arm in a vague manner to somewhere behind me. 'Spaxton's about twenty miles over that way,' he says. 'Four miles or so past Bridgwater.'

I look behind, then back at him again, and he notices the confusion on my face.

'Bottom of the track,' he says, 'You'll see the milestone for Bristol and Bridgwater. Fifteen miles to Bridgwater, it says. Just keep on the main road an' it'll take you straight there. Anybody in Bridgwater will tell you where to go next.' He scratches his head. 'You planning on walking through the night, are you?'

'I think I will have to,' I say to him. 'You see, I have lost my purse, so have no means of paying for a bed for the night. In fact, I don't like to ask, but could you see your way to sparing me a piece of bread?' My face flushes hot as I ask this question. If Mama could see me now, she would die of shame.

'A piece of bread, eh?' The man looks at his wife and winks. 'Think we can spare a bit for this poor lost soul?'

The woman elbows him in the ribs. 'Oh, leave her be, George,' she says. 'Now listen,' she says to me. 'I can't have you wandering the countryside on your own at night. We can spare you a bit of supper and there's a bed in the attic. I can see you're from good breeding, so once you get to this sister of yours, maybe she'll see a way of paying us back for our hospitality. Now, come on. Let's get you inside.'

And then it is all kindness, as I sit at George and Ada's table and share a simple supper of bread and jam and a glass of beer. The beer is new to me and not to my liking, but I am so grateful that I even accept a second glass. There is no need for me to speak much, as George and Ada do nothing but chatter. They talk of the weather, their pigs, the chickens and a neighbour who has just lost a wife. I think they have forgotten I am here. But then George drains his glass and leans back in his chair. 'So, Spaxton, eh?' he says. 'S'pose your sister's told you about all the goings on there then?'

I shake my head. 'No, no,' I say. 'I don't believe she has mentioned anything. Although . . .' I hesitate for a moment. 'She did mention a place called the Abode of Love.'

'Did she now?' he says. 'Well, I can't say I'm surprised. I hear they've even had the newspaper men from London nosing around down there.'

'And why would that be?' I ask. I am all ears now.

'Well, seeing as though you're asking, then I'll be a-telling.' He takes up a pipe and taps it on the edge of the table. 'Pass the baccy will you, Ada?' he says.

'I'll pass you the baccy, but you can shut up with your gossiping,' she says sternly. 'There's no need for this young lady to be hearing things like that. It's not decent. And anyway, I think it's time we turned in now. Come on, my dear,' she says to me, 'I'll fetch you a blanket.'

I rise from my chair reluctantly. I want to stay and find out more about the Abode of Love. I want to know what George

131

was going to tell me. But the moment has passed, and besides, I am a guest in their house and it is not for me to question.

Ada leads me up some rickety stairs to a tiny room in the eaves of the cottage. 'There you go,' she says. 'I'm sure you'll be comfortable enough.' I turn to thank her, and suddenly she leans forwards and kisses me on the cheek. 'I'm sorry,' she whispers. 'Forgive me for that. Only we had a daughter of our own, your age, up until last year, and it's just so good to have a youngster in the place again.' She blinks quickly. 'Well, goodnight then, my dear,' she says.

The walls of the house are thin, and as I settle under a blanket that smells of horses, I watch through the window as the end of the day slides into night. The last thing I hear before falling asleep is Ada muttering, 'She's dressed in mourning, you old fool, didn't you notice?'

Twenty-three

The sun is high in the sky when I wake. I blink into it and curse Lillie for opening the curtains and letting me lie for so long. Now I will have missed breakfast and Mama will send for a plate of scraps and force me to eat yesterday's peelings and bacon rind, so that I will learn to respect mealtimes and the value of freshly prepared food. My belly shrinks at the thought.

I sigh and drape my arm over my face to shield my eyes from the sun. *Where are the leather straps?* I suddenly think. *Why didn't I wake when Mama came to release me?*

Then it all comes rushing back and I catch my breath as I remember. Papa is dead and buried. Mama has washed her hands of me. I should be locked behind the doors of the madhouse, but instead I am here, in the dusty attic of strangers. *Everything will be all right in the morning,* Papa always used to say to me. But it never was. And it still isn't.

I clamber from the bed and look around for my mourning gown. It is nowhere to be seen. But folded neatly on a stool are a plain wool dress and a clean chemise and petticoat. I pull them on quickly and slip my feet into my boots which I see have been cleaned of mud and polished. I need to be on my way. I have to get to Spaxton and find the Abode of Love. Henry Prince is the only one who can help me now. *Receive me as the Son of God and your flesh will be liberated from sin in this world.*

I *will* receive him, and I will be forgiven. I can start my life again and this time no one will think me bad or send me away to rot in the madhouse.

Downstairs in the cottage all is quiet, save for the gentle simmering of a kettle hanging over the fire. It is all so peaceful and ordered. The floor is swept and the table is scrubbed white. The door is open and a light breeze carries in the scents of stone and earth, the sweet smell of cows and grass and the dust of old grain. I should find George and Ada and thank them for their kindness, but suddenly I am in no hurry to leave. I breathe in the calm of it all. I have walked into someone else's life and I want to live it for a while.

Just then, Ada comes huffing through the door clutching a weight of something in her apron. 'Ah, here you are, my dear,' she says. 'I left you sleeping. Out for the count you were. Thought you must have needed it, mind. I took the liberty of washing out your gown for you. Mud scrubbed off just fine it did. It's hanging outside drying beautifully.' She pauses for breath and carefully empties the contents of her apron into a bowl. A dozen pale brown eggs clack into a pile.

'Now then,' she says. 'I 'spect you'll be ready for some breakfast. Eggs do you?'

I sit at the table and let Ada bustle around me. There's no need to talk. She does enough for both of us. 'It's so good to have some company,' she says. 'Don't get me wrong. George is a dear. Good heart on 'im he has. But he's a man! And they're only good for so much, aren't they?' She chuckles and cracks half a dozen eggs into a blackened pan and adds a dollop of butter. She whisks the eggs briskly and within a moment I can smell hot butter and melting yolks. She winks at me as she splashes some yellow cream into the pan. 'Don't tell George, will you? He only gets cream in 'is eggs on a Sunday.'

Soon, there is a plate in front of me, piled high with glistening scrambled eggs. Ada cuts a chunk of bread and drops it next to the plate. 'Eat up, then,' she urges me. There are no napkins and she makes no attempt to say Grace, so I do as she says and I spoon the eggs into my mouth. They are hot, buttery and delicious and a world away from the cold, tasteless eggs at Lions House. I eat every scrap and the bread too. Ada sits beside me and slurps a cup of tea. 'That's it,' she chuckles. 'You get it down you.'

I feel somehow as if I am doing her a great favour. And it is a good feeling.

After she has cleared the table, Ada asks if I would like to look around the farm. 'If you're not in too much of a hurry, that is?'

I tell her I would love to and her face lights up, like a pauper child who has been thrown an unexpected coin. She natters away, nineteen to the dozen, as she leads the way across the farmyard. I am introduced to all five of George and Ada's cows and every single one of their dozen chickens. There's a goat too, pegged out beside the barn. It is bleating plaintively. Ada fetches a bucket and with deft hands she milks the goat. She dips a cup into the bucket and offers me a taste. The milk is warm and thick with a strong tang of grass in it. I am not sure I like it all that well, but I tell Ada it is delicious anyway.

We walk past the barn to the small garden behind and I help Ada pull some weeds from between the rows of onions, carrots and turnips. 'Our Mary used to do this,' she tells me. 'Before she passed on.'

'Mary was your daughter?' I ask.

Ada nods. 'Such a good girl, she was. I miss her so much'

The words are like a slap in my face. I never knew this Mary and the poor girl is dead, but even so I cannot help but feel envious that she had a mother who loved her.

I stand and shake the soil from my skirt. 'I must get on,' I say. 'My sister will be expecting me.'

Ada face falls. 'So soon?' she says. 'But you must wait for George. He's out in the field today. There's fences need mending. Stay for another meal with us, at least.'

And because she smiles at me so honestly and because she makes me feel so wanted, it is as easy as that for her to persuade me to stay.

The morning winds into afternoon. I help Ada make a pie for supper. 'I've been meaning to wring her neck for ages,' she says of the henpecked chicken that goes into the pie.

Everything is so easy and drowsy. Ada asks no questions. She expects nothing of me, only my company, and by the time we sit down for supper, somehow, it is taken for granted that I will sleep the night again.

I want to ask George more about the Abode of Love, but Ada won't hear of it. 'We'll have none of that talk,' she says. And I think it is because she doesn't want to be reminded that I will soon be on my way.

The evening passes quickly. George and Ada are born talkers

and by the time the candles are lit I know all about how George first wooed Ada when he worked as a farmhand on her father's farm, and how it took him a whole six months and almost a field's worth of violets to persuade her to walk out with him. Ada laughs like a naughty child. 'Still brings me a bunch of violets now and then when they're in bloom. Don't you, you old softy?' Her eyes shine when she looks at him.

I know I will have to sneak away come morning. I won't be able to say goodbye to them. It would be too easy to stay. But they are too good for me; I do not deserve their kindness. And if I stay, I will never get to the Abode of Love and Henry Prince will never be able to forgive me for all my badness.

I yawn behind my hand.

'Look at you,' Ada says. 'Worn to a frazzle. Time to turn in, I reckon.'

I thank her for supper and before I can help myself, I put my arms around her and hug her quickly. 'Oh, get on with you,' she says. But her cheeks turn pink with pleasure.

Twenty-four

It is still dark when I wake. But when I look out of the attic window, I see a smear of light across the horizon and know it is time to leave. I dress in my clean mourning gown and leave the wool dress folded on the stool. I creep down the stairs and into the kitchen. There is the remains of a loaf of bread on the table. I hope George and Ada won't mind if I take it with me. It is a sin to steal, I know. But where I am going, I will be forgiven for it all.

As I close the farmhouse door behind me, I dare to wish for George and Ada to always be happy. It is the smallest of wishes. It is a good wish; a simple wish and I hope with all my heart that no harm will come of it.

I walk briskly, keeping to the fields and hedgerows that flank the Bristol Road. I wonder if anybody is out looking for me. Eli, or Dr Fox and Mrs Abbot. I wonder if anybody has bothered to look for me at all. A coach rumbles past, its oil lamps still glowing in the half -light. But otherwise it is peaceful out here with just the sounds of my boots crunching on the ground and the early morning chatter of birds. It is beautiful to see the sky lift around me, like a lid taken off a cooking pot to reveal a freshly made, untouched day.

I pass derelict barns and small, tight copses, and as I walk, I try not to think of Papa or Eli, or anybody. I only think of what lies ahead and of how I will be made as clean and fresh as this new day. I stop and rest awhile by the side of a stream. I splash my face with weed-green water and eat George and Ada's bread. George said that first evening that newspaper men from London had been to the Abode of Love. It must be a place of miracles then: a place full of love and forgiveness.

I start walking again. I am anxious now that the sun is up, and I can see the first signs of Bridgwater in the distance. It is strange to think that I have to go back to where I started, before I can begin to move on. My feet slow, but my heart starts to clatter as I spy chimney pots and wispy plumes of smoke snaking their way up into the pale blue sky. I am scared to be seen in case someone is out looking for me, so I skirt around the edges of town hoping to find a stranger who will point me on to the right road. I pass a small cottage with an old woman sitting on the doorstep. 'Excuse me!' I shout over to her. 'Can you tell me the quickest way to Spaxton?'

She grins a toothless grin and waves at me.

'The quickest way to Spaxton?' I try again. But it is no good. She is either deaf or simple or both.

Across the lane, outside another cottage, there is a man loading sacks onto the back of a cart. His skin is leathery and brown as the earth. He eyes me as I walk towards him and for one awful moment, I think I see a glint of recognition cross his face. But it passes quickly enough and I tell myself that it is easy to see things that are not there if you go looking for them. 'Morning, missy,' he says to me. 'I heard you asking old

Mother over there the way to Spaxton.'

'I . . . I did,' I stammer. 'But I don't think she heard me.'

'Oh, she'll have heard you all right. Hears everything, that one does. But seeing as how she hasn't left that cottage for going on fifty years, she wouldn't have a clue where anywhere was. In fact, she wouldn't have a clue where her own head was unless it was pointed out to her.' He laughs at himself and heaves another sack onto the back of the cart.

'And . . . and you, sir,' I say. 'Can you tell me the way?'

He laughs again. 'Well. I ain't never been called sir in my life! But for that,' he says, 'you can hop in the back and I'll take you part-way if you like. Never had any cause to go to Spaxton meself, but I'll drop you at the crossroads and you'll see it's not far from there.'

'That would be very kind of you, sir,' I say. 'You see, I'm visiting my sister, and I lost my purse and . . .'

'Don't matter to me why you're going,' he says. 'Your business is yours and mine's mine. As long as I get these taters delivered. Now stop calling me sir, and jump in the back.'

I nestle down between the sacks, feeling the warmth of the man's kindness. I didn't know there were people like him and George and Ada in the world, and it makes me glad that I am part of it now. The man whistles and clucks at his horse and I lie on the sacks, out of view, and watch the endless blue of the sky overhead that is varied only by the occasional smudge of a cloud or a low-hanging branch. I could stay here forever, caught between what was and what is going to be. I smile to myself to think that a cart full of potatoes is the one place that, so far in my life, I have felt the happiest.

140

But it ends soon enough, as the man slows his horse and the cart judders to a halt. 'There you go, missy,' he shouts over his shoulder. 'That's as near as I can get you.'

I climb down from the cart and look around. There are two dusty lanes crossing each other and a thicket of trees on all sides. It is not what I expected and it feels as though we are nowhere. The cart driver clicks his tongue at his horse and waves his arm to the left. 'Up that lane there, missy,' he says. 'Just keep going. You'll get there in the end.' Then he is gone, in a rumble of stone and dust, and I don't even think he hears the *thank you!* that I call after him.

The lane is steep and narrow with high banks on either side that are shaded by a canopy of greenery. It seems to go on forever, and I am out of breath by the time the lane flattens out and winds sharply around to the left. I keep walking and the lane keeps winding, this way and that, and I just want it to end. I just want to find this place so the churning in my stomach will stop. Then at last, the lane opens up and I find myself on a quiet village green with a cluster of cottages and a low, white building with a painted sign declaring it to be The Lamb Inn. It is all so ordinary. I look about nervously. There is nothing to tell me I am in the right place.

Then the door of the inn opens and two men step outside. They eye me suspiciously and whisper to each other. 'Lost yer way, girl?' one of them shouts. I don't like the way they are looking at me, as though I have done something wrong just by standing there. I carry on walking, but I can sense they are watching me and judging me. I want to shout back at them, to leave me alone, to mind their own business. But that is not me

141

any more. That is only the girl they see with their eyes. They can't see inside me. They can't see how much I want to change.

Just past the inn, the lane widens and on one side is a high red-brick wall. I remember Sarah's words: 'He has a place in Spaxton,' she'd said, 'surrounded by high walls and guarded by bloodhounds.' I am excited and eager now. The wall is almost twice my height, but I can see from the glimpses of fancy chimney pots and tiled roofs that there are buildings behind it. I come to a small wooden gate, but when I try to open it, I find it is locked. I walk on, and the wall never varies in height. I wonder what it is trying to keep in, or trying to keep out. Further along, I come to another gate, an enormous studded carriage gate with stone pillars on either side. Across the top of the gate is a row of lacy iron spears and, right in the centre is a large metal cross. I know then that I have found where I need to be.

I know I have found the Abode of Love.

Twenty-five

I do not know how to get in. I have walked around the entire perimeter of the wall and there are no other entrances save for the two gates I have already seen. I try banging my fists on the main gate, but soon my knuckles are sore. I walk back to the smaller gate and pick a small stone from the ground. I knock it against the wood, over and over again. Then the barking starts, loud and ferocious, and my blood turns cold at the thought of sharp yellow teeth and mad-dog eyes. But I won't let them stop me. I kick at the gate in a fury. 'Let me in!' I shout. 'Let me in!'

I slump to the ground in frustration. The barking turns to low growls and then to silence. I lean against the gate. It is warm on my back and I think I might have to stay here forever. There is nowhere else for me to go. Then I hear a scrape, a scratching. Just the tiniest sound. I think for a moment the hounds are back. But there is no growling or sniffing. It is a different sound I hear, a gentler sound. I jump to my feet and put my ear to the wood. 'Hello?' I say. 'Hello. Is there anybody there?' I hold my breath and I am certain that I can sense a shift in the air. There is somebody behind the gate and whoever it is, is listening to me. 'Please,' I say. 'I know you are there. I just want to talk to somebody.'

I wait, and wait. Then just as I am about to bang on the gate again, there is a voice, a woman's voice. 'Who are you?' it says.

My relief is so great that my words come too quickly, tumbling out over each other. 'I am Alice Angel. And I've come to see Henry Prince!'

'Are you another from London?' asks the voice.

'No, no,' I say. 'I am from Bridgwater. That is where I first saw him. In the town square.'

'And what business might you have with Our Beloved?'

I don't know what to say. I did not think I would have to give a reason to see him. I thought he would be here himself to welcome me. 'I . . . I heard him in the town square,' I say again. 'He said . . .' I think hard, trying to remember the right words. 'He said, "Follow me and I will show you paradise on earth." So I am here. I came.'

There is silence again, save for the pounding of my heart. '*Please,*' I whisper.

Then the gate rattles. There is the sound of metal on metal and a woman's face peers out at me. She is young and soft-looking and as she gestures for me to follow her, I see that she is with child. 'Alice Angel,' she says. 'What a beautiful name.' She smiles at me. 'My name is Glory.'

She closes the gate behind us and I stare in astonishment at the sight that meets my eyes. There is a whole village spread out before me, a tiny but perfect village. There is a cluster of pretty cottages, a majestic mansion and even a chapel, covered in stone carvings of the strangest creatures I have ever seen.

There are lawns and flower beds and white gravel pathways gleaming in the morning sun. 'I will take you straight to him,' says the woman called Glory. 'He will decide if you can stay.' We walk through a central courtyard and pass a couple of women who are kneeling to tend the flower beds.

'Good morning, Glory,' they say. 'We have been blessed with another magnificent day.'

'Every new day we are blessed with is magnificent,' Glory replies. She leads me along a narrow gravel pathway, lined with neat box hedges. The pathway winds around the side of the mansion and stops outside a white-painted door that is hung with a large golden cross. Two huge bloodhounds are spread out across the doorstep. They growl deep down in their throats, but Glory just pats them casually on the head. 'Hush, now. You have done your duty,' she says. We step over the hounds and Glory opens the door and beckons me inside.

We enter a large, dark hallway. The air is hushed and still and smells of wood smoke, fresh linen and the pungent perfume of freshly cut flowers. It takes a moment for my eyes to adjust from the glaring sunshine outside to the dimness inside. Then I see thick rugs on a polished wooden floor and oak wall panels that gleam in the light of the handful of candles that are dotted about. Soft green fronds of pot plants spill out of ornate vases, and the walls are covered in flocked paper of red, green and gold. And everywhere there are flowers, of all colours and types. It would put the comforts of Lions House to shame. Glory stops and taps lightly on a door which is framed by long, red velvet curtains. 'Wait here a moment,' she says as she disappears into the room.

145

My legs are trembling. A thought comes to me that maybe this is what it is like to stand at the gates of Heaven. Will I be admitted? Will Henry Prince permit me to stay? There is a large mirror on the wall opposite. I look at the girl standing in it. Against the blackness of her gown and hair, her face is whiter than white. She looks exhausted and in need of pity. I know that I would help her if it were within my power.

The door opens and Glory reappears. Her eyes are glittering and she runs her hands over the protruding shape of her child. 'He will see you now,' she says, and stands aside to let me pass. I grab her hand, urgently.

'But what shall I call him?'

She frowns briefly, as though I should already know the answer to this, as though the answer is as simple as saying the sky is blue. 'Why, Beloved, of course,' she says, before walking away.

I take a deep breath and step into the room. My eyes start to sting and as I rub at them and blink, I see horizontal clouds of smoke hovering, from wall to wall, across the room. The walls are red, a deep, crimson red, the ceiling too, and the curtains and the carpet. I have never seen a room like it. The colour folds around me and thrums inside me like a heartbeat. The room is breathing, as though it has lungs of its own. I want to reach across and touch the walls to see if they are real.

'Welcome,' says a voice. My hand flies to my mouth to quell a startled yelp. I peer through the smoke to the other side of the room, where half a dozen chairs are grouped around an enormous marble fireplace. 'Come here, my child. So I can see you.' His voice is as soothing as fat drops of sunlight and honey, just as I remember it to be. I walk towards him, my heart fluttering like a moth in my throat. He is sitting in a high-backed chair, so carved and ornate that it looks like a throne, and he is blowing great plumes of cigar smoke towards the ceiling. 'So, my child,' he says, and he looks at me for such a long while that I fear the moth in my throat will soon shoot from my mouth and hit him between the eyes. 'What have you to say for yourself?' he asks me.

There is so much I want to say that I don't know where to begin. *I am Alice Angel,* I want to tell him. *I am sixteen years old. I am not mad. But I am a bad person. I have done some terrible things lately. I want to be forgiven. I want to be a good person, the person they all expect me to be. I have seen you and I have heard you talk. I think you understand. Can you help me?*

But his eyes have silenced my tongue. I had forgotten how shocking they are in their intensity.

'Well?' he says, at last. 'I believe you wish to join us?' I think he must have seen through the hair, skin and bone of my head, straight into my mind, to read my thoughts.

I nod dumbly.

'Have you brought anything with you?' he asks.

This time I shake my head.

'What? Nothing?' He tosses his head and his ringlets, as black and glossy as a horse's coat, fall about his shoulders.

I stretch out my arms and show him my open palms. 'I have nothing other than what I am standing in,' I manage to say.

He looks at me sharply and his blue eyes turn dark and hard as granite. 'You know that all property and riches are as dirt?'

I nod, not sure of what to say. But there is a sinking feeling inside me. I am doing it all wrong, and I am sure that any moment now, he will throw me out of the door.

147

He settles back in his chair and regards me thoughtfully. He strokes his beard slowly, as if it is a favourite cat. 'You cannot enter the Abode unless you are prepared to give up all your earthly riches.' His voice is softer now and I think that maybe all is not lost yet.

'But I have no earthly riches to give up,' I say. 'I have nothing.' I think of Mama's jewellery box and how it is crammed with all manner of gems and brooches and pearls. If I had been better prepared, I would have stolen a pocketful.

Henry Prince sighs.

My chest is tight with panic now. 'Please!' I say. 'If I had any riches at all, I would be more than happy to give them *all* up!' I lower my head so he cannot see the tears in my eyes. I put my hand to my throat to try and still the frantic beating of my heart. It is then that I feel the chain around my neck and I quickly close my fingers around the gold locket.

'Riches, great or small, must be sacrificed,' he says. 'The more you are prepared to give to God, the greater your reward will be here in this life,'

He means me to give up my locket, I know it. The only thing I have left of Papa. I lift my head, meaning to protest, but there is such a look of sadness on his face, that the words die on my tongue. I squeeze my eyes shut, ready to hear the worst of news.

'Very well,' he says eventually. 'If you have no riches to give up, you may give up your labour to us instead. You will join the Parlour, if that suits?'

'What . . . what is the Parlour?' I ask, my voice shaking with relief.

'Glory will show you. Go and find her. She will be in the gardens.' He stands, and he is like a giant towering over me. 'Now, child.' He places a hand on my head. 'You are blessed, and you have started the journey to forgiveness in this world. Go now, and I will see you in chapel tonight.'

I cannot believe it. I cannot believe he has said yes to me. I feel as though I have been given the greatest gift of all and, just as I saw the girl in the town square do, I want to fall to my knees and kiss his bare feet. But instead I just whisper, thank you. Then another word rises up from inside me and fills my mouth, and I say, louder now, 'Thank you . . . Beloved.'

Twenty-six

Glory is happy to see me again. At least she does not seem unhappy. She does not say it, but I think she has been waiting for me to come back out into the gardens. 'So, Alice Angel,' she says. 'Are you staying with us?'

I nod, shyly. 'I am,' I say. 'I am to join the Parlour. He . . . he . . . Our Beloved, said you would explain it all to me.'

'Of course. I thought as much.' She smiles. 'Come. I will show you.'

I follow her through the gardens, and I notice how finely she is dressed, despite her condition, in a lemon gown so beautiful that even Mama's Paris creations could not compare. Her ears are splashed with pearls and she has a jewel-encrusted cross hanging from a silver rope around her neck. I am puzzled. Do these things not count as earthly riches? But there is no time for me to wonder any further, for Glory has led me into the kitchen of one of the cottages, and she has flung her arms open wide, as though she is presenting me with a palace.

'Your new home!' she exclaims brightly. 'The others will be back for their midday meal soon. They will know better than me what your duties will be.'

The kitchen is small, and although scrubbed clean, it is furnished in the most basic manner, with only a wooden table, an assortment of chairs, a shabby dresser stacked with plates and teacups, and a large black range. I force a small smile. I do not want Glory to see my disappointment. But I think that even the lowliest maid from home would not think much of this place.

'Who are the others?' I venture to ask.

'Why, the Parlour, of course. They are like you. They had no worldly goods or riches to give up, so they have given up their labour in order to follow Him.'

'What . . . what sort of labour will I be expected to do?' I ask.

'As I said,' says Glory, 'the Parlour will show you exactly what is expected. But it will be the usual servants' duties: washing, cleaning, cooking . . .' Her voice trails off, then her face lights up again as she thinks of something else. 'I expect you will bed down with Beth. She is about your age, I think.'

I do not know what to say. The joy that filled me just a moment since is seeping away now, like a pail of fresh, creamy milk that has sprung a leak, and it has left me with a cold, empty space inside. Suddenly, I am confused. Have I done the right thing in coming here? I think of Eli, alone in Lions House with Mama, and the missing of him hits me in the stomach and makes me flinch.

'You have turned quite pale, Alice,' says Glory. 'Sit a while. The others won't be long.'

I fall into one of the old wooden chairs, suddenly exhausted. I remember Eli's last words to me as I was dragged from my chamber. 'It is for your own good, Alice.' I press my hands to my stomach to quell the pain. Even Eli, at the very last, did not reach out to me. What choice did I have then? To be locked away in the madhouse and left to rot? Or to do what I could to become the sister and daughter I am expected to be? I look up and Glory is gazing down at me. 'You are safe here,' she says as though she has read my thoughts. 'Our Beloved will take care of you, I promise.'

There are voices then, and clattering footsteps. Half a dozen women crowd into the kitchen, bringing with them the scents of sunshine, freshly dug earth and the musky sweat of labour. They are dressed plainly in grey linsey frocks and white aprons that are smeared and splashed with soil, grease and soot: the evidence of their various activities. Their chatter stops when they see me. One of the group, the oldest by far, places her hands on a pair of ample hips and says, 'So, who have we here, Glory?'

I am taken aback by her tone of voice and her familiarity. She has addressed Glory as an equal! I wait for Glory to react, to give the woman a sharp dressing-down, as I remember Mama's fury if a servant were to ever speak out of turn. But Glory seems not to notice. 'This is Alice Angel,' she says, as she rests a hand on my shoulder. 'She has come to join us.'

The older woman nods. 'It is good, the word is spreading.' She looks at me directly. 'Welcome,' she says. 'You are most welcome.'

I smile at her gratefully and then I notice a young woman hovering in the doorway. I recognise her large green eyes and the freckles that are scattered across her face. It is like seeing an old friend, and the fears and doubts that have been growing in my mind like creeping ivy are brushed aside by the brilliance of her smile. 'Hello, again,' she says. 'My name is Beth.'

Beth shows me around the cottage. It is, she tells me, where all the women and girls of the Parlour live. Other than the kitchen, all the rooms are divided into bedchambers. I am to share a bed with Beth, in a chamber at the top of the cottage. The room is all scuffed wood with shabby rugs, a rickety washstand and a stained bowl and ewer. The bed looks barely big enough for one person, but when I pull back the thin blanket, I see that at least the sheets and pillows are snowy white.

Beth drags a small trunk from under the bed and rummages through the contents. 'There!' she exclaims. 'I knew I should find you something.' She hands me a grey frock, identical to the one she is wearing. 'You do want to change your dress, don't you?' she says, when I look reluctantly at her offering. 'You will not be wanting as gown as fine as this here, will you?' says Beth as she fingers the black lace at my cuffs.

'I suppose not,' I reply.

'I'll leave you to it then,' she says. 'When you're ready, come and join us in the kitchen.' She clasps my hands in hers and plants a small kiss on my cheek. 'I am so glad you have come to join us, Alice. So glad.' She skips out of the room and I hear her tip-tapping down the stairs and the murmur of voices from the kitchen.

Alone for a moment, I stare out of the small bare window which looks out over the grounds of the Abode. My new home, I think. It is all so neat and ordered; the lawns cut short and sharp around the edges, a stable block with tidy piles of hay stacked outside, pink velvet pigs snuffling in a sty, and geese, as clean and white as fresh linen, waddling and flapping along the pathways. I look to the grey frock in my hand. Wearing it is not too much to ask, I suppose.

I strip quickly and then fold my mourning gown and tuck it into a small carpet bag that I find under the bed next to Beth's trunk. Then I go to the washstand and rinse the dust from my hands, face and neck. I slip the grey frock over my head. There. It is done. There can be no more doubts now. As I am about to leave the room, I remember one more thing. I unclip the gold locket from around my neck and hide it in the folds of my mourning gown, then I push the carpet bag back under the bed.

Beth has saved me a seat. She pats it with her hand and beckons me to sit. I sidle in between her and a mousy-looking creature who is so slender her collarbones jut like knife edges above the scoop of her neckline. The women pause in their dining to glance at me or to nod, and some murmur, 'Welcome, Alice.' Heat stings my cheeks, but I manage to nod back and say thank you.

Beth passes me a dish of potatoes. 'From our own gardens,' she says. I spoon a couple onto my plate. 'And some pork?' she asks. 'From our own pigs.' I take only one thick, pink slice, although my stomach is so hollow with hunger I could eat the whole platter. As I chew the first salty bite, the chatter around the table starts up again, and I feel that the worst has passed and it was not so very bad or awkward at all. With just a few nods and words of welcome, I have been accepted, with no questions asked. I fork another piece of pork from the platter and take a generous spoonful of applesauce.

Afterwards, I help Beth carry the dirtied plates out to the scullery. 'You haven't done this sort of work before, have you?' she says.

'Is it that obvious?' I shudder, as my thumb slides through a slick of pig grease left on the side of a plate.

Beth laughs. 'I'm afraid so. Your hands . . . look at them. They're as soft as kid leather! See, look at mine.' She holds her hands out to me and I see how the skin is red and raw and how her fingernails are torn and ragged.

'No matter,' I say, not wanting her to think I am weak or unwilling, 'I am sure I can wash plates as well as anybody else.'

'Only if you have water,' she teases. She hands me a pail and reaches to the back of the scullery door to unhook an apron. 'Here, take this too,' she says. 'And you'll find the well just around the back there.'

It is not so bad, this washing of dirty plates, especially once the water has been heated on the range. 'You see?' I say to Beth, as I dry the cleaned plates to a squeak and stack them neatly on a shelf. 'There is nothing to it.'

By the time evening falls, I am having second thoughts. My back aches, my legs ache and my hands are so sore it feels as though they have been trampled upon by horses. Under Beth's instructions, I have swept and scrubbed floors, heaved countless pails of water from the well, beaten the dust from a dozen rugs, scoured tables and flicked a hundred cobwebs from the dim corners of every cottage.

I have learned, by listening to Beth's continuous chatter, that the Parlour is responsible for the smooth running of the Abode. Although we have our own cottage, we must also

155

attend to the other cottages and the mansion. 'The work is shared equally,' Beth explained between grunts, as we beat one of the larger rugs together. 'Some of us do the household chores and others attend to the gardens and the animals.'

'And what of the others?' I ask her. 'The ones who do not belong to the Parlour. What work do they do?'

'They have done their work already,' she tells me. 'They have given up all they own to the Abode and to Our Beloved.'

I do not understand. I have seen a few of the others, strolling around the gardens, sitting in easy chairs with books on their laps, or clustered in small groups taking tea and cake. They are all dressed as Glory had been, in fine gowns and jewels, and would not look out of place in Mama's drawing room. But before I can question Beth further, a bell tolls loudly and she beams at me. 'Tis time for chapel,' she says.

Twenty-seven

It is not like being in a church at all. Although the air is as solemn as it was at St Mary's, and although a brilliant stained glass window throws rainbows of colour upon us, everything else is peculiar. The chairs are not the hard wooden ones I am used to, lined up in regimental rows, instead there is a gathering of wing-backed chairs, covered in velvet and chintz, and a few equally comfortable-looking sofas. There is also, strangest of all, a billiard table standing next to the altar.

I take a seat next to Beth, near to the back, and watch as the rest of the Parlour and at least thirty other finely dressed women, and a dozen children of all ages, stroll in to take their seats, all the while gossiping and laughing gaily. One of the others, a haughty-looking creature with lips pulled tight as a buttonhole, seats herself at the organ and begins to thump out a tune. It is no hymn that I recognise, but I stand with everyone else and listen as the whole congregation sings as heartily as factory workers clocking off after a hard week of labour.

As the final notes die away, there is some coughing and clearing of throats. Then a gold velvet curtain hanging behind the altar is pulled aside, and Henry Prince emerges. I am surprised to see Glory too, with her arm hooked through his.

The chapel stills. It seems even the flies that were buzzing around the ceiling beams have frozen their wings mid-flight. I hold my breath and the moment stretches as taut as piano wire. Then Glory drops her arm from his and moves to sit in a chair by his side.

He is wearing a long white gown which pools at his feet and unfurls like giant wings when he slowly, slowly spreads his arms wide.

'MY FLOCK!'

His words hover in the air above us and then float down and settle on each and every shoulder. I imagine the words to be white feathers, soft and pure. I look around and see that every eye is upon him and every face is flushed with pleasure. I look back to him and my skin prickles with heat as his eyes lock with mine.

'OUR NUMBERS HAVE SWELLED!'

He scoops an armful of air and throws it in my direction. Every eye is upon *me* now, and my skin is on fire. I want to shrink into the floor and melt into the flagstones. Then I feel fingers reaching for mine. Beth curls her hand around my hand and squeezes.

'ANOTHER HAS JOINED US. ANOTHER WHO, COME THE DAY OF JUDGEMENT, WILL NOW BE SAVED.

ANOTHER WHO WILL BOW DOWN BEFORE GOD
HIMSELF AND BE MADE CLEAN IN THIS LIFE.'

My arms goose pimple. I wish they would all stop staring at me.
Suddenly, Henry Prince drops his head to his chest and holds
out his arms. There is silence again, thick and expectant. Beth
nudges me. 'Go to him,' she whispers. 'He is waiting for you.'

I swallow hard, my mouth suddenly dry.

'Go on,' urges Beth.

I move slowly. The others, standing alongside me, move back
to let me pass. Some of them smile and nod at me encouragingly.
My footsteps echo on the flagstones as I walk towards the altar.
I bow my head as I stand in front of him because it seems the
natural thing to do. He moves close to me, so close that I can
feel the heat of him, and I can taste the bitter aroma of stale
cigar smoke. For a moment I am back in Papa's study. *I am
doing this for you*, I say to him. *So you will forgive me.*

Then Henry Prince lays his hand on the top of my head.

'Are you ready to give yourself up to the worship of your
Lord?'

The heavy warmth of his hand seeps through my skull and
coats my mind. 'I am ready,' I whisper.

Henry Prince sighs deeply, and his hand trembles and presses
harder on my head, so I sink to my knees. He begins to talk,
to pray. His words are long and flowery and complicated and
they drift away from me. I try to catch them, like butterflies in
a net. But the ones I do catch do not make sense on their own.

'Immortal'

'Judgement'

159

'Salvation'

'Lamb of God'

'Reckoning'

'Anointed'

Then the whole chapel is filled with voices and the organ starts up again.

'You may get up now, my child.'

I look up and he is smiling down at me with eyes that are soft and sparkling. He offers me his hand and helps me to my feet. I feel as though I have done something wonderful, but I don't know what. The feeling stays with me as I walk back to my seat and it carries me out of the chapel with Beth and all the others.

'You are truly one of us, now,' Beth says, and she hugs me tight to her chest. I think she is right – I already feel the weight of guilt being lifted from me. I hope that wherever Papa is, he will begin to forgive me for my selfish wishes and I hope that one day too, Mama will be able to love me.

Twenty-eight

It is night now, dense, black, muffled night. Beth blew the candle out an age ago, but I cannot sleep. I lie here next to her in the scratchy nightgown that she found for me, and although every part of me feels like a dead weight, sleep just won't come.

I listen for a while to Beth's shallow breaths, envious that she could drift away like that, as soon as her head touched the pillow. It is a strange sensation to have someone lying next to me in bed. I dare not move, in case I wake her. I think it is almost as bad as being tethered to the bed with Mama's leather straps.

I try listening to the night. But here in the thick of the countryside, there is nothing. Just heavy silence. Not even a wind to rattle the windows. At Lions House something always made my ears prick: a late-night carriage rumbling down the street, the whistle of the lamp-lighter, the distant hum of the mill. I try to picture Eli and Mama tucked into their beds. Eli, still reading a book by candlelight, perhaps, Mama in the depths of sleep, her face and lashes shining with a slick of castor oil. Are they wondering where I am? For surely they know I never made it to the asylum. I think of Papa's bed, empty and cold. I think of my bed too, cold and empty. Has Sarah stripped it of sheets? Has she washed the smell of me from them? Has she covered the furniture in my chamber with dust sheets? I think of my gowns hanging in the wardrobe. Will Sarah remember to check for moths? Or has Mama already ordered them to be sent to the poorhouse? Is my journal still lying open on my desk? Has Mama read my most private words?

Questions slither through my mind. Endless questions, slipping and sliding in and out of my thoughts. I feel as though my head might burst.

Beth stirs in her sleep. She turns on her side and her arm flips across my chest. I let it lie there. It is comforting. I wonder where she came from. How did Beth end up here? I realise that despite all her chatter, I have not learned a thing about her.

I decide that I have two choices. I can carry on fighting the night, or I can wake Beth and ask her. I lift her arm away from me and turn onto my side. We are face to face now. Her steady breath warms my cheek. 'Beth,' I whisper. 'Beth. Wake up.'

She stirs again and mumbles. I touch her shoulder and gently shake it.

'What . . . what?' Her voice is thick with sleep.

'I'm sorry, Beth,' I say. 'I'm sorry for waking you.'

'What is it?' she says. 'What's the matter?'

'I can't sleep,' I tell her. 'Would you mind . . . would you mind if we talk for a while?'

She groans. 'Seeing as it's your first night. But I'm telling you, you'd best not be making a habit of this.' She yawns loudly. 'So, what do you want to talk about then?'

'Tell me about you, Beth,' I whisper. 'How did you come to be here?'

She tugs the blanket over her shoulder and wriggles her head into the pillow. 'Nothing much to tell,' she says. 'What went before doesn't matter now.'

'But you must have come from somewhere,' I say. 'Where are your parents?'

She is silent for a while. 'We have no need of parents here, Alice,' she says eventually. 'Only of Our Beloved. He is father to us all.'

'But your real parents,' I press. 'You must have a mother somewhere, who gave birth to you. And a father.'

'I told you,' she says, impatiently. 'Our Beloved is my father. My true father. I don't need any other.' She turns over, onto her back, and yawns again. 'What else did you want to talk about?'

I am sorry that I woke her now, but I try again, nonetheless. 'Glory,' I say. 'Tell me about Glory. She is Our Beloved's wife?'

'No,' says Beth, her voice heavy with sleep now. 'Our Beloved has no need of a wife. Not a mortal wife. Glory is his new spirit bride.'

'New?' I exclaim. 'Have there been others then?'

'Many others,' she says. 'But please don't ask me to remember them all.'

'But I don't understand,' I say. 'Glory must be his wife if she is with child.'

Beth laughs softly. 'You have to learn not to question so much, Alice. You'll see in time how it is here. Our Beloved is God Himself made flesh and you are lucky to be one of the chosen.' She turns over again, and this time she has her back to me. 'Sleep now,' she says. 'You will be glad of it come morning.'

163

But I am more awake than ever. For a thought has just struck me: a strange thing that I had not considered until this moment. We are all women here, women and girls. I have not seen one man, save for Henry Prince, the whole day I have been here. I think of the dozen or so children that were there in the chapel; children of all ages, from a babe in arms to a girl of about ten. Where are their fathers?

He is father to us all, Beth said. I shiver and pull the blanket around me. Children of God, I think. Are they all children of God?

I must sleep, eventually, for the next thing I know, Beth is shaking me awake. I see by the sliver of moon framed in the window that it is barely morning, and as I pull the grey linsey frock over my head, there is a heaviness in my chest and a quiet longing for the comforts of Lions House and the tray of morning tea that always came unbidden to my chamber.

Twenty-nine

'Where is she? You must find her!' Temperance Angel screamed. Eli stood white-faced in the doorway of her bedchamber. He had spent three days looking for Alice. Three days searching the back alleys, the lodging houses and the poorhouses of Bridgwater. He had ridden out to the place where Alice had jumped from the carriage and searched barns and ditches and village inns. But there was no sign of her. No one had seen a thing. She must have headed to Bristol, Eli decided. And if she had been swallowed up in that city, there was little chance of him ever seeing her again.

Eli had never seen his mother like this. She was shaking with rage. Her face had twisted and contorted like some demon. His beautiful, composed mother had gone, and he didn't know how to deal with the creature that had taken her place.

'I will find her, Mama,' he said. 'I will keep on looking until I do.'

'The disgrace! The disgrace! If someone should see her!' Temperance ranted.

'But it would be good news if someone were to see her,' said Eli, trying to soothe her. 'We would know where to find her then.'

'It would be better if she were dead!' screamed Temperance. 'Already they are shunning me. I am the woman whose daughter jumped into a grave! They only come now to mock me and to scorn and to walk away all high and mighty. They do not come to pay their respects. They come to gawp! If they knew she was walking the streets . . .' Temperance collapsed into her chair, the thought too terrible to contemplate.

Eli tried again. 'It is Alice we must think of now, Mama. She is all alone out there, and unwell. She has no money . . . nothing. If you would agree to put a notice in the *Bristol Gazette*, I think we might have a chance of finding her . . .'

Temperance glared at him; sinews throbbed in her neck, the skin stretched tight across her face and for a brief moment, Eli glimpsed the hard outline of her skull and the gaping holes of her eye sockets. She bent suddenly and pulled the slipper off her foot. 'Get out!' she screamed. 'Get out!' And the slipper flew across the room and hit Eli squarely on the jaw.

He stumbled into the corridor and stopped to catch his breath. His jaw throbbed, but his pride hurt even more. He'd always been Mama's favourite, and although he'd felt sorry for Alice, he had secretly relished being the one Mama loved. Eli rubbed his jaw. Was this what it had been like for Alice? And would Mama truly wish her dead rather than it become known that she had run away? No. Surely not. It was grief talking. That was all.

Eli made his way slowly down the stairs. What would Papa do? he wondered. The answer was easy. He would be out there now, still searching. He would be doing everything in his power to find Alice.

Eli hovered outside the study. It was time, he decided. He couldn't put it off any longer. He took a deep breath and opened the door. It was dark inside, the curtains drawn, and just as

166

he had feared, there were shadows of his father everywhere – hovering over the leather chair, brushing against the bookshelves and whispering in the corners of the room.

Eli strode quickly to the windows and tugged the curtains open. Daylight flooded in and helped to ease the ache in his chest. It was only a room, he told himself; it was only a desk and a chair and a pile of papers.

He moved to the chair and sat down. The leather creaked and settled, adjusting itself to a new occupant. Eli placed his hands palms down on the desktop and saw how they left imprints in the dust. He picked up a glass, sticky with the remains of brandy, and put it to one side. Then he gathered the strewn papers and put them in a neat pile next to the ledgers that he knew were filled with neat rows of figures and letters. With the space in front of him clear now, he selected a clean sheet of paper and picked up his father's pen.

I'll do my best, Papa. I'll do all that I can.

Then he dipped the pen in the ink pot and began to write.

Personal Notices

INFORMATION concerning whereabouts of Alice Elizabeth Angel, missing since July 27th, 16 years of age, 5 feet 2 inches, dark hair, dark eyes, fair complexion, will be thankfully received. E. Angel, Lions House, Bridgwater.

He blotted the ink and blew it dry. Then he reached over and rang the servant's bell.

Thirty

It is September now. I cannot believe I have been here for over a month already. The heat of the summer has passed and the days have taken on a steady pattern. Beth and I wake early, before the sun has quite risen, and we stumble down the stairs by the grey light of dawn. The first task of the day is to clear the ashes and sweep the grates clean, before we lay the fires in the cottages and the mansion. Then we fetch water from the well to fill all the coppers, and the kettles are put to boil. We lay out the breakfasts for the others, who rise much later than we do, and then, after all these things have been attended to, we go to the kitchen with the rest of the Parlour to eat our own breakfast.

I cannot imagine life without Beth now. If I had ever wished for a sister, I would have wished for one exactly like Beth. It is such a comfort to lie next to her every night and fall asleep to the sound of her steady breaths.

The work is hard and I have done things I would never have thought possible. The worst of these is the black leading of the grates. It is a task I loathe; the hours on my knees, the aches in my fingers and wrists as I rub and rub and rub. The black lead stains my hands and I have to scrub them raw to clean it off. I have hands like Beth now. They are cracked and bleeding. Sometimes I look at them, turning them over and over in wonder. It is strange to think they belong to me. But I am proud of them all the same. They make me feel even closer to Beth; it is something else for us to share. Sometimes, if a goose has been slaughtered for Our Beloved, Beth will bring some of the fat with her to our room and we will rub it into each other's hands. It soothes our chapped skin, but we have to laugh and wrinkle our noses at the terrible stink.

Of all the things I have learned to do, it is the bread making I like best. Beth has taught me well. Every evening after chapel we dust the kitchen table with flour and thump and stretch piles of billowing dough, before shaping it into loaves and pressing it into tins. I imagine the flour comes from Papa's mill, and I am glad to think that maybe Eli has kept it running. I mentioned this to Beth one evening as we clapped our hands together and sent clouds of flour flying into the air.

'You should not think such things,' she said. 'The world outside these walls should not concern you. Everything we have in here is given to us by Our Beloved. We are the chosen ones, Alice. Have you not understood that yet? When the day of reckoning comes, we are the only ones who will be saved. Our Beloved has blessed us with this flour, no one else.'

She said all this with a smudge of flour on her nose and a smile on her lips. But I knew at once that I had done something wrong. I bit my lower lip and carried on pummelling the dough. It was the first time since coming to the Abode that I had put a foot out of place. I did not want the old Alice to come back and ruin anything. So I promised myself I would not speak of

169

those things again. I would shut my words away in a box inside my head. I would not talk of Eli or Papa, or even Mama. They were part of before, they belonged to the outside and as Our Beloved told us every night in chapel, those who were outsiders and did not believe in him were destined for the Devil.

Beth laughed at my sullen face. 'Don't look so vexed, Alice,' she said. 'Be happy. We are in Paradise after all.' Then she threw a sprinkling of flour over my head and soon we were hooting and squealing and chasing each other around the kitchen table throwing handfuls of flour until we both looked like pale ghosts of ourselves.

It is a pleasant, early autumn morning, and I am happy to be sitting polishing boots on the front step of the cottage. I like it that I am able to take a muddied boot and with a few strokes of a brush and a few wipes of a cloth, I can buff the leather to such a shine that I can see the blur of my face. There is something pleasing about the work, and it feels good that I can do something well and that I can make a difference, even if it is only to a dozen pairs of dirty boots.

The children are playing in the gardens with Beth. It is her turn to mind them today and I smile as I watch how she chases them and catches them and then tumbles around on the grass without a care. She is good with them.

I still do not know if the children belong to the women of the Parlour or to the others. I have learned not to ask too many questions. It seems that the children belong to all of us, and I cannot decide whether that is a good thing or a bad thing. But I suppose it is better to have a dozen or more mothers to love you than to have only one who hates.

The children stop in their play to watch the horses and brougham as they are brought around from the stables. Every other day Our Beloved leaves the Abode and travels to nearby towns and villages to spread his teachings. Beth comes to sit next to me. 'He has not asked me to go with him today,' she says. 'He is taking Glory and Ruth.'

Her voice is flat and when I turn to look at her I am surprised to see tears glinting in her eyes.

'I think I have displeased him,' she says. 'It is weeks now since he has taken me with him.'

'I am sure you have not done anything wrong,' I say. 'How can you have?'

She doesn't answer. Instead she turns to me and grabs my wrists. 'Look at me, Alice,' she pleads. 'Look at me and tell me truthfully . . . Am I pretty?'

It is a strange question, but before I can answer her, Our Beloved appears from the mansion. He is wearing his long black travelling cloak lined in purple silk and he looks magnificent as he sweeps along the pathway towards the carriage. I feel the familiar stirring in my stomach that happens every time I am near him. I cannot decide if it is fear, excitement, expectation or love. But I am nauseous with it, and when I stand, my legs almost betray me.

Everyone gathers to send him on his way and I am caught up in the feeling of belonging to something that is much bigger than anything I can explain. He climbs into the carriage and Glory, her face flushed and glowing, climbs in after him. Ruth climbs up to perch next to Agatha, who is holding the reins as well as any driver I have ever seen. We follow the carriage as

171

it is pulled towards the main gates. Some of the women place their hands on the retreating rear of the brougham, needing a final touch of him. For a brief moment, I see through the open gates to the lane beyond and I am reminded how close we are to the outside. I am glad when the gates are closed and bolted. I turn back to Beth, remembering that I have not answered her question yet, but she is not behind me. I look amongst the gathered faces but I cannot see her anywhere.

I find her eventually, lying face down on our bed. 'What is the matter?' I ask. 'I thought the outside world did not concern us? Why are you upset not to have gone?' She doesn't answer, so I try again. 'Beth,' I say. 'Please tell me what is wrong.' There is silence still, so I reach out my hand and stroke her hair. 'You are pretty, Beth,' I whisper. 'You are the prettiest thing.' But when she still does not answer me, I give her hair a final stroke and leave her to her woes.

Our Beloved does not return in time for chapel, so we sit around the kitchen table instead. The women of the Parlour seem at a loss without him and they fidget with their sewing and their darning. He must have travelled to Bristol or Bath, they guess. He will be tired when he returns. We must have something hot waiting for him.

I look around at them all. Because they never talk about a life before here, I have made up their stories in my head. There's Lizzie with the jutting collarbones, who I decide was once a seamstress in Bristol with a brood of children who all died, one by one, of cholera. Then there is Polly who is careworn but pretty still, and I decide she was once a painted lady that Our Beloved found on the streets and taught to change her ways. Then Esther: maybe a governess who fell on hard times and was rescued from the poorhouse. May is easy. She has coarse features, pale watery eyes and meaty arms. When she talks her voice is loud and sharp. I decide she sold fish from a barrow at Bridgwater market. I think of Agatha and Ruth who are still with Our Beloved somewhere in the outside world. Agatha is pleasantly plump but has a livid scar on her face that runs from the corner of her eye to her ear lobe. She had a wicked husband, I think, and she ran from him before he could murder her in her bed. With Ruth, I cannot make up my mind. *She is like me*, I think, *not used to hard work*. She has a way about her and she holds herself upright as though she was once tight-laced.

She has her secrets, as all the others do. The air is thick with them, all those lost sorrows and joys. But I am glad the secrets are not told. For then I would have to tell my own.

I wake in the night to the sounds of carriage wheels crunching on gravel and voices muffled by darkness. Beth is standing by the window with her face pressed to the glass. 'He is back. He is back,' she is saying over and over again. She turns from the window and by the light of her candle, I see the tears streaming down her face.

Thirty-one

Eli Angel looked out of the study window onto a damp and chill October morning. The sky was a patchwork of sullen clouds and pale blues. Every now and then, a shy sun would inch its way out from behind a cloud, only to be smothered again almost immediately. The day looked like Eli felt inside, miserable and uncertain.

Things were not going well at the mill. The workers were unsettled and had not taken too kindly to the news that their futures were now in the hands of an eighteen-year-old boy. The mill manager, a fastidious little man called Ernest Wraith, was of the same opinion.

Although Eli had grasped the rudiments of running the business from evenings spent at his father's side in the study, out in the real world, the day-to-day management, the bickering, the negotiations, and the finer points of it all, were just a fuddle in his brain. It didn't help that since his father's untimely death, his mother had taken to her room and as each day passed she was becoming more and more difficult. Whenever he was in the house, she demanded every moment of his attention. She would have him sit for hours at her bedside, holding her hand

174

and reassuring her that she was still beautiful. She didn't want to hear about the mill, or about Ernest Wraith, or the workers, or the stack of bills that were sitting accusingly on the desk in the study, waiting to be paid. All she cared about was the fading lustre of her hair and the lines on her face and how many calling cards had been left that day. If there were none, which was often the case, she demanded to know why, or she would weep and lament her disgrace and console herself with a draught of laudanum.

And then there was Alice. There was always Alice. She hovered on the edge of Eli's thoughts all day and every night. She gnawed at his dreams, so he awoke bad-tempered and tired, and he couldn't pass the door to her room without his heart contracting.

Temperance, however, seemed to have wiped Alice from her memory. Eli had learned weeks ago that it was futile to even mention Alice's name in front of his mother. She would set her mouth in a tight thin line and turn her face to the wall, or worse, she would begin to shake and spit obscenities at him. It shamed him to his very core, but Eli had to admit to himself that he had been blind.

Alice had tried to tell him so many times. Since she had first been able to talk, she had tried to tell him. But he had never seen it. He had never seen the truth of it. He had bathed in the adoration of his mother. He had thought she was perfect. He had thought she was the most beautiful woman in the world. But he saw her now for what she really was. As Alice had *always* seen her.

Eli sighed heavily and turned from the window to look at the pile of letters on the desk. The advertisement that he had placed in the *Bristol Gazette* had elicited a number of responses during the last few weeks. At first, it had seemed promising. A young woman answering Alice's description had been seen in a lodging house in St Philips, Bristol. Eli had set out, full of hope and apprehension, to meet the writer of the letter. He had met the man, who gave his name as Samuel Wakefield, in a dingy inn on the outskirts of the district. He had been obliged to purchase a jar of ale and to furnish Mr Wakefield with a handful of coins before he would agree to take Eli to the lodging house.

They had set off walking through a network of courts, alleys and side streets, with Eli struggling to keep pace. He had never seen such places before. It was all so dim and filthy and the ground was thick with rotting vegetable peelings, stinking offal and ashes. The stench was unbearable and Eli had to pull his handkerchief from his pocket and hold it over his nose, just to stop himself from retching. Mr Wakefield had laughed and told him it was only the stink of the scavengers' yards and the nearby alkali works, and he should be glad it was not a hot day.

Eli became distracted by the filth that was sticking to his shoes, and had stopped to scrape some of it off on the edge of a brick wall. When he looked up, Mr Wakefield had disappeared. Eli had not realised at that point that anything was wrong. He assumed they had just lost each other in the tangle of alleys. Eli had pressed on and had enquired of an old beggar woman as to the whereabouts of the nearest lodging house. She had pointed to a nearby doorway and Eli had taken a deep breath to ready himself for the state he might find Alice in.

The lodging house keeper made no effort to hide his scorn. After Eli had finished describing Alice, the man held out his fingers one by one. 'We have a pedlar, a cordwainer, a laundry maid, a splint maker and a horsehair weaver, but I'm afraid I don't recall no *young lady*.' He'd winked at Eli and chuckled to himself.

It was only then that Eli realised he had been duped. He had been led on a wild goose chase and had been left with nothing but empty pockets and shit on his shoes.

After that, he'd been more careful. He'd kept his money in his pocket, refusing to hand over a single coin until he had proof of Alice's existence. But of course, the letter writers had all been charlatans, snakesmen, vagabonds and thieves.

The worst of the lot had been the young girl with the head of tatty yellow hair who had sworn she was his long-lost sister. He had met a large-bellied man in a greasy suit on a street corner in Totterdown; a man who had written to say he had Alice. The man led Eli to a small room at the top of a crowded house in a place called Fox Court. On his way up the dark, winding stairs, Eli had to step over a least a dozen drunkards.

The girl had been sitting on the edge of an unmade bed and when Eli entered the room, she flung herself at him and begged to be taken home. 'Brother. Dear brother,' she kept saying. 'You've come for me at last.'

Eli had to wrench her from him, and in his hurry to get away he had pushed her too hard and she had fallen backwards and hit her head on the iron bedstead. She didn't scream or make a sound, but the man had roared at him and Eli had run, tripping and stumbling over the slumped bodies on the staircase until he was back out on the stinking streets. The sound of the girl's head hitting the bedstead, the dull thud of bone on iron, had haunted him for days.

It had been the last time he had gone to look for Alice, and although the letters kept arriving, he couldn't bring himself to open any more.

Eli picked up the letters from the desk and weighed them in his hands. Was Alice in there somewhere? Was he about to throw away his only chance of ever finding her? There was a knock on the door, and the maid, Sarah, came into the study and bobbed him a small curtsey. 'Mr Wraith is here to see you, sir,' she said. 'And the mistress has been asking for you too.'

Eli sighed. Could he never have a moment to himself? 'Thank you, Sarah,' he said. 'Please show Mr Wraith in. And I will attend to Mama shortly.' As Sarah closed the door behind her, Eli tightened his grip on the letters until they bent and crumpled in his hands. Then he threw them onto the fire and watched for a moment as flames blackened the edges of the paper and the lies and deceits of strangers were turned to smoke and ashes.

Thirty-two

I am sitting in the cottage kitchen with a pile of mending at my side. I remember how I hated to embroider those pointless stitches on handkerchiefs and coin purses. I remember how Mama would make me unpick the stitches over and over again until the fabric was mottled with my blood and the piece was only fit for a cleaning rag. It is different now. There is a purpose to the work and Lizzie often praises the neatness of my stitches and the deftness of my fingers. Her words swell my heart with pride.

I am sliding my needle through torn linen and frayed silk, hemming and cross-stitching, when Glory comes into the kitchen. 'Alice,' she says, her voice breathless with the heaviness of her belly. 'Our Beloved wishes to see you. Come quickly.'

My mouth drops open as the sewing slides from my lap. The tightness of my throat squeezes my words to a whisper. 'Have I done something wrong?' I ask.

Glory's laugh tinkles like the row of teacups hanging from hooks on the dresser. 'Why would you think that? It is an honour that he has summoned you. Come now. We must not keep him waiting.'

It is wet outside from the recent rain and a low mist hangs over the Abode like a damp dishcloth. The women of the Parlour hurry about their duties with their heads bowed low and their shawls pulled tight across their shoulders. Beth is struggling across the courtyard with two pails of water. She rests them on the ground and watches me closely as I follow Glory to the mansion. I smile as I walk by, but there is a faraway look in her eyes and she does not return my gesture.

Glory leaves me in the hall of the mansion. 'You know your way,' she says. 'I must rest now.'

I wait until she has climbed the stairs and disappeared into the shadows of the upper floor before I turn to the mirror. I see a different person from when I stood here last. The girl in the mirror has a bloom to her cheeks now. Her eyes are bright as jet and her hair, which is pulled into a loose knot at the back of her head, shines like a pool of ink. I smooth my frock and check that my apron is clean, and then with my heart skipping in my throat, I open the door to the red room.

'Ah, Alice,' his voice greets me as soon as I enter. He is standing with his back to the window and the watery October light quivers around him like a silver lake. 'Come and sit with me,' he says, and he gestures towards the chairs that are pulled close to a blazing fire.

I sit opposite him and stare at the floor. I know that if I were to look him in the eye, I would blush furiously.

'You are looking well, Alice,' he says. 'A far cry from when you first came to us. Life here agrees with you?'

'It does, Beloved,' I answer. 'It agrees with me very well.'

'I am glad to hear it,' he says. He reaches out then, and takes my hands in his. His fingers are warm and soft and he moves them in small circles over my skin. 'You have been working hard, I see?' he says gently.

'I am doing my best,' I reply, trying to stop my hands from trembling

'Your efforts for the Lord have not gone unnoticed,' he murmurs. 'Look at me, Alice,' he says suddenly.

I slowly lift my eyes and can already feel a tide of crimson rising up my chest. He is wearing a fine woollen suit and I stare at the weave of it as my eyes travel the length of his pinstriped trousers and over his frock coat and black vest. He is wearing a patterned silk scarf at his throat and I stare at the intricate swirls of blues and greens and gold before I finally dare to lift my eyes to his.

'Don't be frightened, Alice,' he says. He must hear the terrible thumping of my heart. The blues of his eyes are ringed with black. He continues to stroke my hands. His lashes are long and silky. He blinks slowly and they sweep to his brows.

He is God made flesh.

The enormity of it all fills me to the brim and I want to stay here forever, with his hands on mine and with his eyes smiling down on me. It is only when he reaches out to wipe a tear from my cheek that I realise I am crying.

'Hush now, my child,' he says. 'There is just one thing you need to do, if you are ready.'

I nod, to let him know I will do anything for him.

'Confess your sins to me,' he says. 'All that blackens your heart, you must tell me now. I will forgive you and you will be made fresh and clean as a newborn.'

181

So I tell him. I tell him all of it. It babbles out of my mouth like a fast-running stream. I tell him how I was born so bad my mother hated me, and I hated her in return. How I didn't know it before, but I know it now that I have the power of the Devil in me and I can make wishes come true. But they are terrible wishes and my Papa died because of it. And I want the power to go away and I want my mother to love me and I want my Papa to come back from the dead.

By the time I finish telling him, I am sobbing wildly and my apron is sodden.

He takes me by the hand and pulls me to standing. 'You have done well, my child. It is good you have unburdened your soul. And I will forgive you, as I said I would.' He puts his hand under my chin and lifts my face to his. Then he presses his lips on mine and I taste the smoke and fire of him and the salt of my own tears.

He lets go of me and I am trembling terribly. I understand now what he meant when he said I would be made clean and fresh as a newborn. I feel like a lamb testing its legs for the very first time.

He sits back in his chair and crosses his legs. Then he takes a cigar from an inside pocket and runs it under his nose. 'Delightful!' he sighs. He points the cigar towards the fire and glances up at me. 'Would you?'

I am confused for a moment. But then I notice the jar of spills on the mantelpiece. I take one and hold it into the centre of the fire. When it catches, I turn back to him and hold the flame to his cigar. But I am shaking so much, the flame quivers madly and he has to hold my hand to steady it.

He blows a plume of scented smoke into the air.

'Thank you, Alice,' he says. 'You may go now. But tomorrow you will travel with me. We are to go to Bath to spread the teachings. We will leave just after dawn, so please be ready.' He leans back in his chair and sucks deeply on his cigar.

My insides are burning as hot as the spitting fire and my lips, where he kissed me, are bruised and throbbing. I toss the used spill onto the fire, and then I walk from the room as though in a dream. I wander across the courtyard with no mind to where I am going. All I know is that something miraculous has just happened. He has forgiven me everything. I told him my secrets and he forgave them all.

Bad Alice has gone, kissed away by God himself.

I touch my lips with my fingertips. No one has ever kissed me there before. Only Eli or Papa has ever kissed me at all, but on my cheeks or on the top of my head. It is a wonder, I think. Our Beloved must love me very much to kiss me on the lips. I want to tell someone how wonderful I feel, how astonishing it is to have all the darkness driven away and to be left as spotless and fresh as a newly laundered sheet.

I find Beth outside one of the cottages, on her hands and knees scrubbing the front step. As I walk towards her she sits back on her heels and stretches her back. She glances up at me, but then quickly looks away. Before I can reach her, she has risen to her feet and is carrying her brush and pail back inside the cottage. 'Beth!' I call out. 'Wait a moment!' She doesn't stop, and when I catch up with her, she is in the scullery emptying the pail of dirty water down the sink.

'Leave me be,' she says, before I have a chance to say

anything. She clanks the pail to the floor and begins to scrub the sink furiously.

'What is wrong, Beth?' I ask. 'Has something upset you?'

'Nothing that is any business of yours,' she answers tersely.

Her words smack me in the face, like a jug of cold water.

'But . . . but what has happened?' I try again. 'Why are you being like this?'

She sucks in a breath between clenched teeth and throws the brush into the sink. Then she whips around and glares at me. 'What were you doing in the mansion, Alice? What did he want with you?'

It is a strange question, but I suddenly understand why she is acting like this. I can almost see the green tinge of envy blooming along the set line of her jaw.

'I had to go to him, Beth,' I say gently. 'He asked for me.'

'Why?' she asks. 'What did he want?'

I sigh. 'Do not be like this, Beth,' I say. 'He loves you too. We are all his children. You told me so yourself.'

She picks up the brush and starts scrubbing at the sink again. There is a horrible silence between us then. The moments pass and I cannot bear it any longer.

'I am to go with him tomorrow, to Bath,' I say carefully. 'Perhaps you could ask to come too?'

She stops her scrubbing and there is another moment of silence. Then she turns to me and suddenly she is all smiles. 'No, Alice,' she says. 'There is no need for me to ask. It is your turn now. And I am glad for you.'

She wipes her hands on her apron and throws me a last tight smile before she turns and walks away.

It is cold in the scullery and I rub my arms where they have goose pimpled. Where I was shining before, now I am tarnished. Because I know, that despite what she said, Beth is *not* glad for me at all.

Thirty-three

It is still dark when I rise the following morning. I slept only lightly, not wanting to sleep on and be late for Our Beloved. I am tired and jittery but my heart is banging away with the thought that soon I will be with him for the whole day or more. I know Beth cannot bear the thought of that. She was restless in the night too, tossing and turning for hours, as though she was struggling in some nightmare. Then she woke and scrambled over me and pulled the pot out from under the bed to heave into. 'Can I help?' I whispered to her. 'Are you ill? Shall I fetch you some water?'

'I'm fine,' she snapped. 'Go back to sleep.' She crawled back into bed and curled into herself. I don't understand why she is so angry with me. I have done nothing but worship Our Beloved, just as she does and just as everybody else does.

I thought that perhaps there was something else nagging at Beth, so I reached out my hand and stroked her back in small comforting circles. *Everything will be all right in the morning,* I whispered to her. She said nothing in reply, but she let me keep my hand where it was. And that was something at least.

Beth doesn't murmur when I ease myself out of bed and pull on my clothes. But she is awake. I know she is. I can tell by the way her breaths are so shallow and uneven. She doesn't wish me a safe journey or even turn to say goodbye. So be it, I think. Let her stew in her own juices.

I have borrowed a hooded cloak and I wrap it around myself as I step out into the cold dawn. Agatha has harnessed the two horses to the brougham, lit the lamps and taken her position on the driver's seat. Our Beloved sweeps out of the mansion and I open the brougham door for him. As he brushes past me, the smell of him, warm from his bed, sets my skin tingling. While he settles in the carriage, I walk ahead with May to help with the gates. We swing them open and wait while Agatha drives the horses through. Then I jump up onto the dickey box next to Agatha and wave to May as she closes the gates behind us.

Out in the lane, the quiet of the hour unsettles me, and without the walls of the Abode to protect me, I feel I have been stripped naked. I pull my cloak around me as tightly as I can, and watch how my breath clouds in front of my face.

There is no one about at this hour and nothing much to see, save for the shadows of trees and the grey outlines of the few scattered cottages in the village. The carriage bumps over the rough ground and I hold tight to my seat to stop myself from slipping. It is going to be a long journey.

There is a faint ribbon of pink light stretched across the horizon and I fix my eyes upon it and watch as it turns gradually to scarlet. We pass through small hamlets and by a silvery snaking river and lonely farmhouses. I think of George and Ada and their kindly faces and how good they were to me. I promise myself I will find them again, one day soon. I will tell them of Our Beloved and of the coming Day of Reckoning, and I will bring them back to the Abode with me so they too can be saved.

I wonder, would Eli listen? Or Mama? I imagine the looks on their faces if they were to see me standing next to Our Beloved as he spread his teachings. Mama would choke on her own tongue, I think. And Eli would follow behind her to catch her when she swooned. They would never listen to me, or to Our Beloved. And Eli could never worship anyone other than Mama.

The sky has lifted now. But the day is grimy and damp. Mournful crows group on bare branches or stand shrieking in the middle of bare fields. At least it is not raining. I pull my hood further over my head so it catches the warmth of my breath.

Agatha has gloves to keep her fingers warm and a thick rug tucked around her knees. I am sorry I did not think to do the same. I watch how she holds the reins so easy between her fingers and how she controls the swaying backs of the horses. She is so skilful that I think I was wrong about her when I imagined her life before. Instead of escaping from the grip of a murderous husband, I think now, that perhaps she lived as a man. She was a farmhand, and slept in a stable, pressed up against the warm flanks of a horse. Perhaps she slaughtered the pigs and drove the farm wagon to market. And perhaps she earned her scar in a drunken brawl at a country dance. I smile to myself. I wonder what she would say if she knew what I was thinking?

I sneak a glance at her, but she catches me looking and takes it as an invitation to talk.

'There's the Tor over there,' she shouts over the racket of wheels and hooves. I look to my left and see the tower-topped hill in the distance, rising up majestically from the Levels. I have heard of the town of Glastonbury and the mystical Tor, where once an abbot and his monks were hanged on a gallows, and I am all eyes now to see it. Agatha tells me it is possible to climb to the very top of the Tor and that the view from the top is the best you could ever wish to see.

Glastonbury is a small town, but very smart-looking. The houses are of a good size and the main street is bustling with traders. We pass by a bootmaker's, a draper's, a chandler's, a cooper's and then a staymaker's. I flinch when I see that one, and I cannot help but rub at my wrists.

At the bottom of the main street, the road winds around to the left and we drive by a huge jagged stone ruin that Agatha tells me was once an ancient abbey. I am more taken by the sight of the Abbots Inn, which sits squat and inviting by the side of the road. But we drive straight past it. My stomach rumbles and I wonder when we will stop for refreshment.

We journey on, leaving the Tor behind us. We pass through a village called West Pennard and through a wood so thick it blocks out the sky. By now, I feel faint from lack of nourishment and sore from the constant jolts and bumps of the carriage and the strain of holding tight to my seat. 'Will we stop soon?' I shout to Agatha.

'Shortly!' she shouts back. 'When we reach Shepton Mallet.'

We roll through another sleepy village, and my eyes grow heavy and my chin falls to my chest. Then suddenly, Agatha is pulling back on the reins and I lift my head to see the welcome sight of a large white painted inn bearing the name of The Highwayman.

It is good to stretch my legs. I walk up and down the grass verge while Our Beloved disappears into the inn and Agatha organises water for the horses. There is a wooden bench outside the door to the inn and when Agatha brings out two glasses of beer and some bread and cheese, we sit there and eat our meal in hungry silence. Agatha sighs and wipes her mouth with the back of her hand. 'It's all talk of witches in there,' she says eventually, nodding her head towards the inn door. My eyes widen as Agatha tells me that a local woman has just been sent to the house of correction for putting a spell on a poor farmer's wife. 'Gave her a box, she did, with a painting of the Devil inside, some strange verse and the legs of toads.'

The wind has risen now and crows are circling the chimney pots of the inn. I am glad when Our Beloved climbs back into the carriage and we can be on our way.

It is mid-afternoon by the time we reach the outskirts of Bath. The city lies below us and from where I am sitting, high up on the dickey box, it looks like a giant bowl of smoke, confusion and honey-coloured buildings. As we draw nearer, the road becomes busier and soon Agatha is battling through a swarm of carts, omnibuses, carriages and people. The noise is overwhelming: the tremendous racket of wheels rattling over the pitted road, the heavy rumble of carts, the beat of footsteps, the shouts of hawkers, and the ringing of bells. But it is the stench that surprises me the most. Bridgwater was not the sweetest of towns, but here the air is thick with the smells of gas, coke, sweat and the stink of rotting meat. But for all that, I feel a flickering in my stomach, a thrill as sharp as a needle and the delicious promise of the unknown.

We leave the horses and brougham in the care of a groom in the courtyard of a small hostelry named the Saracen's Head. It is where Our Beloved stays when in Bath, Agatha tells me. He is friends with the proprietor and there is always a ready and warm welcome for him.

I am travel-weary and dazed by it all, but there is no time to rest. Our Beloved emerges from the carriage looking as fresh as if he had slept the whole journey on a feather pillow. He hands me a wooden box to carry and tells Agatha and me that he wants to fill the remaining hours of the day with teachings. 'There are souls out there waiting to be saved,' he says. I follow him closely, petrified of getting lost in the hustle and bustle. But he is so broad and tall, and he slices through the crowds as easily as a knife through butter, that soon I am just happy to watch the elegant sway of his back and the way that people stop in their tracks and turn to watch him pass.

We make our way to the very heart of the city. The buildings are beautiful here. They are built of soft yellow stone with rows of columns holding up roofs that drip with fancy carvings. The thin October sun washes over the spires of the looming Abbey, turning the stone from yellow to golden. I have never seen such a place before and I twirl on my heels breathing in the wonder of it all.

I set the wooden box in the middle of the Abbey churchyard, which is more like a busy town square. It is filled with fashionable ladies and gentlemen wearing well-brushed hats and glossy boots. They are all admiring the beauty of the Abbey and listening to the faint strains of orchestral music that is seeping out from inside.

Our Beloved slips off his shoes and climbs onto the box. He looks magnificent. His dark frock coat and the blackness of his hair is a shock against the mellow backdrop of the Abbey. I clasp my hands to my chest and listen as his powerful voice booms out across the churchyard.

A crowd gathers at once. I feel so proud, that I am tempted to shout out and tell them all that I already belong to him, that I am already saved and that they should listen carefully if they want the same thing for themselves.

Instead, I watch their faces. I see how some of them stand with their mouths open and their brows furrowed. I see how some whisper to each other and quickly walk away. I see how some of them laugh, as if they are watching a tumbler or a clown from a circus. As some people walk away, others take their place. But none stay for long.

Gradually, the crowd thins until there is only me and Agatha left. But Our Beloved carries on preaching regardless. My heart aches for him. If there was only one soul for him to save, just one, it would make all his effort worthwhile. I look around, desperate to help. A gentleman in a green coat is strolling by. He is not taking a blind bit of notice of Our Beloved. *How dare he*, I think. *How dare he not even spare a moment of his time*. I run after the man and tug on his sleeve. He whirls around, grabbing my wrist as he does.

'Try to lift my purse, would you?' he splutters.

'I would not!' I say, fury stinging my cheeks. 'Do I look like a pickpocket?'

The man glares at me. 'Well, who are you then?' he asks, pulling down the cuffs of his coat. 'What do you want with me?'

I plant my hands on my hips and stare him straight in the eyes. 'The Day of Reckoning is coming,' I say. 'Do you think you will be saved?'

He rolls his eyes. 'What are you talking about?'

'Why don't you listen to him?' I say, nodding towards Our Beloved. 'He saved me. He could save you too.'

The man looks over my shoulder towards Our Beloved. 'Him?' he says.

I nod. 'Yes. Just stay awhile and listen.'

The man snorts. Then without any warning, he spits at my feet and strides away.

I look down at the glistening gobbet, and I shudder. *He has the Devil in him*, I think. I watch his back disappearing into the distance and the hairs rise on the back of my neck.

'What are you doing, Alice?' Suddenly, Our Beloved is by my side and his voice is hot in my ear. I turn to him and see how his eyes are glinting with anger. My stomach drops.

'I . . . I just wanted to make him listen to you,' I say.

Our Beloved takes me by the elbow and leads me away, steering me through the fast-darkening streets. Agatha trots behinds us with the box under her arm. 'I am sorry,' I say. 'I am sorry. Have I done something wrong?'

But he doesn't answer. And I dare not chance to look at his face, in case the anger is still there. He is taking great strides, and I have to half run to keep the pace. The sights around me pass by in a blur. There is nothing but my boots skidding over cobbles and muck and the tight grip of his hand on my elbow.

Finally we reach the Saracen's Head. The windows glow with warm, yellow light and a great tiredness washes over me. I long for a soft pillow and clean sheets. We stop and Our Beloved spins me around to face him. I am breathless from the walk, but he is calm and unflustered. 'Never do that again, Alice,' he says fiercely. 'It is for me to save souls. Not you. Do you understand?'

I nod meekly. But I do not understand at all, and I am overcome by a dreadful disappointment, something that I haven't felt since I was a small child trying my best to please Mama. 'I am sorry,' I say. 'I only wanted to help.'

He looks at me carefully, as if he is trying to make a decision. I can't bear it. I can't bear it if he thinks badly of me.

Then he sighs and turns away from me, as though I am not there any more. 'We have had a long and tiring day,' he says. 'We will eat now and then we will rest.'

He walks into the belly of the inn and Agatha beckons me to follow. It is bright inside and the reek of stale beer and old tobacco smoke stings my nostrils. But there are other smells too, of roasted meats and gravy, which make my stomach curdle. We are greeted by a pock-faced man with a slick of grey hair combed over his head. 'Mr Gantrot,' says Our Beloved. 'We are ready for our supper now. And if you could show my companions to their rooms?'

'Of course, of course,' simpers Mr Gantrot. 'My wife has already turned the beds down, and I have given you the best rooms, of course. As always.' He shows Our Beloved to a small table in the corner of the room, where a fire crackles, orange and inviting. 'Ladies,' he says to me and Agatha, 'if you would follow me.' He takes us to a side room. There is no fire, just a dusty floor and a stained wooden table. 'My wife will bring you supper,' he says. 'Then she will take you to your rooms.'

I feel like a piece has been torn from my heart. I have disappointed Our Beloved. I have angered him. I have done something wrong. I hold my head in my hands and stare at the stains and gouges in the table top.

Agatha nudges me. 'Don't look so woeful, Alice. We will have a good supper now, to fill our bellies. And no clearing up.' She winks at me and takes a large gulp of the beer that has been set before us.

But I have no appetite. My stomach is too full of regret. I manage only a mouthful of potato soup and a few bites of a chop. 'You are not ill, are you?' asks Agatha as she scrapes my leftovers onto her plate.

I shake my head. How can I explain to her how I feel? I cannot explain it to myself. I only know that since I saw the anger in Our Beloved's eyes I feel as though I have lost something precious. 'I am just tired,' I tell her.

Mrs Gantrot clears the table and asks if we would like to be shown to our rooms. We follow her ample backside through the bar and I see Our Beloved still sitting at the table in the corner. He is leaning back in his chair waving a fat cigar in his hand. There are the remnants of a meal and half a dozen bottles of spirits on the table. He is surrounded by a knot of gentlemen, their faces all flushed with drink. Some of them have richly dressed women sitting on their laps and they are all laughing uproariously. I want to walk over there and push my way through the heat of bodies and the fog of smoke to where he is sitting. I want him to smile at me and stroke my hand and tell me that everything is all right. But as Mrs Gantrot leads us past the table towards the back of the inn, he doesn't even look my way.

I had expected to be sharing a bed with Agatha, so I am surprised then, when Mrs Gantrot shows us into separate rooms. It is a relief to wash the dirt of travel from my skin, and even though the sheets still smell of the sweat of strangers, my limbs are so heavy that a bed of straw would have been just as welcome. I lay my head on the greasy pillow and try not to think of him. I try not to think of anything other than the hours ahead of blissful sleep. The street outside is noisy with the yelling, fighting and cursing of drunkards, the noise of organ grinders, carts on cobbles, and the hollering of street performers. It all rolls into one great confused racket which sings in my ears and eventually lulls me into an exhausted sleep.

'Alice? Are you asleep?' The words are soft like feathers in my ear.

'Papa?' I murmur. I can smell the hot fruitiness of brandy and the stale tang of cigars on his breath. I reach out my hand in the darkness to touch his face. My fingers find the soft bristles of his beard and I burrow them into the familiar depth of it. 'Papa,' I sigh.

It is so warm in my bed that I don't want to think that morning has come so soon. I wonder if Lillie will be long with my tray of tea. I slide back into the comfort of sleep. Eli is there. He is laughing at something I've said. 'Oh, Alice,' he says. 'You are so beautiful.' He strokes my hair and lifts tresses of it from the pillow. He presses it to his face. Then his breath is hot on my neck. 'Alice. Alice,' he is saying over and over again.

Suddenly, I am awake. Something is very wrong.

I open my eyes and for a moment I am lost. The room is all darkness, save for the faint glow of a gaslight out on the street. This isn't Lions House. In a rush, I remember. I am in Bath. In a room. In an inn. I push the face away from my neck in a panic. 'Who's there? Who is it?'

'Shush, Alice. Don't be frightened.' The hands are on my hair again, stroking gently. 'Do you not recognise me?'

My heart flips. It is Our Beloved. I see him now, silhouetted against the window. He leans towards me again and puts his mouth to my neck. His beard scratches my skin. 'Alice,' he breathes. 'Have you forgiven me yet for talking to you so harshly?'

The closeness of him overwhelms me. I cannot move, or speak. He brushes his lips against my neck. 'You are very special, Alice,' he whispers. 'I needed to tell you that.'

Still, I cannot speak.

'You are one of the chosen ones,' he says. He runs a hand over the blanket, along my side and over my hip. 'Soon, you will know how very special you are.'

A shiver runs through me. Something does not feel right. But all I can think is that he has come to me, and he is not angry any more.

'Sleep now, Alice,' he says. 'Sleep well and dream well. Tomorrow is another day and there will be much to do.'

Then he is gone.

The damp wool scent of his coat and the fruit of his breath linger on my pillow. I lie rigid as a statue. The street outside has quietened now, but there is still the odd shout and whistle and the banging of doors. My ears strain to every sound. I hear someone coughing in the room next door and, from further away, an insistent grunting. I imagine I hear footsteps and with every creak of a floorboard my heart jumps into my mouth.

Calm yourself, I think. *Everything is all right now. He has come to you and he is not angry any more. And you are special. Very special.*

You are one of the chosen ones, he said. I say the words out loud, over and over again, and slowly, my limbs relax. My breathing comes easy again and I roll over, pulling the blanket tightly around me.

But I cannot close my eyes. I watch the shadows on the walls, stuttering in the faint light. I see the outline of a picture that I hadn't noticed when I came to bed hanging above the tiny fireplace. And I watch how the thin curtains billow out every now and then when a gust of wind finds its way through the window frames.

A church bell in the distance strikes the hour of three. But then it seems like only a minute has passed before Agatha is banging on my door telling me it is time to wake up.

Thirty-four

Eli had never travelled to Bath before. In truth, he would be glad never to have to do so again. But there was the business of a bank loan his father had taken out, and Ernest Wraith had insisted that it was a necessary for them both to meet with the owner of the bank to ensure the future of the mill.

It was all so tedious, the whole business was. As the weeks had passed by, Eli hated his father more and more for leaving him with the dreadful responsibility of it all.

They met with the bank owner in his plush offices in the centre of the city. Eli understood little of what was said. His mind kept wandering back to Lions House, and how he hated it there too. It was like a mausoleum. A dark, empty, silent tomb of a house. His mother rarely left her chamber now. And when she did, she stalked through the house like some wild animal on the hunt. She would suddenly and silently appear in a room and pounce, and it was usually Eli who fell victim to her attacks. It seemed that he could not please her these days. Nothing he did was good enough. If he did not constantly dance to her tune, or reassure her endlessly that she was beautiful and the very best of mothers and that he loved her above all else, then she would threaten to disinherit him and throw him out of the house.

'What have you ever done for me?' she would scream at him. 'You deserve nothing! Do you understand? Nothing!'

He realised how much he had taken being her favourite for granted, and now that he wasn't, he missed it terribly.

Eli began to spend much of his time in the servants' quarters. There was life down there at least, and cheeriness, and always an offering of something tasty to eat. But he knew it wasn't right. He knew he was crossing the line. He could sense that the servants were taking liberties. But he did not have the heart or the strength to do anything about it.

Ernest Wraith cleared his throat pointedly and Eli became aware of a sheet of paper being placed in front of him. 'Your signature, please,' growled the bank owner. Eli picked up the proffered pen and scrawled his name onto the bottom of the page. He had no idea what he was signing, but he did not care in the least.

Eli drifted away again. He had been thinking lately how he should like to go abroad. He should like to see something of the world. Isn't that what all young men were supposed to do? The Grand Tour? The thought of staying in Lions House and enduring his mother's tirades, along with the thought of having to master the complexities of business, filled him with a heaving terror.

But how could he ever get away from his mother? She could hardly bear it when he left the house for a few hours. And when he'd told her that he had to travel to Bath and it would entail an overnight stay, she had been seized by a sudden fit of apoplexy and Dr Danby had had to be sent for.

If only Alice hadn't disappeared. It was *her* duty, the *daughter's* duty, to be at home. It wasn't right that everything had been left to him. It should be her at home in Lions House, helping to organise the servants and overseeing the running of the household. And although he hardly liked to admit to the thought, he knew that if Alice were at home, it would be her on the receiving end of his mother's moods, not him. Maybe he should look for her again, Eli thought. She must be somewhere. But where to begin? He had no idea.

Ernest Wraith was thanking the bank owner. It seemed as though business was concluded for the time being. Eli left his thoughts simmering in the back of his mind and stood and shook hands too. He was sure he must have been told the man's name, but it had slipped his mind completely.

Wraith and Eli left the office and made their way back on to the street. Wraith suggested they should perhaps take an early supper in one of the fine eating establishments tucked away down the lanes behind the Abbey. The White Post, he said, was famous for its rump steaks and fine wines. As Eli had developed a taste for wine of late, he agreed to the suggestion, thinking that a few glasses would at least soften the painful experience of an evening spent in Wraith's company.

Wraith led the way, his chest puffed out with self-importance. 'Come,' he said to Eli. 'I will show you some of the sights on the way.'

But Eli had already seen some sights. When Wraith tried to point out the splendid façade of the Assembly Rooms, Eli's attention was focused on a line of girls walking arm in arm along the opposite pavement. Eli had seen girls like these before, of course, on a certain street corner in Bridgwater. He had seen glimpses of them at least: a pair of cherry red lips, a battered bonnet worn at a jaunty angle and layers of petticoats lifted above a shapely ankle. But he had never seen their kind walking about so brazenly before. There were four of them, all twittering away merrily like a row of sparrows. Eli felt a stab of envy. They seemed so carefree.

The girl on the end of the row, nearest to the road, had on a blue silk bonnet studded with roses. The blue of the bonnet was pale against the blackness of her hair and when she tilted her chin towards one of her companions, Eli saw her skin was as creamy as the top of a rice pudding. For one dreadful moment, he imagined the girl might be Alice. Is this what she might have turned to, to survive out on the streets on her own? The girl in the blue bonnet laughed then, and Eli saw the blackened stumps of her teeth. He shuddered. Of course it wasn't Alice. How could he even think such a thing?

The White Post was crowded, but Wraith managed to secure a table away from the main bar. He had been right about the rump steak. It was as soft as butter. And the wine was rich with spices. Eli let the woozy warmth of it run through him. Wraith started a conversation with a gentleman at the next table. They seemed to be trying to outdo one another with their knowledge of the delights of Bath. Eli didn't mind. It let him off the hook.

He looked around the heaving hostelry and imagined himself to be in Paris, or Venice perhaps. He would be in the company of other young men his of age. There would be jollity and laughter and plenty of pretty girls to teach him the art of flirting. He poured himself another glass of wine.

By the time they left the White Post, to make their way back to the hotel, Eli was somewhat the worse for wear. The afternoon was teetering on the edge of dusk, but the streets seemed busier than ever. Eli concentrated on his feet, putting one boot in front of the other. It was not far to the hotel. He would make his excuses to Wraith and retire to his room straight away. If Wraith wanted to indulge in a nightcap, then he would have to do it on his own.

They cut through a small lane at the side of the Abbey and walked across the churchyard. Eli glanced up from the ground every now and then to check the way forward was clear. His head was starting to thicken and tighten around his temples and he could feel the chewed morsels of steak churning around in his stomach. He stopped for a moment to steady himself and to take a deep breath. Just up ahead, he noticed a large, distinctive-looking man bending down to talk to a girl in a dark cloak. It was the man's hair, though, that drew his attention – long, jet-black ringlets that fell below his shoulders – and the fact that he wasn't wearing a hat.

Wraith came to his side. 'Are you all right?' he asked.

'Yes, yes,' said Eli impatiently. 'I just needed to catch my breath.' He looked back towards the man and Wraith followed his gaze.

'Well, I never,' said Wraith.

But Eli didn't hear him. Because at that moment the man grabbed the girl by the elbow and her hood fell from her head. Eli swallowed hard. It couldn't be. He blinked hard. The man was dragging the girl away now and Eli couldn't see her face any more, just a loose knot of dark hair bouncing against the base of her neck.

He started to follow, quickening his pace as the two of them wove in and out of the crowds ahead. 'Where are you going?' shouted Wraith. 'The hotel is this way.'

Eli started to run. He could see the man's head, bare amid the sea of hats. He was turning left on the main street, Eli was sure of it. Keeping his eyes fixed on the man's head, Eli stepped into the road.

'Watch out!' The words rang in his ears and he was wrenched backwards, away from the road, just as an omnibus rolled in front of him, the horses snorting and its wheels racing perilously.

'What do you think you're doing? You could have been killed!'

Eli turned to see Wraith standing there, his face red and indignant. Eli looked across the road, his eyes flitting backwards and forwards. But there was no sign of the man now, or the girl.

'Did you not see the omnibus?' asked Wraith.

Eli sighed. 'No, I didn't,' he said. 'But I thought I saw Alice. I could have sworn it was Alice.'

'I think maybe you have had too many glasses,' said Wraith. 'You are seeing things.'

'But it looked so much like her!' Eli protested. He turned to Wraith. 'Did you see the man in the churchyard just then? The tall one with the head of black ringlets?'

Wraith nodded. 'Well, yes. I was just about to point him out to you, when you ran off.'

'She was with him,' said Eli. 'The girl I saw was with him.'

Wraith narrowed his eyes. 'In that case, Mr Angel, we will have to hope that it was *not* your dear sister you saw, because that man, if I'm not mistaken, was Henry Prince: a dangerous madman by any other name.'

Thirty-five

It has been two weeks now since we returned from Bath, and there have been some changes. The routine of the day is the same, the work is the same and the meals on the table are the same. All that hasn't changed. But it is all better somehow. I feel as though I truly belong. It was my destiny to come here. Our Beloved called to me and I came.

He asks to see me every day now. I go to him in the red room, most often. He spends long hours writing his sermons and he likes to read them out loud to me. 'You understand me so well, Alice,' he always says.

It is a wonder to me to know that I will never die, nor suffer grief or sickness, because the Lord has come in his own person to redeem my flesh. That is what Our Beloved tells me every day. And I believe him.

He takes me with him when he journeys out into the world to preach his sermons. We have been to Taunton, to the port of Watchet and along the coast to the town of Minehead. I have never seen anywhere so pretty as Minehead. We stood on a pebbled beach looking out across the great expanse of water that Our Beloved told me was the Bristol Channel, which flowed into the great North Atlantic Ocean, and I felt as though I was standing on the edge of the world. We brought a lady back with us from Minehead. She is a widow named Martha Wright. She was moved to tears by Our Beloved. She said she had seen the light and has promised to sell the house she was left by her late husband.

I have learned my proper place now, and I always stand by his side and never speak to the crowds. 'If they have heard me,' Our Beloved says, 'then they will come to me of their own accord.'

Glory gave birth today: to a boy. Our Beloved has named him Power. Agatha assisted in the birth. 'Slipped out easy, like a little piglet,' she told us as she washed her bloodied hands at the sink.

We celebrated at chapel. Mrs Holloway (with the buttonhole lips) thumped extra hard on the organ and we sang until we thought the stained glass windows would shatter. Our Beloved sang the praises of his new son and also of our newest member, Martha Wright, from Minehead. With her kind donations, he said, a new carriage was to be purchased, the Queen's old equipage no less, and four new horses. For the Lord should travel to spread the word in the finest comfort. Then we all sang 'Hail to the King of Kings' until our throats were sore.

Afterwards, we feasted together in the great dining hall of the mansion. There were roast meats and fruits and jellies of all colours. We sat with the ladies and Our Beloved, all as one, and drank to his health with rivers of wine. Only after Our Beloved had retired and the ladies had drifted away to their rooms, did we have to begin our work again.

But it is all done now, and we are back at the cottage resting our weary feet. Agatha has supped too much wine and is goading us into singing again. There is much laughter and warmth. I sit in a chair in the corner and I watch it all. I hug myself tight because I cannot believe how happy I am.

My only sadness is Beth. She is still so cold with me. No matter how often I tell her that Our Beloved cares for us all, she still looks at me with disdain in her eyes. And every night she sleeps with her back to me.

Tonight, as I climb into bed next to her, I try again. 'It has been a wonderful day, hasn't it?' I say. 'Are you not happy that we have another child among us now?' But she doesn't answer. And when I wake, much later, in the thick of the night, I hear her quietly sobbing.

Thirty-six

I am preparing Our Beloved's breakfast. I do this for him every day. He says that no one prepares it better than me. He likes his bread cut very thin and barely toasted. He will only have the two slices and these have to be spread with Gentleman's Relish and topped with two softly poached eggs.

I go to the mansion's kitchen at seven each morning. Mrs Holloway supervises my cooking and always checks the tray before I take it to the red room. Our Beloved likes me to sit with him while he eats and to pour his tea. He never talks while he is eating and he expects me to be silent too. After he has mopped up every last smear of yolk from his plate, I fetch him one of his cigars and light it for him. If he is moved to talk, it is when he blows the first plume of smoke into the air that he will begin. But otherwise he will motion for me to leave and I am left with a terrible craving for him that is only satisfied when he calls for me again.

Yesterday was a good day. Yesterday I spent over an hour with him at breakfast.

'I knew it from the moment I first saw you, Alice,' he said to me. 'I knew you were different. I knew you belonged here with us.'

He sucked deeply on his cigar and blew another spiralling cloud into the air. 'Even among all the chosen ones here, you stand out,' he said. 'You rise above them all.' He looked at me questioningly. 'Where you came from – they did not understand you, did they?'

I shook my head. How did he know these things? How could he see so deep inside me?

'They didn't understand you, because they know no better,' he said. 'How could they? They are the ignorant ones. But you, Alice – you heard the calling and you came.'

He reached out for my hand and he enclosed both of his around it. His hands were warm and strong, his knuckles smooth and white, and the strings of veins that ran towards his fingers were a pale violet. I stared at them for so long that I saw the blood pumping through them. Holy blood – that would run through his veins forever. I was trembling with the glory of it all when he finally bid me to leave with the tray of dirtied breakfast dishes.

I spoon the last poached egg onto the plate now, and arrange it on the tray with the silver teapot and the thin china cup and saucer in which Our Beloved likes his tea to be served. Mrs Holloway places a silver dome over the eggs and toast and moves the teapot an inch. 'There,' she says. 'That will do very well.'

I carry the tray carefully through the mansion towards the red room, my heart beating wildly as it always does when I am about to be with him. I as walk through the hall, I see Beth on her hands and knees running a duster along the thick wooden skirting boards. As she sees me, she scrambles to her feet and brushes a stray hair from her face. 'Morning, Alice,' she says. Her eyes dart to the tray I am carrying.

I am surprised she has spoken to me, considering how she has behaved towards me of late. But here she is, twisting her duster around in her hands and smiling. It warms my insides at once to see her and I realise how much I have missed her friendship.

'Beth!' I say, my voice light with pleasure. I smile back at her, wanting her to see how glad I am that she has bid me a good morning. I wish I could stop and speak with her, but Our Beloved is waiting and his eggs must not grow cold.

I keep my eyes on Beth's face as I walk past and I keep my smile wide. That is why I don't see her foot shoot out in front of me. But I hear her snort of satisfaction as I stumble to the ground and the tray crashes heavily beside me.

By the time I have cleared up the mess and cooked Our Beloved some more eggs, I am nearly a half hour late with his breakfast. 'I am sorry,' I say as I place the tray by his side. 'I had an accident and I had to cook for a second time.'

He looks up from the book he is reading and nods at me to sit. But he says nothing about my lateness and I feel stupid for even thinking he would be concerned with such trivia. As he eats his food the usual silence feels heavy today and painful. I sit in agony waiting for him to finish and praying that he will ask me to stay.

He eats slowly and thoroughly, every mouthful takes forever to slide down his throat. Eventually there is only one forkful left, so I stand quickly to fetch his cigar.

'No,' he says suddenly and my footsteps falter as I stop.

My heart falters too at the tone of his voice.

'Leave my cigar,' he says. 'Go to the kitchen and bring back a bowl of warm water, some soap and a towel.'

I hurry to do as he asks. I do not stop to wonder why he might want these things, I am only too glad to do his bidding.

When I return to the red room he is already sucking on a cigar that he must have lit for himself. 'Over here,' he instructs me, and I place the bowl of water on the floor at his feet.

'Is your faith strong, Alice?' he asks.

I nod. 'Yes,' I manage to say.

'You believe in me? You believe I am God made flesh?'

Again, I nod. 'Yes . . . yes, I do.'

'And yet, when you are trusted to serve me, you abuse that trust and you are late.'

'I . . . I am sorry,' I say. 'It was just an accident . . .'

He holds his hand up to silence me. 'Kneel, girl,' he says. 'Kneel at my feet and wash them clean.'

I drop to the floor and with shaking hands I pick up the soap. I dip it in the water and rub it to a lather. *He is angry with me. He is angry with me.* The thought stabs at my heart and hurts as much as any knife. I lift one of his feet and lower it into the bowl. As it is his habit to go barefoot, his feet are black with grime. I soap first one foot and then the other. I rub over his soles and between his toes and soon it is the water that is black with grime. I soap his feet again, sliding my fingers across the now clean skin, all the while hoping that he will forgive me. But he doesn't speak. He just sucks on his cigar. I cannot bear it any more. It is like all those times I was locked in my chamber at Lions House feeling the weight of Mama's displeasure closing in around me. I rest his feet on the towel in my lap and carefully pat them dry. There is nothing more I can do now. His feet are clean and dry and still he has not forgiven me.

There is only one thing left to do. I lower my face to his feet and I kiss them in turn; first one and then the other, and all the time I murmur, 'Forgive me, Beloved. Forgive me.' I am crying and my tears mingle with my kisses so his skin grows damp with my remorse.

Eventually, he places his hand on the back of my head. 'Rise, child,' he says. 'You have done enough. You may go now.'

His voice is soft again and although he does not say the words, I can tell by the gentleness of his touch that he is with me again and all is not lost.

As I carry the bowl and towel back to the kitchen, my thoughts turn instantly to Beth. It is her doing. All of it is her doing. Her envy has turned sour. She doesn't want to share Our Beloved with me, or with anyone. A flash of anger strikes at my insides. She needs to learn a lesson. She needs to know what it is like to lose something precious so she can be grateful for what she still has. Before I know it, I am wishing this on her. But it feels like a good thing to wish. To cure someone of selfishness cannot be a bad thing, can it?

Thirty-seven

I awake to the sound of frightened cries. The back of my shoulder is cold so I know that Beth is not in bed beside me. She must be having a nightmare, I think. Part of me is glad. I still cannot bring myself to forgive her for the other day. At night, in our room, we ignore each other completely and lie back to back in bed like a couple of statues.

The crying grows louder. She sounds more in pain than frightened. 'Beth!' I whisper into the darkness. 'What is the matter?' As my eyes grow used to the darkness, I see her shadow slumped in the corner of the room.

She groans, then, 'Help me,' she suddenly gasps. 'Help me, Alice.'

If this is another of her tricks, I think as I reluctantly climb from the bed, then I will scratch her jealous eyes out. Lizzie appears in the doorway with a lighted candle in her hand.

'What is wrong?' she asks. 'What is all the crying about?'

I shrug my shoulders and point to Beth in the corner.

Lizzie brings the candle closer and the light from the flame catches on Beth's face. Her eyes are huge and pleading. 'Help me,' she pleads. Lizzie bends down to pull Beth from the floor and as she does, the candle lights up the whole of Beth's huddled form. I let out a half scream, half groan and Lizzie stumbles backwards. The candle flame flickers wildly, from Beth's waxy face, then down again to her blood-soaked nightgown and the black pool on the floor that is spreading out from beneath her.

I don't know what to do. I feel my own blood drain from my face as my heart pounds in my throat. It is like the other times, with Lady Egerton and Lillie and Papa. But I didn't do it this time, I know I didn't. I would never dare to wish for anything like this.

Lizzie is suddenly all efficiency and she calls for May and Agatha. I stand frozen by the bed and watch them lift Beth and carry her out of the room. She is whimpering like an injured dog. 'It is nothing,' they reassure her. 'Calm yourself now.'

'I didn't do it,' I shout after them. 'I promise it wasn't me!'

Lizzie turns to me, a puzzled expression on her face. 'Well, of course you didn't do it,' she says. 'It is God's will that this has happened. Our Beloved's will. It must have been the Devil's child inside her, and the Devil's child cannot be born into this world.'

They disappear down the stairs and I am left in the darkness with only the sounds of their murmurings from below. I try to understand what has just happened but my thoughts are moving too fast for me to catch. I move to the bed and lie down. The blanket is still warm and I think of the blood on the floor in the corner and wonder if that is still warm too.

I wait for them to bring Beth back to bed. They will have washed her, I think, and given her a clean nightgown and will already have put the bloodied one to soak. But they don't come . . . and they don't come. And soon my eyes grow heavy and I have to close them. I see Beth with a belly swollen and taut. She is screaming silently. Then I see, in her arms, a child all slippery with blood and its hair is black with it too. I see above the child's forehead there are two strange marks. I look closer. I put my hand out to touch, then I recoil in horror as I realise they are stumps, tiny, bony stumps. The child opens its eyes then and they are blacker than oil. *I can see inside your soul*, says a cold, little voice.

I wake suddenly. Shivering. My heart pounding. Grey morning light cloaks the room and there is rain spattering against the window. My hands are stinging. When I open them and turn my palms to my face, I see they are pitted with small red crescents where I have clenched my fists in the night. *It was only a dream*, I tell myself.

But I am still alone in the bed, and when I look across the room there is a dark stain of blood on the floorboards. I throw back the blanket and open the window. Cold air and splinters of rain hit me in the face. I am awake now, wide awake. But none of it makes any sense. How could Beth have been with child? Did she lie with someone on one of her journeys outside with Our Beloved? My teeth are chattering now, my bones chilled through. I close the window and dress quickly. I must find Beth.

May and Agatha and Lizzie are bustling around the kitchen. There is fresh bread on the table and cups of steaming tea. The fire has already been lit and the room is warm. 'Where is Beth?' I ask. 'How is she?'

Lizzie smiles at me brightly. 'She is quite well,' she says. 'She is at the mansion, resting now. Our Beloved is praying for her. So do not fret.'

I sit at the table, my limbs heavy with relief. Lizzie pushes a cup of tea towards me. 'Do not worry so,' she says gently. 'Beth will be back here with us soon.'

The first sip of tea scalds my throat, but the question on my tongue burns more, so I ask it. 'How did she come to be with child?'

Lizzie presses her lips firmly together and lifts the teapot from the table. She takes it over to the range and fills it with more hot water.

'How did Beth come to be with child?' I ask again. I look to May and Agatha, but they have their backs to me. I slam my teacup onto the table and the tea spills out and creeps across the table to drip on the floor.

'Will none of you answer me?' I shout.

Lizzie brings the cloth that she had used to pick up the kettle and begins to mop up my spilled tea. 'It is no concern of yours, Alice,' she says firmly. 'It was the Devil's child.' She sighs. 'That is all you need to know. It was the Devil's child and it has come out of her now.' She leaves the sodden cloth on the table and wipes her hand on her apron. 'Right,' she says. 'You must put it all from your mind. There is work to be done. There are grates to be cleaned and fires to be lit and time is getting on.'

She hurries out of the kitchen and May and Agatha follow her. *Perhaps Lizzie is right*, I think. *Perhaps it is no concern of mine. Let Beth have her secret, as I have mine. Perhaps it is better that way*.

I fill a pail with clean water and I take a brush and a cloth. Then I climb back up the stairs and I scrub at the blood on the floor until the water in the pail is the brightest red. Although I try hard to do as Lizzie said, and put it all from my mind, there is one question that keeps buzzing around inside my head like a persistent fly.

If it was the Devil's child, then who is the Devil?

Thirty-eight

A week has passed since I found Beth bleeding on the floor. She is back to work now, and back in our bed. Although quieter than usual, she seems much herself, and we are back to how we were before with each other. I have allowed myself to forgive her, for in my heart I know that it was me who wished it all upon her. But I do not feel any guilt this time. For if it was truly the Devil's child inside her then Our Beloved would have wished for it to be out of her too.

We never speak of it, but at night, when all is quiet and Beth is breathing steadily next to me, I think of the Devil child I saw in my dream, all slippery with Beth's blood, and I am filled with a breathtaking terror. I pull the blanket tightly around my shoulders, close my eyes and search desperately for my meadow.

It is not easy to find. There are too many thoughts and feelings blocking my way. All the ordinary nonsense: the pile of mending still to be done, the eggs to be gathered, the last slice of apple pie hidden behind a pitcher in the scullery. And the darker thoughts too; of Mama and Eli and Papa, now rotting in his grave. I have to pick through them all and toss them to one side. But eventually, I stumble into it, my beautiful meadow, hidden in a deep, dusty corner of my mind. It is the same as always. It is wild and green and peaceful and I am free to run in any direction I care to. Except now there is someone to run to. I see him in the distance, waiting for me, his white gown fluttering in the breeze. He is smiling his beautiful, calm smile; the one that crinkles the corners of his eyes. He reaches out to me and I run like the wind. Only when his arms have folded around me and I am safe in his embrace, do I allow myself to go to sleep.

A strange thing happened today as me and Our Beloved and Agatha were on our way back from Minehead. The light was just fading as we came into Spaxton. I was sitting as usual, on the dickey box next to Agatha, and I was looking forward to a hot drink and the plate of warming supper I knew would be waiting for us on our return. As we passed by the little row of cottages just down from the Lamb Inn, I saw a girl opening the gate to one of the front gardens. She was carrying a jug in her hands and I thought perhaps she had just fetched some ale from the inn. She stopped to close the gate and watched us as we drove by. There was something very familiar about her, so I turned my head to see her all the better. She dropped the jug then. It crashed to the ground and she cried out as it shattered into pieces. Her hand flew to her mouth. But she did not look down at the ruined jug or the spilled contents. She stared straight at me with eyes as round as peeled eggs.

It was Sarah.

I looked away quickly, my heart thrumming hard against my ribs. For a brief moment, I felt a surge of anger towards her. What was she doing here, spying on me? I glanced back and saw an old man had joined her at the gate. Her father. I remembered then, how she had told me that her father lived in Spaxton.

The carriage turned into the gates of the Abode, and the hairs on the back of my neck crisped as I imagined her running after me. Only when the gates were closed and locked again, did I dare to breathe easily. 'You look like you've seen a ghost,' Agatha said to me as we climbed down from the carriage.

And I thought that perhaps she was right. It was a ghost I had seen. Just a ghost from the past. And it was left outside the gates now. Where it belonged.

Thirty-nine

It was a cold, wet afternoon. Eli sat in the dust and gloom of the study listening to the muffled sounds of his mother on the rampage again. The study was the only place he could get away from her and hide behind the pretence of work. She had started on him first thing, at breakfast. 'Do you have to make such a noise chewing your food?' she had begun with. 'Have you no manners? Perhaps you had better eat with the servants in future.'

'I am sorry, Mama,' Eli said. 'I didn't mean to offend you.' He had pushed his plate away, thinking it would be better if he didn't eat at all.

'I see!' Temperance had said, throwing her napkin onto her own plate, 'Even the food in this house isn't good enough for you any more. Or are you just a wastrel? Like your father was.'

'Don't be silly, Mama. I have just had my fill. That is all.'

'Had your fill?' Temperance had said. 'Just as you've had your fill of me? That's right, isn't it? You've had enough of me, just as your father had.'

'Oh, Mama.' Eli could see her colour rising and the edges of her nostrils beginning to quiver dangerously. 'You know that's not true. Papa loved you and so do I.'

'Pah!' Temperance spat. 'You are a liar. A pathetic liar. Look at you. You are not even man enough to fill your suit. At least your father knew how to run the business and provide for us. You are just a useless little boy, Eli. Do you hear me? A useless little boy.' She picked up her napkin and wiped the flecks of spit from the corners of her mouth. Then she pierced a chunk of devilled kidney with her fork and placed it in her mouth with a satisfied sigh.

Eli had sat for a moment watching the precise way his mother's jaws worked the offal in her mouth to a paste. He had never noticed before how fragile his mother's beauty was. As her jaws clenched and unclenched, he saw that from a certain angle and with the mottled light of the morning catching on the powdered mask of her face, she was actually quite ugly.

She glanced up at him. 'Are you still here?' she asked quite pleasantly. And before Eli could answer, 'Please leave me. You are disturbing my appetite.'

Eli had been only too glad to slink away. But from inside the safety of the study he could hear the hurried footsteps of servants skittering this way and that and knew his mother was making their lives a misery too.

He sighed and put his head in his hands. At once, Alice came to mind, as she always did. In the month since Eli had returned from Bath, he had been unable to forget the girl he had seen outside the Abbey, or the strange man with the jet-black ringlets. For a time, he managed to convince himself that it had been the wine skewing his vision. With a skinful of alcohol was it not likely that his imagination had run away with him?

223

However much he tried not to think of her, Alice's face kept creeping into his dreams and into his waking hours. He saw, over and over again, the hood fall from her head to reveal her black hair and the familiar line of her nose and jaw.

Wraith had told him the little he knew about the man he called Henry Prince. 'I have seen him once, preaching in Bridgwater,' he had said. 'He proclaims himself to be the Messiah. Belongs in the madhouse if you ask me. But somehow he has managed to persuade a good many wealthy women to believe him, *and* to pay for the building of his *Abode of Love*.' Wraith pursed his lips in disgust. 'They say,' he had whispered, 'that he has fathered a child with at least a dozen of them. There is always some piece of scandal written about him in the newspapers.'

Eli decided he needed to find out more about this Henry Prince. He couldn't imagine for one instant that Alice would be caught up with someone like that, but his curiosity was piqued. And any chance to find Alice would be a chance worth taking. If he could just bring her home, how much better things would be. He would be free to travel; Wraith would take care of the business, and Alice? Well, Alice would be back where she belonged.

He looked at the pile of newspapers mouldering by the side of fire; the ones his father had kept to roll into spills. There must have been dozens there. Arthur Angel had never thrown anything away.

Eli picked up an armful of the newspapers and spread them out on the desk. He blew the soot and dust from the covers and settled down to read. Most of the papers were copies of the *Bridgwater Gazette*, but there were a few copies of *The Times*, which Arthur Angel used to send out to London for.

Eli idly flicked through the pages. He wasn't interested in current affairs or foreign affairs or the court circular and soon his mind began to wander. So much for Wraith's assertion that Henry Prince was always in the newspapers. An hour passed, and Eli was about to give up, when his eye caught upon an unusual word. *Agapemonites*. He quickly scanned the article below, and there at last, he found the name, Henry Prince.

It has been reported that on Tuesday last, a certain Mr Lewis James of Charlinch, Bridgwater, staged an attempt to rescue his wife from the clutches of the self-styled 'Messiah', Henry Prince of the notorious Abode of Love in Spaxton, near Bridgwater. Determined not to lose her and her fortune of £5,000 without a struggle, he travelled to Spaxton the night preceding the adventure in the company of three assistants, there to protect him from the fury of the Agapemonites. He slept at the Lamb Inn, which adjoins the institution, and early in the morning he scaled the gates, entered the grounds and secreted himself behind a conservatory to await a sighting of his wife.

Time wore on and nothing particular transpired till about nine o'clock, when his three assistants heard James exclaim, 'I will have you, Harriet!' This was followed by a piercing shriek of 'Murder!' uttered by a female voice. The trio immediately jumped over the gates into the grounds of the Agapemone where they were met by some 30 or 40 women and children. In a few minutes Mr James himself was forcibly ejected and the four invaders had to come away crestfallen, their enterprise having failed. But Mr James remains undeterred. He is convinced that if he can release his wife from the influence of Henry Prince, he can shake her belief in the delusion she now credits.

It will be remembered that the relatives of another inmate of the Abode of Love, a certain Louisa Jane Nottidge, tried every means to disabuse her mind of the monstrous notion that Prince was God Almighty, and had eventually to place her in a lunatic asylum, for the two-fold purpose of dissipating her mad belief and keeping her out of his clutches. They were unsuccessful.

It was a strange story indeed, thought Eli. And that it should be happening just a few miles away. It was odd that he had never heard any whisperings about it before. But then, why should he have? It was a scandal, he reminded himself, and as such, did not concern the likes of him.

There was knock on the door. Eli sighed. He knew already who it would be, and he knew what the rest of his day would entail. He straightened up the rifled newspapers into a neat pile on the desk. The knock came again. Eli clenched his fists and banged them hard on the desk. He couldn't carry on like this for much longer. With a heavy heart he opened the door to Jane. 'Your mother wishes to see you,' she said.

'Yes, yes,' said Eli. 'Tell her I will be with her in a moment.' He went to the window and looked out at the dismal afternoon.

He could be sitting outside a café in Rome right now, he thought, or strolling through a park in Prague. But instead, he would have to spend the rest of the day enveloped in the lavender fog of his mother's chamber, dodging her criticisms and put-downs and spiteful words.

He turned from the window. But before he left the room, he swiped at the pile of newspapers so the pages flew from the desk into the air and landed scattered about the floor like a flock of angry birds.

Forty

They waited until morning to tell Master Eli. The evening before had been too full of questions and disbelief for a decision to be made. When Sarah had run into the kitchen in a flap after returning from her monthly visit to her father in Spaxton, Jane and William had been sent for. 'Are you sure it was her?' they had asked Sarah. 'Are you sure it was Miss Alice?'

Sarah's cheeks had been as pink as the slices of ham sitting on the table waiting to be eaten. 'I have seen her!' she had squealed. 'I have seen Miss Alice!'

They had asked her the same questions over and over again. Maybe it was someone who just resembled Miss Alice, they suggested. Maybe the light played tricks with your eyes? Poor Sarah was reduced to tears.

'Why would I make it up?' she sobbed. 'I tell you. It was Miss Alice. I saw her. Clear as day. And she saw me too.'

'It is late now,' William had said. 'We will sleep on it, and I will decide what to do in the morning.'

And so it was, that along with his morning tea and jug of wash water, Eli received the news that his sister had been seen riding atop a carriage in Spaxton. And that the carriage had entered the grounds of the mysterious Abode of Love.

Eli, his head still foggy with sleep, thanked William for the news and dismissed him with a wave of his hand. 'Oh . . . But say nothing to my mother!' he shouted, as the old valet closed his chamber door. Eli sat propped up against his pillows until his tea grew cold in its cup.

So, I have found her at last, he thought. And she was never that far away. It had been Alice he had seen in Bath. It *had* been her, and not some wine-induced apparition after all. But the Alice he had seen that day was being dragged through the streets. Had she been taken to this Abode place by force then? He didn't like to think that. He didn't like to think what she might have been doing to survive out on the streets by herself all this time.

What should he do? He rubbed the sleep from his face. He would have to get her out. That much was certain. He needed her back at Lions House. He had had more than enough of Mama. It was Alice's turn now. He would have to go about it discreetly though, tell the servants to keep quiet. He couldn't let Mama know yet. God only knows what she would say or do.

He would ride out to Spaxton today, he decided. Have a look at the place. Go to the inn he'd read about in *The Times*. Talk to a few people. Make some plans. He rang for more tea. Then he jumped out of bed, suddenly full of something much better than the gloom and drudgery of the last few weeks.

He whipped the curtains open and saw it was a perfect day for riding out. A little misty perhaps, but that would soon lift, and if he hurried, he could be out of the house before Mama finished her morning toilet and began to demand his attentions.

Forty-one

It was good to be back in the saddle. Eli had missed the freedom and the heady scents of polished leather and hay-sweet horse breath. He rode hard, avoiding the roads and lanes and choosing instead to gallop through fields and over farmland until the pulse in his neck beat in rhythm to the pounding hooves of his horse and the wind blew his skin tight across his face.

If he hadn't taken directions, Eli was certain he would never have found Spaxton. It was tucked away in the back of beyond. Only one lane led to it, and it wound around so narrowly and for so long that Eli began to imagine it would never end. But then, as if out of nowhere, a cottage appeared and then another and soon Eli found himself staring at the entrance to the Lamb Inn, wondering what on earth he was going to say. How did you go about admitting to anyone that you had lost your sister?

It was warm and inviting inside the inn. A fire was burning and the low hum of voices filled the air. Some men, farmer types, were gathered around the bar. They gave him a cursory glance before turning back to their drinks and conversation. Eli walked to the bar, pulling nervously at the cuffs of his riding jacket.

The landlord greeted him blithely, as though he were used to strangers walking into his inn. He poured Eli a jar of frothing beer. Eli swallowed a mouthful. It was warm and yeasty and he tried not to grimace. After a few more mouthfuls, Eli found his nerve. He cleared his throat. 'Excuse me,' he ventured. 'Could you tell me something of the Abode of Love and the man they call Henry Prince?'

The landlord sighed. 'You look a bit young to be a journalist,' he said.

'I'm . . . I'm not a journalist,' said Eli. 'Only I did read about this place in *The Times*, and I wanted to come and see it for myself.'

'And why might that be, young sir? You looking to join his flock?' The landlord laughed and winked at the gathered men. They sniggered into their beers and Eli felt his face grow hot.

He took another gulp of beer. 'No,' he said. 'But I should like to know where I can find him, this Henry Prince.'

'You have found him,' said the landlord. 'The Abode is next door, behind the walls. But actually seeing him is another matter.'

'Does he not receive visitors?' asked Eli.

Again the landlord laughed. 'Not unless you are a woman,' he said. 'And a rich one or a good-looking one at that.' He poured himself a beer and leaned his elbow on the bar. 'Why are you so interested anyway?'

Eli looked at the landlord, grinning away as if it was all a great joke. He didn't want to tell him. But he couldn't think of any other way. Eli took a deep breath. 'It is my sister,' he said. 'I think she is inside the Abode. I think Henry Prince has kidnapped her.'

The grin dropped from the landlord's face. He looked into his beer for a moment, then lifted his eyes back to Eli. 'I'll tell

231

you one thing,' he said. 'All the women and girls in there, are there because they want to be. He tells them he is God, you see. And they all believe him. They're a strange lot to be sure. But they keep themselves to themselves. They don't bother us. Most bother we get is from folk like you, and journalists, of course. They can't get enough of it.'

'My sister doesn't want to be in there,' insisted Eli. 'She was kidnapped. I'm telling you.'

'That's what they all say,' said the landlord. 'People like you, who come looking for their wives or mothers or sisters.' He lowered his voice to a whisper. 'But I'm telling you, none of them want to leave. Only one, I remember, was ever taken away. And she weren't ever right in the head again. Had to put her in the madhouse, they did.'

'I don't believe you,' said Eli, although he remembered the newspaper article he had read, only the day before, that spoke of a young lady and a lunatic asylum.

'Suit yourself,' said the landlord and he turned to his other customers.

'No, wait!' said Eli. 'Please. There must be a way I can get in there. Just to see her. To see that she is well, and happy.'

The landlord turned back. 'Listen,' he said. 'You could climb the walls if you wish. Or break down the gates. But they'll throw you out as soon as you step foot inside.' His face lit up for a moment. 'Or,' he said. 'You could wait outside the gates. They ride out most days. You might be lucky and catch sight of her then.' His eyes glinted. 'I can do you a good rate on a room.'

Forty-two

I am sitting in the red room with Our Beloved. I brought him a tray of tea and he asked me to stay and share it with him. He is sitting at his desk with his cup by his side and I am in a chair by the fire. It is peaceful in the room with only the scratching of Our Beloved's pen and the spit of the fire to break the silence. I sip my tea, content to be in his presence and away from the daily chores for a while.

I watch as his shoulders shift beneath the fabric of his coat as he moves his pen across the page. I have never felt such love for anyone. Not even Papa. But that is how it should be, I tell myself. Shouldn't everyone love the Lord above all else?

I place my cup back in its saucer and fold my hands in my lap. I would be happy to sit here like this for always as long as he is next to me.

It is a fine day today. One of those rare autumn days when the sun shines bright and lifts the gloom of decay from the world. A ray of sun is slanting through the window now. It strikes the top of Our Beloved's head, lighting the blackness of his hair with a golden halo. It is just a small miracle, but a miracle nonetheless.

He leans away from his work then, and as he does, a grey cloud rolls across the sky and sends its shadow into the room.

He rises from his chair and comes to sit next to me. My heart swells to bursting, as it always does, and I try to swallow the dryness from my mouth. He takes my hand in his. 'Alice,' he says. 'I have some wonderful news for you.' He pushes a stray thread of hair from my forehead. 'It has been decided that you are ready now. Ready to receive the greatest honour of all.'

He pauses and looks at me intently. I try to hold his gaze, but there is such power there that I weaken and lower my eyes.

'You are ready, aren't you, Alice?' he asks. 'I am not wrong about you, am I?'

I lick my lips. 'I am ready, Beloved,' I reply. 'I am ready to do whatever you ask of me.'

He laughs then, and the brightness of the sound chases the shadows from the room. 'It is agreed then! You are to be my Queen! My spirit bride!' He pulls me from my chair and spins me about the room. 'A drink!' he shouts. 'A drink to the Lamb of God and his bride!'

I am breathless and dizzy, my thoughts a tangle of knots that I cannot unpick. He hands me a glass of amber liquid and I drink it one gulp. It burns my throat and stings my eyes, but the warmth of it spreads out from my belly and trickles through my arms and legs until even my fingers and toes are tingling. *His queen. His bride.* I fall back into a chair.

I would never have dared to wish for this moment. I would never have dared to wish to be so happy. But it has happened anyway, without any wishes at all. And perhaps that is how all good things should happen.

* * *

I leave the mansion in a daze. The ceremony is to be tomorrow. Tonight will be my last night in the cottage. Then I will move into a room at the mansion. 'It is fitting,' Our Beloved told me, 'that the bride of the Lord should be by his side both day and night.'

By the time I get back to the cottage, the news has spread throughout the Abode. I hear it being spoken of softly, with bated breath. The women of the Parlour look at me differently. There is respect in their eyes and a certain deference. They tiptoe around me and nod at each other knowingly. I soak it all up. It is the best feeling in the world to know, at long last, that I am truly special. I have been chosen by the Lord to be his spirit bride!

How I would laugh at Mama, if she were here. Look at me, I would say. What do you see now? A wicked and troublesome child that belongs in a lunatic asylum? Or a young woman whose soul has been washed so clean that she is betrothed to the Lord himself? I would spit at her feet if I could. For I know now, that it is she who is vulgar and unworthy and I know that she too will perish, along with the rest of the outsiders, when the Day of Reckoning comes.

And Eli too, I think. How weak he was to have never stood up to her, to have been blind to all her faults. He deserves to perish too.

Only Papa ever understood. Only Papa ever accepted me and loved me for who I was. But he is already saved. He is already in Paradise. And I am thankful for that.

I want the day to pass quickly so tomorrow will come all the sooner. I busy myself with chores to keep my mind from racing. What seemed like drudgery before is nothing – now that I know that today is my last day in the Parlour. I take a basket of wet linen out to the gardens and peg the pieces on the line. It will dry beautifully in the autumn sun. I watch the breeze fill the sheets and set them sailing into the sky. I feel as though I am sailing with them, growing lighter and lighter and flying higher and higher towards Heaven. I stand in the midst of the billowing whiteness and throw my arms in the air. I twirl around, this way and that, and let the wind catch my hair. And then I am laughing, bubbles and bubbles of joy bursting from my mouth.

I see Beth staring at me from across the lawns, her arms folded tightly across her chest. I stop my twirling and lift my hand to wave. She starts, as though I have woken her from some deep dream. Then she turns on her heels and walks away.

It is quiet at supper. The women of the Parlour talk gently to each other and pass around the dishes politely. Every now and then, I catch one of them looking at me from under lowered eyelids. I will miss them all. They have been kindness itself to me. But I was never truly one of them. I always belonged with the others.

Beth is sitting at the end of the table, as far away from me as she can get. I notice that she barely touches her food. She is the first to leave the table and she is quick to take the dirty plates out to the scullery. Her envy has surfaced again, I think, and it pains me that she cannot bring herself to be happy for me.

Beth does not come back to the kitchen, but the rest of us sit awhile by the fire. Lizzie stitches the hem of a nightgown while Agatha dozes gently in her chair. Polly and May split

236

a deck of cards at the table and Ruth sits and stares into the fire, braiding and un-braiding the skein of hair that falls over her shoulder.

I look down at my worn linsey frock. I will have no need of it any more, nor the scuffed boots that have seen better days. *I will need new gowns*, I think, *and petticoats and slippers and all manner of beautiful things. A new cloak too, for when we ride out in the carriage. I will no longer have to sit on the dickey box. Next time, I will be inside with him, sitting comfortably on velvet seats.*

One by one, the women of the Parlour take their candles and bid each other a goodnight. They take special care to kiss me on both cheeks, and I am sure that Polly almost curtsies. For the last time, I climb the stairs and prepare for sleep, next to the still and silent form of Beth. Tomorrow night there will be feather pillows and a thick quilt, and maybe even hangings of rich damask around the bed. And Beth will be glad to be rid of me. I won't be glad to be rid of her though. My heart aches to know that I will soon lose the only friend I have ever had.

I blow out the candle and I lie down next to her. The faint reek of smoking tallow fills the air. But I can smell Beth's hotness too, the anger of her, seeping from her skin. I can tell she is still awake. She is too quiet and her breathing is too shallow for sleep. 'Why do you hate me?' I ask. 'Is it because he has chosen me and not you?'

She sucks in her breath. So I know she has heard me.

'Beth?' I nudge her hard, so the bed rocks. 'Beth?' I will keep her awake all night until she answers me. I nudge her again and push against her legs with my feet until she grunts.

At last, I hear her sigh in defeat and she whispers something that sounds like, 'Come away with me, Alice.'

'What did you say?' I whisper back.

She shifts then and turns over, onto her back. 'Will you come with me?' she whispers. 'I have to leave here, and I think you should come with me.'

It is my turn to be silent. I am confused. 'What do you mean?' I finally ask. 'Why would I want to leave here?'

'You don't know anything, Alice,' she says. 'But you have to trust me. You have to get away from here. Before it's too late.'

'Too late for what?' I ask.

'Just trust me, Alice. Please,' she says. 'We can go tonight. The dogs know me. They won't bark and alert anyone.'

'But go where, Beth? What are you talking about?' I think maybe she is half asleep and doesn't know what she is saying.

'We could be in Bridgwater by morning . . . or Taunton,' she says quickly. 'You have family in Bridgwater, don't you? You could go there. You could tell them this was all a mistake. You didn't know what you were doing. They would have you back, wouldn't they, Alice? They would, wouldn't they?'

She is not making any sense, but she is talking to me at least and I am curious. 'What about you?' I ask carefully. 'If you do leave here, where will you go?'

'To Taunton,' she says. 'I have a sister there.' She pauses. 'At least, that is where she was living when I first came here.'

'When *did* you first come here, Beth?' I ask gently.

'Years ago,' she says. 'I can't remember exactly.' She turns to face me. 'My mother brought me here after my father died. I was only young so I had no choice. She gave everything we owned to

Our Beloved and my sister swore she'd never speak to her again. And the thing is, she never did get to speak to her again.' Beth sighs deeply. 'You see, my mother died not long after we came here.'

'Why have you never told me this before?' I ask.

She shrugs. 'There was no need,' she says. 'I had everything I could wish for here. I never wanted to think of what went before.' She is silent for a moment. 'But now . . .' she says, her voice suddenly strong again. 'Now, Alice, things have changed. I have to leave and you must come with me.' She puts her hands on my shoulders. 'Please, Alice. Please. You must listen to me. You can't stay here.'

I push her hands away. She is beginning to annoy me. Her words are stabbing inside my head like prodding fingers. She is confusing me and spoiling all the joy of the day. 'I don't want to go anywhere, Beth,' I tell her. 'My place is here. Tomorrow is the most important day of my whole life. What is wrong with you? Why are you talking like this? And after the way you have treated me, why should I believe anything that comes out of your mouth?'

'I know I have treated you badly, Alice,' she says. 'And I am so very sorry for that. I thought you were taking him away from me, but now I know how wrong I was. But you can't do it, Alice,' she presses. 'You don't understand. You can't become his bride. Please listen to me!'

But I do understand. I understand very well. And I am furious that her envy has wormed its way so deeply inside her. 'I am sorry, Beth,' I say. 'I am sorry he didn't choose you.'

'It's not about me, Alice,' she says, sharp and bitter. 'Open your eyes . . .' Suddenly her voice breaks and she tugs at the

239

blanket to wipe her eyes. 'It's too late for me, Alice. But it's not too late for you. Please come with me. We can help each other.'

I know what she is doing, and I won't let her carry on. 'I am sorry, Beth,' I say, 'that you have lost your way. Our Beloved would have chosen you, if it was meant to be. But it wasn't meant to be. He chose me instead, and if you love him as you should, you would not say such things or question his decisions.' I pull the blanket aside and climb from the bed.

'Where are you going?' I hear the panic in her voice.

'It doesn't matter,' I say. 'But don't worry, I won't tell Our Beloved how you have betrayed him.' I pull the small carpet bag, which still holds my old mourning gown with Papa's gold locket hidden inside its folds, out from under the bed. Then I take my frock and shawl from the hook by the bed, pick up my boots and walk to the door.

'Don't do it, Alice,' she whispers desperately. 'Please, listen to me.'

'Goodnight, Beth,' I say. I open the door and walk out.

'Alice!' I hear her pleading. 'Alice! Come back!'

I close the door on her poisonous words. I do not need to hear these things.

It is still warm in the kitchen. I poke at the fire to wake the dying embers and throw a few more sticks on. I pull my frock over my nightgown and wrap my shawl tight around my shoulders. Then I settle in a chair and wait for morning to come.

Forty-three

'Alice! Alice!' Somebody is calling my name. 'Wake up, Alice. It is time.' I open my eyes and groan at the stiffness in my neck. Agatha is standing in front of me, looking at me quizzically.

'Have you been here all night?' she asks.

I nod and rub my eyes with the heels of my hands. 'I couldn't wait for morning to come.'

She smiles at me understandingly. 'Well, Alice Angel,' she says. 'It is your day now. You must go to the mansion to prepare.'

'This minute?' I ask.

'Yes,' she says. 'They are waiting for you.'

'Should I not wash first?' I ask in a panic. I can smell the sour night sweat rising from my clothes.

Agatha laughs softly. 'There is no need. They will do all that is required at the mansion. Now hurry. It's not every day Our Beloved takes a new bride.'

I jump from the chair and fling my arms around her neck. 'Thank you, Agatha. Thank you!'

'Go on with you,' she says and a blush reddens the long scar on her face. 'I'll see you later, in chapel.'

I take up the old carpet bag and run from the cottage, although I feel as though I could fly. The morning chill washes across my face and wakes me as well as a jug of cold water. It is misty outside and there is no one about yet. I run across the lawns and only then do I realise that I left my boots in the cottage kitchen. I laugh out loud as my feet fly through the wet grass. I have a vision then. That I am in my meadow running free. My clothes are loose around me and my hair sails behind. I am running to him, and everything is as it should be. Only this time it is not a vision at all. This time it is real.

The bloodhounds are prowling around by the door to the mansion. They growl low in their throats as I climb the steps. I swallow hard and look straight ahead. It is their yellow eyes that frighten me the most. But if I don't look, then they won't see my fear. They will know me better when I am here every day, I think, to calm myself. I enter the hallway and close the door behind me. It is all quiet and muffled inside. But someone has already lit the candles. My feet leave wet prints on the wooden floor as I walk further in, wondering where to go. I cannot go to the red room, surely? It is bad luck for a bride to see her intended on the morning before their union.

'Hello?' My voice echoes above my head and the candle flames flicker. 'Hello? It is Alice.' A door slams somewhere. I shout louder. 'Hello!'

'Alice.'

I look up and see there is someone at the top of the stairs.

'Come on up, Alice. We have been waiting for you.'

I start up the stairs and see it is Mrs Holloway, with her buttonhole mouth stretched into a smile.

'Follow me,' she says. 'We are all here.'

She leads me along the landing, past at least a dozen doors. Up here, there is soft carpet on the floor and rich tapestries on the walls. The air is light and perfumed and I feel as though I should whisper. I hear a small cry from behind one of the doors. 'That is Power,' says Mrs Holloway. 'He is blessed with a strong voice.'

'And is Glory well?' I ask out of politeness.

'Oh, yes,' says Mrs Holloway. 'She couldn't be better. There is no pain or illness in Paradise, is there?'

She opens a door and beckons me into a chamber that would make Mama's chin drop to her feet. There is a magnificent four-poster bed that looks like a ship in full sail, with its hangings of jewel-coloured silks and golden threads. The wardrobes, chests and mahogany arms of the sofa shine with beeswax, and the marble fireplace would not look out of place in the grandest of drawing rooms. The fire is blazing and there is a bath pulled up in front of it.

'Alice!' There are four other women in the room and they clap their hands together and greet me with delight. Although I see them most days in chapel, I am not sure of their names and I hope I do not embarrass myself. They are all dressed in costly gowns and are seated around a table drinking tea. 'Come and join us,' they say. 'You will take some tea, won't you?'

It is a world away from the cottage kitchen and I feel a sight in my old frock with my nightgown bunched underneath and nothing on my feet. But they do not seem to notice. I put my bag on the floor and soon the women are chattering away, deciding which gown I should wear; which, of all the gowns they own between them, is the richest and costliest and would suit my colouring the most.

It is decided that I will try them all on, and every piece of jewellery too. 'You must look like a queen,' I am told. 'A queen that is fit for the King.'

But first I am to bathe. I am shy at first to strip in front of them, but they are so kind to me, and so excited to help, that soon I put myself in their hands and begin to enjoy myself. The bath water is deliciously hot and scented with oils. It slips over my skin like a silk gown. They wash my hair with perfumed soap and rinse it with jugs of clean water. They wash my body too, with soft cloths and gentle strokes. All the while, they tell me how beautiful I am. How they have never seen such skin as mine, nor hair as strong and thick. 'You will make Our Beloved the most perfect bride,' they say.

They wrap me in warm towels and I sit by the fire to dry my hair. They come in and out of the room, bringing with them armfuls of gowns and petticoats which they pile on the bed, and handfuls of jewels which they scatter across the table.

They dress me layer by layer. First a chemise and drawers and then some stays. I begin to protest at the stays. They bring dark memories to the edge of my thoughts and I do not want anything to spoil this day. But the women brush aside my protests. 'Our Beloved would have you properly attired on this day,' they insist. Then come the petticoats, frothing about my ankles, layers and layers of the finest linen and lace. Then, at last, the gown. I step in and out of one concoction and then another, until finally it is decided that the rose-pink silk taffeta complements my complexion the most and fits me beautifully.

Next, they dress my hair. They brush it until my scalp aches, then they coil it and pin it and twist it, and decorate it with silk flowers and pearls. Then they hang my ears with diamonds and my neck with pink coral. Finally, they pin a veil of milky lace to my hair and lead me to a mirror.

I do not recognise the woman I see in the glass. For it *is* a woman and not a girl. She is shapely and elegant with slender shoulders and a pair of bosoms that bloom softly at her décolletage. Her lips are pink and full and her eyes shine with contentment.

The women crowd around me, cooing like proud mothers. Mrs Holloway crosses her arms over her chest in satisfaction and nods her approval. 'Now we will leave you for a while,' she says, 'so you can contemplate your good fortune and so that we can ready ourselves for the ceremony.' They flutter from the room like a flight of fancy doves and a delicious silence settles upon me.

I look to the mirror again, turning this way and that, trying to see every bit of this stranger. I can't get enough of the vision. When, eventually, I have looked a dozen times upon every inch that I can, I sit myself carefully in a chair by the window. It is hard to stay still though. I twist my hands in my lap and tap my feet, now shod in embroidered satin. I wonder if this is how every bride feels, this turmoil of terror and bliss and nerves.

I pull the curtains aside and peer out. The mist has lifted, leaving behind another fine day. I watch the clouds skitter across the pale blue sky and the children chasing one another across the lawns. The mansion is built much higher than the cottages and from up here I can see over the wall to the lane beyond. I see a cart driving by and, further away, the rooftops of the village cottages. It is strange to think of that other world out there, of all the people going about their business, eating and sleeping and fighting, and none of them having any idea of how soon it will all be over for them when the Day of Reckoning arrives. *But if they choose not to listen*, I think, *then how will they ever hear?*

I wonder if I will ever see Mama and Eli again. A tiny part of me would like them to be here now, to witness me dressed as a queen, all ready to wed the King of Kings. How Mama's eyes would bulge. How she would regret all her cruelties. And how Eli would regret his blindness. But I would not forgive them, no matter how much they asked me to. I would let them taste just a small drop of Paradise, then I would send them away, back to the outside, to their horses and their Lady Egertons and to the fates that they deserve.

Suddenly the door opens. It is Mrs Holloway, with a small glass of ruby wine balanced on a silver tray. I uncurl my fingers from where they have been clenched into fists. 'Alice,' she says. 'It is nearly time.' She places the tray next to me. 'I have brought you a little sherry,' she says, 'to calm your nerves and help you relax. Drink up, now.'

'Thank you,' I reply. I am grateful for her thoughtfulness, for my stomach is indeed jumping about like a sack of frightened rabbits. I take a mouthful of the sherry. It is not as sweet as I thought it would be and I shudder as it burns a trail down my throat.

'All of it,' says Mrs Holloway. 'You will need every drop.'

I take a breath and swallow the rest of it. It coats my tongue with a bitter aftertaste.

'Good,' says Mrs Holloway, with a satisfied smile. 'Now, Alice. Are you ready?'

The chapel bells begin to ring out across the Abode as Mrs Holloway leads me from the mansion. I feel like I am floating on air. As if angels are somehow carrying me over the lawns and along the pathway to the chapel. We enter through a side door, into a room that is separated from the main chapel by a pair of gold velvet curtains. It is murky in the room. The only light comes from a slit of a window high above our heads.

I sense his presence before I see him. I can taste the promise of him in the air.

'She is ready,' Mrs Holloway states. She nods to me then, and leaves the room.

I grow hot, all of a sudden, my whole body covered in pinpricks of heat. It is the cursed stays, I am sure. I have grown used to not wearing them, and with the heaviness of my gown and the layers of petticoats, my bridal outfit is proving a burden to bear.

'Come, Alice,' he says, as he appears from the shadows. 'Let me feast my eyes on you.'

I walk towards him, but my feet are unsteady, and for one dreadful moment I fear I will swoon. He holds his arm out to me and I take it gratefully. 'You are a vision indeed,' he says. 'A bride truly fit for the Lord himself.'

I try to smile at him, but my mouth doesn't seem to belong to my face.

'Come now,' he says. 'It is time.'

The thin pipes of the organ strike up and I imagine Mrs Holloway sitting primly before it, with her lips pursed in concentration. Our Beloved pulls the gold curtains to one side, and we walk arm in arm into the chapel. Every member of the Abode is out there. I see them all; the richly dressed ladies and the plainer women of the Parlour and all the children dotted in between. Even Beth is there. After all her talk last night of leaving, she is out there, sitting at the back, with her eyes locked onto Our Beloved.

In front of the altar there are two gilt thrones with velvet and gold-braided seats. Our Beloved directs me to sit in one of them and he takes his place in the other. The sound of the organ swells then. Mrs Holloway is red-faced with fervour. The congregation get to their feet and soon the whole chapel is echoing to the voices of angels. Or so it seems to me. My head has grown light and I have to swallow the urge to giggle.

The voices die away and an expectant silence fills the great space. I want to close my eyes and sleep, but I am also horrified that I should think that. Our Beloved rises to his feet. He turns and bows to me, then he takes my hand and raises me from my throne. I hold his hand tight, because the dizziness has worsened now. The edges of my vision has blurred into soft clouds.

Our Beloved begins to speak and I want so much to hear his words; the most important words that will ever be spoken to me. But he sounds so far away, as though he is in another room and not standing right beside me. His words echo in and out of my hearing.

I take Alice Angel as my spirit bride.
Divine purification.
The Holy Ghost shall take flesh in the presence of flesh.

Flesh upon flesh.

Flesh upon flesh.

Mrs Holloway is beside me now too. I didn't notice her leave the organ. But the congregation are still singing; a strange chanting hymn that makes the inside of my skin tremble. Our Beloved and Mrs Holloway lead me to a table covered in a white cloth. No. It is not a table. It is the altar. Am I to say my vows?

There is a set of small steps next to the altar. Mrs Holloway wants me to climb them. She wants me to lie down on the altar. Am I to go to sleep now? It would be most welcome. *No, Alice,* I tell myself. *You cannot sleep on an altar.* But I am lying down. I am so heavy. I can barely keep my eyes open. The singing-chanting slides over me like a thick blanket. I close my eyes.

Just for a moment . . .

My arms are being held down. Something tight around my wrists. Someone is leaning over me and I catch the sickly sweet scent of lavender. *Mama?* I retch. The bitter sherry rises in my throat. My eyes snap open. *Mrs Holloway? Why is she holding me down?*

I try to move, to wriggle out of her grasp. But there is no strength left in me. What is happening? I open my mouth. But before I can scream, there is a hand clamped over it. I can feel rough callouses against my squashed lips. Mrs Holloway's face is red and contorted. She is breathing hard through her nostrils

I look around, frantically. The congregation are still singing. Can they not see what is happening? There's Beth. She is not singing. She is the only one not singing. She is crying.

I turn my head again. Our Beloved is standing at the end of the altar by my feet. He is looking to Heaven with his arms outstretched. He moves closer to me. At last. He is going to stop Mrs Holloway.

But he doesn't. His head is bowed. He is pushing up my petticoats. He is pressing himself against me. He is doing unspeakable things under my skirts.

And then there is pain.

Red hot.

Splitting.

Inside me.

I scream through tight fingers.

Then there is only darkness.

Forty-four

I am dreaming. But it is a terrible dream. I cannot move. I am tied to the bed. With Mama's leather straps. But it is Mrs Holloway leaning over me. She has stolen Mama's smell. The stink of lavender is suffocating me. I open my mouth to scream, but no sound comes out. But then I am floating. I am gliding down the aisle of the chapel in all my bridal glory. Our Beloved is waiting for me with outstretched arms. I am desperate to reach him, but he keeps moving further and further away. The women of the Parlour are there and all the other ladies and children. They are pointing at me and laughing. I look down into my arms and I am carrying a newborn child, a bloodied, squirming thing with bony horns pushing through its skull. There is blood all over me. My skirts are soaked, my petticoats too. And my thighs are sticky with it. I throw the child to the ground and I look to Our Beloved. I need him to save me. But he has his back to me. He is walking away. 'No!' Suddenly I am screaming. 'No! No! No!'

I wake with a start.

Someone is in the room. They pull back the curtains and the sudden light blinds me. The back of my eyes ache, my head too. I groan and try to sit up. 'Where am I?' I ask, as much to myself as to the person in the room. I hold my head in my hands.

'It's all right, Alice. You're just in your chamber. Your new chamber.'

I lift my head and slowly take my hands away. Beth is standing looking at me, her arms folded across her chest. 'How are you feeling?' she asks.

'I . . . I . . . terrible,' I say. 'I feel terrible.' I press my fingers to my eyes to try and push away the ache. 'What happened?' I ask. 'Why do I feel like this?'

'I'm sorry,' Beth says. 'I did try to warn you. You'll remember soon enough though.' She looks down at the floor. 'It's what he does to all the chosen ones.'

I shake my head. 'I don't know what you mean.'

'You should have come away with me last night.' She turns to go. 'When you remember what happened, come and find me.'

I watch her leave the room, then I look around and try to make sense of things. I am in the four-poster bed, with its high mattress and rich hangings. The bed I hoped would be mine. The hip bath is still sitting in front of the fireplace. There are teacups still on the table by the window. I remember the sweet perfume of the oil in the bath and the chink of teacups as we all sat at the table together. I liked it, I remember. I liked it a lot.

Then there were the gowns. Oh, yes. I remember the gowns. The rose-pink taffeta that rustled when I walked. The bodice that scooped up my bosoms and held me tight at the waist. And the veil. The bridal veil.

I remember the chapel, the thrones, the music and the singing. Our Beloved leading me to the altar.

Mrs Holloway. Her face looms up before me. Her buttonhole mouth stretched wide. A sudden shudder runs through me and my stomach lurches painfully.

I remember.

I remember what he did to me. What Mrs Holloway helped him do to me.

I remember what I felt him doing beneath my skirts.

My breath comes fast and shallow. I don't want it to be true. It was just a nightmare wasn't it? Just a nightmare? I push the bed covers down. I am wearing a thin cotton nightgown. I don't remember who undressed me. Where is the rose-pink gown now? I swing my legs out of the bed. It is then that I feel it. Stickiness between my thighs. My heart stops. I reach my hand down to touch myself and when I bring it back towards my face, my fingers are red with fresh blood. I fall to the floor.

It is true.

It all happened.

He did those things to me in front of everyone.

I curl into a ball and rock backwards and forwards. My insides ache unbearably. What happens now? I can't let anybody see me. I am so ashamed. So ashamed.

There are footsteps on the other side of the bed. My heart stops for a moment.

Beth? Please let it be Beth.

The footsteps stop behind me. 'What are you doing down there?' I recognise the thin tones of Mrs Holloway.

I pull my knees tight to my chest and pray for her to leave.

'Come on,' she says. 'Get up from there. It is a new day. Your first day as Our Beloved's new bride.'

253

I turn my head slowly. She looks as she always has done. There is no evil on her face, just a creased concern. 'Come,' she says again. 'He would like you to breakfast with him this morning.'

'No,' I say, shaking my head vigorously. 'I cannot. I cannot go anywhere.'

'Nonsense,' she says. 'I will help you dress. We must please Our Beloved in all ways. You know that. He has blessed us with eternal life in return for our love.'

I shake my head again. 'But I am bleeding,' I whisper. 'I am bleeding from inside.'

Mrs Holloway bends down and pulls me to my feet. 'Hush, now,' she says. 'That is only to be expected. It is nothing to be concerned about. The first time, blood has to be sacrificed. You will feel better in a while, I promise you.' She pulls me to her and rests my head on her breast. The lavender again. I can smell the lavender. I don't want her near me, with her false kindnesses. Does she think I don't remember what she did?

I twist out of her embrace. 'Can you leave me for a while?' I say, my heart thudding fearfully. 'I will be fine now. And I will dress myself.'

She looks at me closely. 'Very well,' she says. 'But do not take long. He is expecting you in the red room.'

After she has gone, I sit for a long while. It is because he loves me that he did what he did, I try to tell myself. He is God after all. It must be right. But the spasms of fear and loathing that turn my legs to trembling jelly and my heart to a mess of beaten meat, tell me otherwise. Why did he do that to me? Why did he have to spoil everything? I thought he had forgiven me my sins. So why did he have to punish me in such an unspeakable way?

I will find Beth. She will know what to do. She can help me to make sense of it all. Maybe she can put everything back in the right place.

There is water in the jug on the washstand. I pour some into the bowl and begin to wash myself. I wipe my thighs slowly and move the cloth tentatively between them, to the soft hidden part of me. The water in the bowl turns pink when I rinse the cloth. I catch my breath at the horror of it all. I cannot imagine the wound will ever heal. He might as well have ripped my heart out too.

I find my old grey frock tossed over the back of a chair and I pull it over my head. I will not dress as his new bride and I will not go to him. I am too scared to look him in the face. I am afraid that if I see him in the flesh, he will make me think things I don't want to any more.

Forty-five

Beth is in the scullery at the cottage. 'You have remembered then?' she asks as she scrubs the dirt from a bowl of potatoes.

I nod and brush an unbidden tear from my cheek.

'I'm sorry it had to happen,' she says. 'I tried to tell you. But I don't blame you for not listening.'

'How did you know?' I ask. 'How did you know he was going to do that to me?'

She shrugs. 'You are not the first and you won't be the last.' She turns from the bowl and wipes her hands on her apron. 'I have begun to question it all of late,' she says. 'Why he does the things he does. I loved him so much, you see. He is the only one I have ever loved.' She takes a knife and begins to cut the cleaned potatoes into chunks.

'He takes who he wants,' she continues. 'He took me too,' she says. 'As he took you, only not as a bride. He has taken many of us. They are all his children out there. Every one of them.'

I am frightened by what she is telling me, but I know I have to keep listening.

'But when I lost my child, he rejected me. He said it was the Devil's child. But I knew it wasn't. It was *his* child. It

256

could only be his child.' Beth lifts her apron to wipe at her eyes. 'That's when I knew,' she says. 'That's when I knew he was lying. That's when I knew it was *all* a lie. I am only glad I didn't die, like poor Glory.'

My mouth falls open. 'Glory is dead?'

She nods. 'She is in Paradise.' She gives a fierce little laugh. 'It is strange, don't you think? She was promised eternal life, but died in childbirth.'

My temples are throbbing. I don't want to hear any more. It is like a wall in my head is being knocked down, stone by stone. But I don't move. My feet are frozen to the floor.

I suck in my breath. 'What are you saying, Beth?'

'He is not God,' she says. 'It's as simple as that.'

Forty-six

Lions House was full of whispers. No one dared speak out loud in case the mistress got to hear. But the servants huddled in corners when they could, and asked each other what might happen. It was a scandal to be sure. That Miss Alice had been found was a miracle, but to think she was in that place in Spaxton where the unspeakable happened, where a charlatan ruled over a band of heathen women, where illegitimate children ran wild – it was unthinkable. If the mistress were ever to get a whiff of the truth . . . well, it didn't bear thinking about.

Eli returned from Spaxton with his head in a spin. Could he do it? Could he really rescue Alice and bring her home? He would need help for certain. But who could he ask? Who could he trust? It was a tricky situation, and how he would ever explain it to his mother, he didn't know. Would she accept Alice back when she couldn't even bring herself to speak her name?

Eli stopped outside Alice's chamber on the way to his own room. He opened the door and stepped inside. It was a sad sight. The bed had been stripped bare and the furniture was covered in dust sheets. He wondered if Alice's clothes were still hanging in the wardrobe and folded in her drawers, or had his mother tried to erase every trace of her?

If she had, it hadn't worked because he could still see and smell Alice everywhere. The mattress still held the shape of her and every corner of the room vibrated with the memory of her defiant voice. *She was always good at standing up to Mama*, he thought. *Much better than I am.*

Then as though he had conjured her up just by thinking about her, Temperance appeared in the room. 'What are you doing in here?' she demanded. 'You have no business in here. Get out.'

'Oh, Mama. I was just remembering Alice. That's all. Don't you miss her? Wouldn't you like her to come home?'

Temperance put her hand to her throat, as though she might choke. Then in a sudden movement she reached out and slapped Eli across the face. 'Where have you been all day?' she shouted. 'I know you haven't been at the mill.'

She followed Eli as he left Alice's chamber.

'Where have you been? I demand to know. Where have you been sneaking off to? I will not allow it. Do you hear me?'

Her voice vibrated inside Eli's head and poked at his brain. He was desperate to get inside his chamber and shut the door in her face. Why couldn't she just leave him alone?

'Don't forget, Eli,' she said, her voice suddenly calm. 'This is my house. The money is all mine too. Just you remember that.'

Eli turned and looked at her. She reached out her hand and he flinched. But this time she just rested her hand gently on the side of his face. 'My son,' she said. 'Now be good for your mother. You are all I have left now.'

As Eli retreated to the sanctuary of his chamber, he felt sick to the stomach. He had to bring Alice home. There could be no doubt now. He couldn't bear it any longer. Now, he didn't care how his mother would react. With Alice back in the house his mother would surely return to her old ways and leave him in peace. And it would be all right, because Alice would know how to deal with her. She had had a lifetime of practice, after all.

He would speak to Wraith, he decided. He wouldn't refuse to help. Not if he knew what was good for him.

Forty-seven

'Alice?' Mrs Holloway marches into the scullery. She looks me up and down and frowns with annoyance. 'What are you doing?' she barks. 'Why are you dressed like that? And why are you not with Our Beloved?'

Before I can think of an answer, she grabs me by the wrist and pulls me out of the scullery. I glance desperately to Beth. She quickly puts her finger to her lips and then mouths, 'Don't worry, I'll come for you later.'

Then I am being dragged away, out of the cottage, across the lawns and through the doors of the mansion. Mrs Holloway stops outside the red room and releases my wrist from her grip. She folds her arms across her washboard bosom and nods towards the door of the red room. She is leaving nothing to chance, and although every part of me has turned as cold and as stiff as the skin of a plucked goose, I am forced to lift my hand and knock on the heavily varnished wood.

'Come,' says his voice from inside.

I swallow hard and open the door.

'Alice,' he says as I walk into the room. 'Where were you? I sent for you, but you could not be found.'

'I am sorry,' I manage to say. My tongue is thick in my mouth. 'I . . . I was unwell. I came as soon as I could.'

'Unwell, you say? We cannot have that, can we?' He comes to me and catches my chin in his hand. He lifts my face and the blood drains to my feet as I look into his eyes. 'You are a bride of the Lord,' he says. 'And as such you do not suffer from sickness or grief. Are you sure it was not all in your mind?'

My heart smashes noisily against my ribs and I am terrified he will hear it. 'It . . . it may have been in my mind,' I stammer. 'I had a restless night.' I lower my eyes then, so he will not see the flash of hatred in them. 'But I am better now,' I finish.

'Good,' he says. He slides his hand from my chin and lets his fingertips travel down my neck and over my bosom. My skin shrinks from his touch, as though a spider has crawled into my bodice. I shudder.

'Do you write well?' he asks me suddenly, removing his hand.

'Yes,' I say. 'I . . . I believe that I do.'

'Excellent!' He rubs his hands together. 'I am publishing my sermons and I should like you to copy them out for me.' He sits me at his desk with a pile of notes and a sheaf of fresh paper, then he settles himself in a chair by the fire and lights a cigar. 'I shall inspect your work in a while,' he says, 'when the clock strikes one. And I hope you will absorb my teachings as you write.'

I pick up the pen that is lying on the desk and dip it into the pot of ink. My hand is trembling and a drop of black ink falls onto the centre of a clean page. I stare down at the splash. It looks like the sun with its rays spread out around it. I remember seeing my future before in a stain of ink and blood and I am glad it is the sun I see now, at least, and not a dark cloud or a page of tears.

I begin to write, copying Our Beloved's words in neat lines across the paper. They are just words though, and I do not join them in my mind into sentences. I slide my eyes over to where he is sitting, his head in a cloud of cigar smoke and his nose in a book. I keep glancing at him, searching for a halo or a glow of goodness; looking for a sign that he is God made flesh. Looking for something that will make sense of what he did to me. Beth said he is not God. But that is a truth too terrible for me to contemplate.

I look at him again, willing myself to see something divine, to see something heavenly, to see anything. But I see nothing except a beast of a man bent over a book with the stain of tobacco on his fingers.

The clock strikes one. He rises from his chair and yawns. 'Let me see,' he says. He gathers my work in his hands and flicks through the pages. 'You have done well,' he says. 'But tomorrow, I am sure you will manage a few pages more. Go now and ready yourself for chapel.' His eyes flick over my old frock. 'And perhaps something more suitable for the bride of the Lord.'

My hand aches from the hours of writing and I am desperately in need of air that isn't fouled by the stink of tobacco. I slip out of the mansion, thinking I will find somewhere quiet where I can be on my own and calm the storm that is raging inside me. I have only just stepped onto the lawns, when Beth comes running up to me. 'Alice,' she hisses. She grabs my arm and pulls me into the gazebo. 'Have you thought about what I told you?'

'I have thought of nothing else,' I tell her.

Her face lights up. 'Then you will come with me?' She grabs my hands and squeezes them hard.

I nod, although my belly is flipping over and over like a butter churn. 'I . . . I don't know where I should go, though,' I say. 'I don't know anything any more.'

Beth drops my hands and frowns. 'Yes you do,' she says. 'You know the most important thing of all now. You know the truth. You do, don't you, Alice?'

'I wish I didn't,' I whisper.

She laughs bitterly. 'Do you want to be like the rest of them? Do you want to be blind and stupid? Do you want to believe that what he did to you on the altar was in the name of God?'

I shake my head, and the dreadful memory of it all causes my throat to tighten so that for a moment I cannot speak.

Beth grabs my hands again. 'It will be all right, Alice,' she says. 'I promise. You have a home to go back to. And I will look after you until then.'

She looks at me intently, her face trembling with determination. Suddenly, I am so full of love for her, that I pull my hands from hers and fling my arms around her neck. 'Thank you, Beth,' I breathe. 'Thank you.'

She pulls me away quickly and leans her head in close to mine. 'We will go now, Alice,' she whispers. 'While they are all at chapel. We shall walk straight out of those gates and by the time anyone misses us, we will be miles away. We can do this, Alice. You know we can.'

I nod. She is right. Why should we waste another minute in here? And I know I could not bear *him* near me ever again.

264

'Meet me by the gates as soon as the chapel bells start to ring,' Beth whispers. 'Fetch whatever you want to bring with you. But be quick. We don't have much time.' She strides off across the lawns. Then she stops halfway and turns back to me. 'I am leaving here, Alice,' she says. 'I shan't change my mind this time. So hurry. Because I won't wait.'

I watch her walk away and I turn cold. I am as scared as I have ever been. I don't know where we go or what we will do, but I am glad that Beth has the courage for us both, because I know I could never do this on my own.

There is a sharp cough from behind me. I turn quickly and my heart sinks when I see Mrs Holloway standing outside the mansion. She beckons me over. 'You will be late for chapel if you do not hurry,' she snaps. 'You will be changing into a fresh gown, I presume?'

She follows me back to my chamber, so closely I can feel her breath on the back of my neck and her lavender scent catches in the back of my throat. 'Thank you,' I say to her. 'I will be down in a moment.' I leave her outside the room and I lean against the closed door and take a deep breath. My legs are shaking, but I know I must move. I will need a spare dress, a warm shawl. I run to the wardrobe and rifle through the contents. Then I see it. A lemon gown made of silk and muslin and lace. I recognise it at once. It is Glory's. It is the gown she was wearing on the day I arrived. I slam the wardrobe door shut. This was her chamber. This was her bed. These were her clothes.

The thought of it fills me with horror.

The chapel bells start to ring. My heart jumps. Beth will

265

be hiding now, by the gates, waiting for me. I look out of the chamber window and I see the women of the Parlour and all the others, trotting like sheep across the lawns and along the pathways to meet their shepherd. Then I see him. My heart quickens and I grip on to the windowsill as I watch him walk up the pathway to the chapel. It is as though I am seeing him for the first time. Only now he makes my bones shudder. There is something about the way the clouds seem to darken as he moves towards his flock that suddenly makes me turn from the window and look frantically around the room for the carpet bag. My gold locket is still inside it, hidden in the folds of my mourning gown. And I can't leave here without it.

It is now or never. I can't begin to imagine where I will go or what I will do. I only know I have to get away.

I have to meet Beth.

I see the carpet bag lying at the foot of the bed, but before I can get to it, the chamber door opens.

'You are not ready.' Mrs Holloway's accusing voice hits me hard in the stomach.

'I . . . I won't be much longer,' I stammer. 'I will be down in a moment.'

'Then I shall wait for you, if you don't mind,' she says.

Panic floods through me. 'There's no need,' I say. I rush back to the wardrobe and pull out the first gown my hand touches. It is Glory's lemon gown. But I don't care, I just have to get rid of Mrs Holloway. I look at her pointedly. 'I should like to get dressed in private, please.'

'Very well,' she huffs, 'but hurry.' And to my relief, she leaves the room.

I dress quickly, trying to forget I am wearing a dead woman's gown, then I run to the carpet bag and rummage inside until my hand brushes against my gold locket. *Wait for me, Beth*, I chant under my breath. *Please, wait for me.* But before I can wrap my fist around the locket, the chamber door opens again and as I smell the first dangerous whiff of Mrs Holloway's lavender, my heart plummets.

With Mrs Holloway following close on my heels, it takes all of my strength to walk back into the chapel. It takes all of my willpower not to look at the altar as I walk past it to stand by his side. I look out at all the faces. They are shining with adoration and they are singing with joy. Every one of them believes in him. Every one of them has chosen to follow him. I don't understand any more. Not now, when the very air that he breathes sickens me to the stomach.

Then, as if he knows I am fighting with demons, he reaches out to take my hand. My skin crawls as the damp of his flesh sticks to mine. Then I notice the empty chair at the back of the chapel and I know at once that Beth has gone without me.

'Sing!' he commands me. 'Sing, little lamb!'

But I can't. My throat has closed up so tight that I am afraid if I open my mouth the only sound that will come out will be a loud and terrible scream.

Forty-eight

Eli persuaded Ernest Wraith to come with him, and to bring a couple of strong men from the mill. 'But you must promise me your discretion,' Eli had said. 'Your absolute discretion.'

They arrived in Spaxton in time to take lunch at the Lamb Inn. 'So you have decided, I see,' said the landlord gruffly, as he placed jars of ale in front of them. 'Best of luck to you then, I say.'

After they had eaten their fill of the landlord's finest beef pie, Eli took the men for a walk around the walls of the Abode. 'You see,' he said to them, 'the only way in is through these two gates, or over the walls. But the landlord has informed me that Prince's carriage has not left its home for a couple of days now. So if we are lucky, we should catch the gates opening at some point tomorrow. We shall post ourselves in the lane from dawn, and as soon as the gates open, we shall rush in.'

As they walked back to the inn, the chapel bells began to ring out, and Eli thought of Alice. Poor Alice, a prisoner behind those great walls. If only there were some way of letting her know he was there, of letting her know that her ordeal was almost over. He was struck by a sharp thrill. *This is what life should be about*, he thought. *Adventures*. Not following a dry old man like Wraith around a dusty mill all day, or placating a demanding mother. Eli felt like a hero and before he could stop himself, he rushed to the gates and began to shout, 'Alice! Alice! I'm here, Alice!' His only answer was a snarling and a scrabbling of great claws as the bloodhounds jumped at the gates.

If Eli had not run from the barking and the snarling like some frightened deer, if he had just waited a few minutes more, he would have seen the smaller of the two gates open very slowly. He would have seen a pretty, freckle-faced girl creep out onto the lane, and he could have entered the Abode without any trouble at all. But by the time Beth had closed the gate behind her, Eli was back at the bar of the Lamb Inn, drinking a small brandy to calm his nerves.

Forty-Nine

Later that night he comes to my bed. 'My bride,' he slurs as he climbs in beside me. I smell the drink on his breath and the stale reek of his sweat. God shouldn't smell like that. I lie there stiffly, waiting for the touches that I know will come. My insides shrivel. He puts his hand on me. He runs it over my breasts and belly. I bite my tongue to stop myself from screaming. But then his hand stills. It lies there, heavy on my thigh. His breathing deepens and I dare to hope he has fallen asleep.

Then he is snoring and grunting and he fills the bed with the stench of his wind. I lie there all night, not daring to move. I would rather a sleepless night than have him wake.

When the first pale light of morning seeps into the room, I slide quietly from the bed. He has kicked off the blankets and I see he is naked. I look down at him, at his face squashed into the pillow and at the white roll of his belly slumped over the soft worm of his manhood. I want to laugh out loud. Beth was right. Of course he is not God.

He is just a pitiful man.

Fifty

It is wet and gloomy today. I watch from the window of my chamber as the wind whips sheets of rain across the lawns and over the wall to the lane outside. I finish my tea but I leave the buttered toast on its plate. Because even though I am empty, I have no appetite.

I think of Beth and I hope she has found somewhere safe to be. I wish with all my being that I had been able to go with her. But I know that is one wish that will never come true. She is long gone. But all the same, I wish good things for her. I wish for her to find happiness.

I make a wish for myself too. It is a foolish wish really, because I know it is too late for me. With Mrs Holloway breathing down my neck at every turn, there is no chance of escape. There is no miracle left that will free me from this place. I have made my bed. But I keep wishing for freedom nonetheless, because there is still a tiny part of me that believes I can make it happen.

Our Beloved is to travel to Bristol today and to my relief he is taking Ruth with him and not me. They will be gone for two days at least. He has left me a pile of sermon notes to write up for him. 'You are more use to me here, than out on the road,' he said.

I wonder if this will be my life now, hours and hours spent writing down words that I don't believe, or even understand. I have nothing left now and I don't want to feel this empty forever. So maybe if I write for long enough, I think, for a year or even two, maybe the words will seep into my brain and organise themselves into some meaning. Then maybe one day I will believe again and I will have something to live for.

I watch as the carriage rolls towards the gates. Poor Agatha and Ruth. Even their oilskins will not keep them dry in this weather. The gates are opened and the horses nose into the lane.

Then something strange happens. The horses stop, half in and half out of the gates. For a moment I think he has changed his mind. Maybe he wants me with him after all. My heart twists into a tight knot. But then I see four figures running into the grounds. I press my face to the window. The figures are men and I see that two of them have thick sticks in their hands. They are waving them at the bloodhounds to try and keep them at bay. The women have all emerged from the cottages now and they are running towards the men. I hear their angry shouts.

One of the men breaks loose and he is sprinting towards the mansion. He is shouting too. I lift the catch on the window and push it open. Rain spatters on my face, but I hear him clearly now.

My heart stops.

'Alice! Alice! Alice!' I step back from the window, not quite believing what I have seen. Is it really Eli down there? Eli calling my name? Has he come to free me? Has my wish come true?

I dare to look again, but all I can see is a confusion of bodies. The women have surrounded him. They are pushing and pulling him, back towards the gates. 'Eli!' I call out of the window, 'Eli! I'm coming!' I look frantically around the chamber, trying to remember where the carpet bag is. There. Under the chair at the foot of the bed. I pull it open and scrabble inside until my hand closes on the gold locket. With shaking hands I clip it around my neck, then I slam open the chamber door and fly along the corridor and down the stairs.

'Leave my brother alone!' I shout as I run out to the lawns. 'Leave him be!'

'Out . . . Out . . . Out . . .' they are all chanting. 'Out . . . Out . . . Out.'

I push my way through, not caring who I scratch or bruise. The rain is running down my face and into my mouth. 'Eli,' I gasp. 'Eli.' I finally reach him and I grab hold of his hand.

'Oh my god, Alice,' he cries. 'What have you got yourself into?'

'STOP! STOP THIS NOW!'

A powerful voice sails over all of our heads and suddenly the skirmish stops and quietness descends. We turn to the voice and there is Our Beloved, standing on the steps of the carriage with the bloodhounds prowling around his feet.

Eli pulls me towards the gates. The other men are already standing out in the lane, panting fast and adjusting their dishevelled jackets.

'WAIT!' Our Beloved holds out his hand to me. 'Who is this, Alice?' he asks.

'Don't answer him,' Eli hisses. 'Come on. Let's go.'

'Where are you going, Alice? You don't want to leave us, do you?'

I look at Our Beloved as Eli drags me out into the lane. I watch as his lips form the words that are coming out of his mouth. I push Eli away. I want to do this on my own.

'Alice!' Eli shouts. 'Don't. Don't go back!'

'Alice,' says Our Beloved, as I walk towards him. 'You know you belong here. Come back inside now, so we can shut the gates.'

'No, Alice,' yells Eli.

'Come,' says Our Beloved. 'Come, my spirit bride. We are all here for you.'

I look back to Eli. 'Come home, Alice,' he says, sounding suddenly exhausted. 'I have missed you so much.'

I turn again towards Our Beloved, and all I can see is the ugliness of him. There is no shining God, no saviour, no divine being. He is just a man. A mortal man named Henry Prince.

Mrs Holloway walks to his side. Her eyes are spitting flames at me. I step back into the grounds of the Abode while Eli shouts warnings from behind me. I walk straight to Mrs Holloway and I slap her hard, right across her face. Her buttonhole mouth splits wide open. 'You know what that is for,' I say. Then I run back to Eli and grab his hand again.

'Come on!' I yell. 'Take me home!' Then we are both running, as fast as we can, down the lane towards the carriage that is pulled up outside the Lamb Inn.

Fifty-one

The air inside the carriage is heavy with the sound of panting as Eli and I try to catch our breath. I am surprised to see Mr Wraith sitting across from us, but I notice at once that he cannot bear to look at me. He sits as far away from me as the cramped interior will allow. But I don't care. I am exhilarated. I cannot sit still.

The miracle happened. It happened for *me*. My wishes meant something after all. I am not lost any more. I wriggle around on my seat so much, anyone would think I had fallen in a clump of nettles.

'How did you find me?' I ask, as soon as I can speak again.

Eli clears his throat. 'It was Sarah,' he says. 'She saw you being driven through the gates of that place. I didn't want to believe her at first, only I thought I had seen you too, in Bath, in the company of that . . . that Henry Prince. Did he kidnap you, Alice? Is that what happened?'

I don't know what to tell him. What will he think of me if I tell him the truth? If I tell him that I chose to go there? The bubbles of happiness that have been fizzing around inside me begin to burst.

Mr Wraith takes a handkerchief from his top pocket and

blows his nose loudly. Eli glances at him and then, as if he has sensed my discomfort, he puts his arm gently around my shoulders. 'It's all right,' he says. 'You can tell me all about it when we get home. You can tell me how they came to kidnap you. You will be perfectly safe back at Lions House. And when we get there you can tell me everything . . . But perhaps we had better spare Mama the details.'

I look at him sharply. 'Does she know you have found me?' I ask. 'Does she know where I have been and that you are bringing me home?'

The guilt that flashes across his face tells me all I need to know.

Eli turns and looks out of the window. 'Mama will be happy to see you,' he says eventually. 'I must tell you, Alice. She has missed you so much.'

A scornful laugh bursts out of my mouth and I try to disguise it as a cough. The idea that Mama would ever miss me fills me with such a mixture of pain and amusement that Eli has to slap me on the back to stop me from choking.

The carriage rattles on, shaking my bones, and Eli begins to tell me of his plans. 'Once you are home, Alice, and have settled yourself, of course, well, I should like to go abroad for a while. Paris. Rome. You know. Oh, and you must remember not to breathe a word to anyone about where you have been these past months. We will put it about that you've been with relatives. People can choose to believe us or not . . . Mama needs you, you see. A mother needs a daughter close by, don't you think? And with you at home again, I shall be free to travel.' He smiles at me broadly. 'And don't worry,' he says. 'If you behave yourself, Alice, I am sure she will forget any idea she may have had of an *asylum*.'

He whispers this last word as though it is so dirty he cannot bear to have it on his tongue.

'And you will behave, won't you, Alice? After all . . . being where you have just been . . . I am sure you would not like to go anywhere like that again.'

On he goes. Yapping away like some stupid puppy. But I am not listening any more. I know the truth of why he came to my rescue now; it was for his own sake and not for mine. In a strange way the realisation gladdens me. It is as though his selfishness has set me free and an astounding thought occurs to me. I do not want to go back to Lions House, to the place I used to call home. But I do not want to go back to the Abode either. I don't need Mama and Eli, and I certainly don't need Henry Prince. They might need me for their own twisted reasons but I don't need any of them. How blind I have been. I thought there were only two choices, but there is a world of choice out there and it is time for me to find my way now.

I pull down the carriage window and lean my head out. 'Stop!' I yell to the driver. 'Stop the carriage.' The racket of skidding hooves and screeching wheels flies in through the open window.

'What on earth are you doing, Alice?' Eli's eyebrows are arched in panic.

'I just need a little air,' I say.

'But we are almost home,' he complains. 'Can't you wait?'

'I'm afraid not,' I say. I open the carriage door and jump to the ground.

'Will you be long?' asks Eli. He sighs and leans back in his seat. I reach up and push the carriage door shut.

'I will be as long as it takes, dear brother. As long as it takes.'

Then I pick up my skirts and I run. I run as fast as I have ever run. I don't know where I am going just yet. But I know that I will end up somewhere. And somewhere is better than nowhere. The rains pours down, my skirts slap against my legs, Papa's gold locket bounces at my throat . . . and I run and run and run.

I wish to be happy! I shout at hedges and trees and empty fields. *I only wish to be happy!* And the wind picks up my wish and whips it high into the sky and carries it away to the place where dreams come true.

Fifty-two

I am soaked to the skin. But the rain has stopped now, at least, and I have found a lane to walk along. My skirts are thick with wet mud from the fields I first ran through. The rain has got into my boots too, and they are rubbing on my heels. I will have to stop soon and find somewhere to rest.

But this lane seems to lead nowhere. It is just endless hedges and puddles. I walk fast, even though my heels are stinging and the soles of my feet are burning. I am impatient to get to where I am going. I just don't know *how* to get there yet.

It came to me just after I had shouted my wish across the fields. It was as though the wind had heard my cry and blown the answer back to me. *I have been here before,* I thought, *running across this countryside; running away from myself and a life I do not want.* These could be the same fields I ran through before; these could be the same low, sparse hedges that snagged my skirts and the same mud that coated my boots. Except I know this isn't the right place. I will find no barn to shelter in here and no welcome around a farmhouse table.

Where is everyone? I have not come across a soul yet. Anyone will do, a farmer, a traveller, a coach driver or a pedlar.

Anyone who can point me in the direction of the Bristol Road. I tramp onwards, wincing with every step. There is a copse ahead and a fine sycamore with just a scattering of golden leaves left on its branches. I make my way towards it and see there is a bed of sod and fallen leaves covering its roots. I fall onto it gratefully and lean back against the flaking trunk. I close my eyes and allow my breaths to slow. I had not realised I was so tired.

I am cold now that I have stopped walking. I left the Abode in such a hurry that I have not even a shawl with me. I rub my arms briskly. I won't stay here long. I have to get on. But I feel so heavy now; it is as though all the strength has seeped out of me and into the roots of the sycamore. Just a few more minutes. Just a few more minutes . . .

I am in my meadow. It is more beautiful than ever. The grass is so green it hurts my eyes. Every blade of it slides across my bare legs like the finest gossamer. The sky is hushed and peaceful and never-ending. I turn around and around. The meadow is empty. But there is somebody here with me. I know that for a certainty. I look again – to the very edges of where the grass meets the sky. Nothing. *How odd*, I think. Then I feel something; the tiniest of movements, a fluttering of life. I hold my breath. It is coming from inside me. Whoever is with me in the meadow is deep inside of me, and the strangest thing is, I am not frightened by it at all.

There is a rumble and a clattering. My eyes fly open. Cartwheels are splashing through puddles and mud. I jump to my feet. The cart rolls on down the lane and I chase after it. There is a thick blanket stretched over the top of an assortment of furniture. I can see table legs and chair backs and the doors of a worm-eaten cabinet. 'Stop!' I shout. I run as hard as I can with my skirts held up in one hand and the other hand waving in the air. 'Stop!'

The cart slows and the tables and chairs knock together as the wheels jerk to a standstill. I dash to the front and crouched over the reins is a pock-marked old man buried in a weathered overcoat. Next to him is a woman with a scowl on her face and a battered bonnet on her head.

'Whadda you want?' barks the man. His eyes have barely any colour to them and they slide over me, taking in my muddy boots and the wet hair that is sticking to my face.

'Please,' I say. 'I need to get to the Bristol Road. How far is it from here?'

'Not too far,' grunts the man. He is staring at me in a way that makes me want to run back the way I came.

'Are you going that way yourself?' I ask.

'Yup,' he says. He is not making this easy for me.

'Could you . . . would you mind . . . could I please come with you? I could squeeze in the back there. I won't damage anything, I promise.'

He screws his eyes up at me. 'Can yer pay yer way?'

'I'm sorry,' I say. 'I can't. I have no money. I have nothing. But I would be so grateful if you would help me.'

'No money, no ride,' he says and he clicks his tongue at the horse and takes up the reins.

'No! Wait. Please!' I put my hand down the front of my bodice and pull out Papa's gold locket.

The man's eyes light up and he puts the reins back in his lap.

I unfasten the chain from around my neck and hold out the locket towards him. 'Now will you take me to the Bristol Road?'

He nods and licks his lips. I push the locket into his outstretched hand. 'One more thing,' I say. 'I need to go to the milestone on the Bristol Road. The one that reads Bridgwater, fifteen miles. Do you know it?'

Again, the man nods. He tucks Papa's locket deep into his coat pocket. 'Hop on, then,' he says.

I find a space between a dusty wooden trunk and a three-legged stool. It is comfortable enough. I can just see over the back of the cart as the lane stretches further and further behind us and I know in my heart that this is the most important journey I will ever make. *Thank you, Papa*, I whisper. But I think he knows already, and he will be glad that his gift has helped me on my way.

I stand by the milestone on the Bristol Road. *Bridgwater 15* is carved into its granite surface. There's the track that runs beside it. And a way up the track, if I squint my eyes, I can see a feathery whisper of smoke rising from the chimney of the farmhouse in the distance. Although I am tired to the bone, there is a wonderful lightness inside me now and I barely feel the blisters on my heels as I hurry as fast as I can along the track.

I know they will not turn me away.

I think of the strange dream I had under the sycamore tree and I put my hand to my belly. A curious warmth seeps through my fingers. Could it be true? A new life? Someone for me to truly love forever?

If it is true, I am not frightened. Because I know that where we are going they will not turn *us* away.

Four years later . . .

The sun is warm on my skin. I notice how, after a summer spent outside with the sleeves of my blouse rolled up, my arms have turned the pale brown of freshly baked biscuits. I put the basket of wet washing on the ground and pick out a garment to peg on the line. It is one of Eve's little smocks and I smile to see it hanging there, so tiny next to my own. I hear her giggles from across the yard. She is running circles around George again.

I finish pegging out the rest of the washing, and I stand for a moment with my hand shielding my eyes from the sun, looking out across the fields. I see a figure in the distance and my heart begins to dance in my chest. It is Tom. I can tell by the lazy sway of his hips and the assured swing of his arms. I quickly brush my fingers through my hair and check that my apron is clean.

I pick up the empty basket and turn back to the farmhouse. Ada is standing in the doorway watching me. 'Don't fret,' she says, and then winks at me. 'You look a picture.'

Tom has been coming over from the neighbouring farm for months now to help George out. But this is the first time he has ever come to supper. I have never felt so nervous.

Then Eve runs around the corner, with George hobbling behind, pretending to chase her. 'Help me, Mama. Help me!' she squeals. 'He is going to eat me up!' She flings herself at my legs. I drop the basket to the ground and lift her into my arms. I nuzzle my face into her neck and breathe her in. I don't think I will ever tire of the hot, sweet, straw and dirt smell of her.

'I will save you!' I laugh into her neck. 'I will always save you.' I swing her around in my arms and she squeals louder and louder. George has admitted defeat and is standing by Ada's side, both of them smiling at us broadly.

Then Eve catches sight of Tom and she wriggles out of my arms. 'Tom! Tom!' And she's off, her black ringlets bouncing off her back. And he already has his arms open to catch her.

I stand there for a moment and I look around at all of it: the farm, the fields, the sun, the sky. George and Ada who took me in without a question. George and Ada who love me like a daughter. George and Ada, who when Eve came along, instantly loved her too.

And Tom, of course. There are no promises and no wishes. It will be what it will be.

Once a month, George takes the cart and rides out to Bridgwater for candles and suchlike. He brings me snippets of news and gossip when he hears it. It was him that told me Mama had passed away last summer. A sickness of the brain, it was rumoured. There was a good turnout at her funeral, a dozen carriages at least. I was glad for her; she would have liked that. But I am not the least bit sorry that she is dead. Eli is married now too, with a child on the way. He still has the mill, although business is not as good as it once was. And it is said that he frequents the lowest parts of town more often than is decent. I hope that he has found some kind of happiness.

A few weeks back, George took us all for a ride out to Taunton to buy Ada a new bonnet. Taunton is not a small place, so I went with little expectation of coming across Beth. Nevertheless, as we climbed back into the cart to leave for home, with Ada balancing her new hatbox on her lap, a heavy disappointment lay across my shoulders. But then, as the cart trundled by a fancy goods shop, I happened to look behind as Eve pointed at something in the window. And there was Beth, tidying the display of ribbons, buckles and snuff boxes. She looked just the same, only softer and brighter. I put my hand up to wave, but of course she didn't see me. But it didn't matter. Just to see her was enough. Perhaps George will take me back to Taunton another day and I will walk into that shop and buy some ribbon for Eve, and Beth and I can talk to each of ordinary things, as if that is what we have always done.

George told me that the last time he was in Bridgwater he saw Henry Prince preaching in the town square. I was peeling onions at the time and when I heard his name, the knife slipped and sliced into my finger. I put the finger in my mouth and sucked on it. The sweetness of the blood mixed with the bitter sting of onion juice that had collected under my nails, tasted to me at that moment of life itself. Bitter and sweet all at once.

For out of the bitterness of it all, I now have the sweetest thing imaginable. I have my Eve.

And she is my Beloved.

I remember the last wish I ever made, on the day I left the Abode, the day I left my brother far behind. I remember tramping through the fields, the mud splashing my skirts and the rain stinging my face. *I only wish to be happy!* I'd shouted to the world. *I only wish to be happy!*

And as I look around me now, at all the faces that I love, and who love me back, I realise that it came true.

I wished it, and it came true.

Historical Notes

The Agapemonites (from Agapemone – meaning Abode of Love) was a religious sect founded in 1846 by a defrocked clergyman named Henry Prince.

Prince declared himself the 'Holy Spirit' and managed to persuade a number of believers, mostly rich widows and spinsters, to sell everything they owned for the Lord. With the proceeds, Prince set about building the sect's headquarters in the tiny Somerset village of Spaxton. These headquarters consisted of a twenty-bedroom mansion, a chapel, cottages, stables and a gazebo. The whole site was surrounded by fifteen-foot walls and was guarded by ferocious bloodhounds.

Prince's followers were divided into hierarchies. Those who had given the most continued to live a life of luxury, spending their days reading, playing hockey and billiards and, of course, worshipping Prince during the daily sermons in the chapel. Those women who had no riches to give to the Lord, gave their labour instead and lived as servants. They were known as the Parlour.

The very existence of the Abode of Love caused moral outrage in the society of the day, with its strict Victorian values of propriety, modesty and virtue. The newspapers were full of the scandal of it, and readers lapped up stories of brainwashing, sexual outrages and attempts to kidnap various family members. It was said that Prince took advantage of his exalted position to take many 'spirit brides' and to even rape a young kitchen maid on the chapel altar in front of his congregation.

In 1896, at the ripe old age of 85, Henry Prince initiated the building of a church in Clapton, North London. It was a vastly ornate building (still standing today) that included a stained glass window which depicted the submission of womankind to man.

Prince died in 1899, causing panic amongst his followers who had truly believed he was immortal. They buried him standing upright, in readiness for the Day of Reckoning.

Prince was succeeded by a man called John Smyth-Pigott who declared himself the second Messiah. Incredibly the Agapemonites grew from strength to strength, with the number of women at the Abode swelling to nearly one hundred. It was reported that Smyth-Pigott took at least seven 'spirit brides' a week.

It wasn't until the death of Smyth-Pigott in 1927 that membership of the sect started to decline. By the early 1950s only a handful of 'disillusioned old women and frustrated young women' were left.

The last member of the sect, a sister Ruth, died in 1957. The following year, the Abode was sold and the chapel went on to be used as a backdrop for the children's television series *Trumpton* and *Camberwick Green*.

Alison Rattle

Alison grew up in Liverpool, and now lives in a medieval house in Somerset with her three teenage children, her husband – a carpenter – an extremely naughty Jack Russell and a ghost cat. She has co-authored a number of non-fiction titles on subjects as diverse as growing old, mad monarchs, how to boil a flamingo, the history of America and the biography of a nineteenth-century baby killer. She has worked as a fashion designer, a production controller, a painter and decorator, a barmaid, and now owns and runs a vintage tea room. Alison has also published two previous YA books about young Victorian women with Hot Key Books – *The Quietness* and *The Madness*. Follow Alison at www.alisonrattle.com or on Twitter: @alisonrattle

HOT
KEY
BOOKS

Thank you for choosing a Hot Key book.

If you want to know more about our authors
and what we publish, you can find us online.

You can start at our website

www.hotkeybooks.com

And you can also find us on:

We hope to see you soon!